Let These Bones Live Again

A Christopher Worthy/Father Fortis Mystery

DAVID CARLSON

coffeetownpress
Kenmore, WA

For more information go to: www.coffeetownpress.com
www.DavidCCarlson.net

This is a work of fiction. Names, characters, places, brands, media, and incidents are either the product of the author's imagination or are used fictitiously.

Cover watercolor by Kathy Carlson
Cover design by Aubrey Anderson

Let These Bones Live Again

ISBN: 978-1-60381-393-8 (Trade Paper)
ISBN: 978-1-60381-394-5 (eBook)

Library of Congress Control Number: 2018945985

Printed in the United States of America

He asked me, “Son of man, can these bones live?”

I said, “O Sovereign Lord, you alone know.”

Ezekiel 37:3

☩

ACKNOWLEDGEMENTS

I AM INDEBTED TO ALL THOSE IN my life who let me enter the world of imagination. When I was young, imagination saved me when I encountered problems I couldn't fix. At other times, I would enter the world of imagination when I found schoolwork, especially math and science, boring. I know I worried my parents and some of my teachers—but not all of them, thank God—with my daydreaming.

It was only as an adult that I realized how important imagination would be to my life as a teacher and as a writer, a vocation that developed slowly. I have been blessed to be married to a fellow writer who is also a painter and a gifted editor. Kathy has always accepted that my need to spend time with paper and pen or, now, computer screen is not some hobby, but what I need to do to feel fully alive.

My sons, Leif and Marten, as well as my daughter-in-law, Mandy, are all artists and thereby kindred spirits. Over the years, they have encouraged me, as I hope I have encouraged them, to stay close to the child within, the one who loves to play, imagine, and create.

My grandchildren, Felix and Freya, bless me in so many ways. Felix has become my mentor as he shares the richness of his imagination, and I can only imagine what is going through Freya's mind, as she is now old enough to hold in her tiny hands her brother's toy cars and study them intently.

I am also grateful to my friend and agent, Sara Camilli, and my publishing friends at Coffeetown Press: Jennifer McCord and Aubrey Anderson, who have given me the greatest gift a writer can receive: the request to write more.

Finally, I wish to thank all the colleagues and students I have had over the decades at Franklin College, a gem of a liberal arts college. Their creativity, expressed in so many ways, has constantly fed and encouraged me.

Chapter One

Allyson Worthy inhaled the salty air deeply and smiled. Yes, I really am in Venice, she thought. She watched as a seagull rose from the Grand Canal, landed near her on the promenade, and plucked up a piece of bread dropped by a passerby.

She looked to her left and saw the corner of the Doge's Palace, its pink and white marble glistening. Over the rooftops she could also see the cupolas of the Basilica of San Marco. In front of her was the church of Santa Maria della Salute and beyond, across the Giudecca Canal and catching the late afternoon rays like a lazy sunbather, was the pure whiteness of the church and monastery of San Giorgio Maggiore.

"It's more than perfect," Allyson whispered to herself. She was thinking not only of the scene that surrounded her, of the architecture of Palladio that she studied in art and architectural history back at Franklin College, of the deep blue of the water, but of the entire semester abroad that she was beginning.

Venice had been her dream destination for so long that she couldn't remember when she first laid eyes on pictures of the famous city. During her parents' divorce, when she was fifteen, she would open a *Time-Life* book on Italy and stare at the pictures of Venice's palazzos, her churches, her islands lying off in the lagoon, and her canals. She would close her eyes and imagine the sounds and smells of Venice and find that her imagination could indeed give her some relief from the pain around her in Detroit.

Her parents' divorce was the quiet kind, full of sadness and few words. Both her father, Christopher Worthy, a noted homicide detective with the Detroit police department, and her mother, Susan, took the divorce as a tragedy foisted on each of them from some invisible third party.

After the divorce was finalized, Allyson chose to punish mainly her father, but did not completely spare her mother. Four months after the divorce was finalized, she ran away from home, taking only her makeup, some clothes, and the book on Italy, imagining that she could somehow wash up on the shores of Venice and survive on sheer longing for the city.

The reality was far different and far less romantic. For months she was out of contact with her family as she stayed above the garage of a summer-camp friend who had an extremely understanding divorced mother. But later, Allyson wondered if the mother didn't see her as an insurance policy against her own daughter similarly running away.

Then one day, she walked back into her home and sat down at the dinner table. She never explained where she had been, just in case she needed to leave again. And she didn't trust her father who would very likely find some way to press charges against the mother who shielded her.

But the dream of Venice never left her. And now she was here, not as a runaway without resources for survival, but as a college student taking the fall semester of her sophomore year abroad. She had a great roommate, Sylvia, a Venetian whose English was very good and who promised to help Allyson with her Italian. She also knew that she had not only an internship, but a great internship, one actually in her academic major of criminology. She would start the next day at the Venice police department, or the *Questura di Venezia*, as she loved to repeat to herself. She would be working with the "*Carabinieri* for the Foreigners" on cases in Venice that had an American or English connection. Her contact in Venice, *Ispettore* Ruggiero, indicated in his butchered English emails that Allyson would primarily be interviewing American and English tourists who had been pickpocketed or swindled in some other way in the city. Through those interviews, Allyson would log into the computer the *sestieri*, neighborhoods, and *albergi*, hotels, of Venice where such crimes were trending. The department could then deploy their policemen and policewomen more strategically.

Venice, she learned through research, had a very low serious crime rate, with virtually no homicides. That was despite the tendency of movie makers to set horror films in the dreamy and sometimes fog-shrouded city. Pickpockets and swindlers are fine with me, Allyson thought. I don't need murders like my father does.

Yes, it's perfect, she whispered again. As she turned to head back to her apartment for a light dinner with Sylvia, she slowed her pace and consciously avoided gawking at the buildings and calendar-worthy vistas that she was passing.

I am not technically a tourist, she reminded herself. I am a college intern, someone with almost a job. I will not get lost like a tourist on my way back to my apartment. I live in the Castello *sestiere*, and I will not have to ask directions like a tourist. This is my home for three delicious months. I will wear what the fashionable young women here wear and pack away my Nikes and baggy jeans. I will get a short haircut, like that woman's over there.

I am almost Italian, she thought.

Father Nicholas Fortis also felt that he was experiencing something close to perfection. Yes, *saltimbocca alla Romana* may be on every tourist menu in Rome, but this *ristorante* in the Roman neighborhood of Trastevere, chosen by Dom Philip, Benedictine, was off the main piazzas and filled with Italians.

For a moment, Father Fortis wondered about the ethics of eating veal. Certainly calves had a right to a future other than to be slaughtered for their tender flesh, but would a calf have any awareness of the adult bovine life that would be missed?

"Father Fortis, thank you, thank you for your role in our conference's success. As you know, this is our third international meeting of Christian monastic renewal, East and West, and I think it was by far the best. I'm not exaggerating when I say that your paper on the relationship of Roman and Byzantine chants was more than academically interesting. I heard many positive comments about your very open spirit, from both our side and yours."

He means the Catholic contingent and the Orthodox, Father Fortis thought.

"And I want to commend you on this restaurant," Father Fortis returned the compliment. "Every course has been, what shall I say, *magnifico*."

The elderly Benedictine abbot and organizer of the conference sighed heavily as he wiped the corners of his mouth with the cloth napkin. "Ah, if only everyone in your church and mine could break bread together as we are doing tonight."

"Our Lord called twelve followers, my friend, and I think that we would both agree that they must have all been very different," Father Fortis replied. "I mean, think of a tax collector like St. Matthew eating with Galilean fishermen like Saints Peter, James, and John. Let's just say that they probably didn't eat off the same menu."

Dom Philip smiled. "So maybe our differences, you Orthodox and we Catholics, are not as great as those of the apostles?"

"We are meant to be together, as our Lord prayed," Father Fortis replied as he reached for another piece of bread. "But we shouldn't worry about becoming the same. Perhaps we're coming to a time—finally—when we will begin to love our differences."

Dom Philip looked down at this plate. With his fork, he dragged the few remaining pieces of linguini together, but then seemed to lose interest.

"I have a confession to make, Father Fortis," he said, pausing for a moment before adding, "Maybe the best way of explaining what I mean is to say that the Vatican is picking up the check for our meal."

"Then by all means, let's order another bottle of this *Frascati*," Father Fortis said. "From what I hear, we won't come close to breaking the bank. The Vatican bank, that is."

The smile left Dom Philip's well-worn face as he wiped his mouth with some finality and folded the napkin before him. "Father Fortis, the Vatican would very much appreciate your looking into some nasty business in Venice."

Father Fortis laid the piece of bread down. "You will have to explain, my friend."

"There have been at least three break-ins at Venetian churches in the last five weeks. By itself, that isn't unusual. Venice is peppered with smaller churches, and the security at them as elsewhere in Italy is quite inadequate. But there are two features of these burglaries that are very troubling. And I must warn you. Some of what I am going to tell you is already common knowledge, while some is strictly confidential. Do you understand?"

Father Fortis' thoughts were spinning. To visit Venice before returning to his Ohio monastery was always part of his plans. He promised his close friend Lt. Christopher Worthy that he would visit his daughter Allyson, who was beginning an internship in that city. In addition, he knew Venice to be the most Byzantine of the Italian cities and suspected that he would never again have such a chance to see the treasures of the famous city.

"I have no problem keeping confidences," Father Fortis replied. "But I still don't see how I can be of help."

"What is very soon to be common knowledge, if it isn't already, is that the objects targeted by the thief or thieves are not works of art or even altar pieces, even though some are gold, silver, or encrusted with precious jewels. No, what was taken in each case is hard to understand. I am talking about relics, Father."

"Relics? But why?" Father Fortis asked.

"That's exactly what the police are wondering. The reliquaries that hold the relics—many of the reliquaries are gold or silver, some encrusted with precious stones of some considerable value—have been left open. Missing are pieces of bones."

"Important relics?"

Dom Philip shook his head. "Certainly not the relics of St. Mark from San Marco. But relics of early Christian saints, all, and perhaps this is important, from the Christian East. A foot bone of St. Lucia would be the most prized."

Father Fortis took more than a sip of the wine and considered what Dom Philip was saying. The stealing of relics was a major activity in the Middle

Ages, as was the false "finding" and selling of relics associated with famous saints. But in a secular age that found holiness to be far less important than success, relics became, at best, curiosities for tourists.

Dom Philips leaned forward and lowered his voice. "So now I will share the confidential part. This comes from what I shall call a friend in the Venice police."

"A friend of the Vatican, you mean."

Dom Philip nodded. "Scandals of late have certainly hurt the Holy See, but we still know how to gather information."

Father Fortis imagined that the Vatican has about as many "friends" around the world as the CIA.

Dom Philip cast a furtive glance at the tables near them. At one, two young children were being restrained by their parents and spoiled with candy by their grandparents. At another, lovers were holding hands across the table while lifting their wine glasses for a toast. Their section's waiter was leaning against a far wall while watching women walk by outside.

"About seven weeks ago, three Russian monks, Orthodox, of course, arrived in Venice," Dom Philip whispered. "Their leader, one Brother Sergius, purports to be an ecclesiastical historian. That was easy to check out, of course. He does have an advanced degree from St. Petersburg. His specialty is the Fourth or Fifth Crusade, depending on how they are numbered. But that crusade is the most ignoble one, where largely Venetian troops forgot about the Holy Land and pillaged Constantinople instead. The long and short of it is that Brother Sergius has given a few talks for the Orthodox community in Venice. His theme has been the widespread ransacking of Constantinople and the transferring, shall we say, of many sacred objects to Venice at that time."

Father Fortis pondered how the Vatican learned what a Russian monk said at a small gathering of Orthodox folk in Venice. What didn't the Vatican know?

"Did this Brother Sergius specifically mention relics from Constantinople that ended up in Venice?" he asked.

"Yes, but no more than altarpieces, bronzes, or icons. And there have been no thefts of those. Just the relics."

"So the concern is that the Russians may be 'stealing back' the relics of Eastern saints taken by the Venetians in the twelfth century. But if the Vatican and the police suspect that, then surely their rooms have been searched."

"Unofficially, yes, of course," Dom Philip admitted. "But the searchers found nothing suspicious. Just monastic robes and books."

Although Father Fortis was sure of the answer, he asked the question anyway. "And just what do you want me to do?"

"Please don't be offended, Father Fortis, but we already know that you are traveling to Venice after the conference."

"Yes, but that is for a short layover to visit the daughter of a close friend."

"Yes, of course. But if you agree, we would like you to stay longer, at the Orthodox Center, in fact. You would be there as a scholar in residence, continuing your research on Byzantine chant in the West. From there, you could assess the Russians without raising suspicions."

"That can be arranged?" Father Fortis asked.

"If you agree—again, I want you to know that you can refuse—but if you agree, it has already been arranged."

How long *has* this been in the works, Father Fortis wondered.

"As you know, Dom Philip, I have taken a vow of obedience to my abbot. I am not in charge of my comings and goings. And, as with you, my personal preferences are not considered."

Dom Philip grimaced.

"Ah," Father Fortis understood. "That has also been arranged, I see."

"Only if you agree," Dom Philip assured him. "But yes, we used the proper channels to receive your abbot's permission. And please don't assume false modesty here. We, that is to say, the Vatican, knows of your part in solving crimes with a Detroit police officer named Christopher Worthy."

The amazement that Father Fortis felt at the Vatican's tentacles of informants was giving way to irritation.

"And was my invitation to speak at the conference also part of the Vatican's plan?"

Dom Philip sat back as if struck and shook his head. "Absolutely not, Father. I know the Orthodox sometimes accuse the papal bureaucracy of trying to play the part of the Holy Spirit. And sometimes that criticism has been well-founded. But from our point of view, all the branches of the Vatican, even the more clandestine ones, exist only to cooperate with that same spirit. So please believe me on this, Father. Until we saw the program for the conference, we did not realize the opportunity that your being here in Italy afforded both of us."

"Both of us?" Father Fortis asked.

"I use the term 'us' deliberately. The increasingly cordial relations between both our churches, Orthodox and Catholic, could experience a major setback if the Russian monks are up to mischief in Venice."

Dom Philip looked all of his seventy years, his bald head creased with wrinkles, as he gazed pleadingly at Father Fortis over his folded hands.

"I believe that we are both men of faith, Father Fortis. So let me say what I strongly believe, that your being in Italy at this very time is nothing short of divine providence. The only remaining question is this: do you also believe that God wants *you* to help?"

Chapter Two

The next morning, in slacks that fit fashionably tight to her hips and thighs, Allyson arrived at the *Questura*. She approached the uniformed woman at the desk and announced in her practiced Italian, carefully rolling her r's, that she had a meeting with *Ispettore* Ruggiero.

She was somewhat disappointed when the woman informed Allyson in more than passable English that her supervisor would be waiting in the second doorway on the left.

As she knocked on the door, she wondered what *Ispettore* Ruggiero would look like. Would he be handsome like Al Pacino and Robert DeNiro, someone whom she would have an instant crush on, or someone short like Danny DiVito? The man who opened the door to her knock looked instead like a tall German, with fair hair that was turning to grey at the temples and even some pink in his cheeks. But his lavender shirt and deep purple tie, with glasses frames to match, were pure Italian. He looks kind, she concluded, but not "crush material."

With the one inadequate window, the metal filing cabinets and what appeared to be framed commendations on the walls, the office was oddly like her father's in Detroit. Would *Ispettore* Ruggiero remind her of her father in other ways?

The inspector pointed to a seat and in English less polished than the woman's at the desk, said, "Please, please sit. Welcome to Venezia."

Seating himself behind a desk burdened with files, Ruggiero asked if her travels were acceptable and if she found acceptable lodging. He pronounced each syllable of "acceptable" slowly, as if he practiced the word that morning as much as Allyson practiced her Italian.

Once the acceptability of Allyson's domestic situation was established and once Allyson provided her cell phone number to her supervisor, Ruggiero rose to stand up behind his chair.

"Things have changed a bit since we last communicated," he began.

Allyson's heart sank. Had the internship washed out for some reason? Was she, after all, little more to Ruggiero than a tourist?

"I hope that you will find the new situation acceptable. It will seem very odd, I am sure, even when I explain."

That sounds better, Allyson thought. A "new situation" hinted that she still had an assignment, maybe even a more challenging one.

"You will still be our, what you call it in English, our 'point person' with American and British visitors. The duty to investigate fraud, as I presented them in our emails, will remain the same."

Ruggiero paused to push his glasses farther up his nose. "But we will need you also for reasons that have risen, or maybe the word is 'arisen,' in the last four weeks."

So more responsibility, Allyson thought. Why doesn't he just tell me?

"You have no reason to be following the recent news of our city, have you?" he asked.

"No, I haven't," Allyson replied, feeling a bit guilty. Was she being tested by her supervisor?

"Maybe you remember the name Lorraine LaPurcell?"

Allyson thought for a moment. "I know I've heard the name before, in the States, but I can't recall why."

"Ms. LaPurcell received a medal of honor at last year's Film Festival here in Venezia. For her outstanding acting career, I am told."

"Now I remember," Allyson replied. "She's an actor from the seventies or early eighties."

Ruggiero offered a brief smile. "Long ago for someone your age."

The smile just as quickly left his face. "Her body, it was found in one of our smaller canals four weeks ago, over in the *sestiere* of Dorsoduro. She fall, maybe, from her third story hotel window."

"How awful! No, I hadn't read that. You said that she received an award here in Venice. Had she remained in Venice for the past year?"

Ruggiero tapped his fingers on the back of his chair. "No. No one seems to know why she return. She check into the hotel two weeks before her death under another name, her real name—Linda Johnson. And this hotel, well, it is far below acceptable standards for movie stars. Especially for American movie star," he added.

Allyson's heart jumped again. Is he telling me this because I will be involved in the case?

"Suicides are not uncommon here in Venice," Ruggiero said. "Thankfully, murders are rare."

"Did she leave a note?"

"No, no note. But the autopsy, it reveals two very odd, what I would call unacceptable, things," he said. "Her liver had much cancer, so there, perhaps, is motive. And she also had a recent scar on her abdomen."

"Surgery, then," Allyson concluded.

"Except that no one, not her American family, her doctors in your country, or the medical community in Venice has any record of the procedure."

Allyson had a sudden desire to channel her father's genius, his ability to pose the right question in the case of a suspicious death. But I am not my father, she thought.

"As I said, suicides we have in Venice. But then last Thursday, we had happen something that maybe in English is a coincidence too much."

"Another movie star?"

"No, but another body. This also an American, but an auto maker general—no, that is not the word—a boss from your Detroit. Do you know the name James Kuiper?"

"I think everyone in Detroit has heard of him. You say he died last week here in Venice?"

"By an overdose of sedatives. No note, but again strange findings in the autopsy. Cancer of the bladder, in this case."

"And a recent scar?" Allyson asked.

"Yes, just above one of his kidneys. And again, no record anywhere of hospital stay or visit to clinic."

So what do they expect of me, an intern, Allyson asked herself again.

"No doubt you are wondering why I tell you these things, yes?" he asked. Without waiting for an answer, he continued, "The family in Detroit has made a request of us. Ordinarily, I would not hesitate to accept such an offer. What they request is perfectly… acceptable. But as it involves you, Ms. Worthy, I wanted to ask, no, consult with you before I decide."

"How could it concern me?" Allyson asked.

"Because they have asked that your father, Lt. Christopher Worthy, be accepted by us as a consultant or partner in the investigation."

Allyson felt her heart sink. She would be in her father's shadow. In Venice. In her city. It wasn't fair.

"Of course, my father should come if that is what the Kuiper family wants."

"But is it what you want, Ms. Allyson Worthy?"

"I don't think that should matter, one way or another, *Ispettore*," she said, the last word uttered with perfect Italian inflection. "I will concentrate on the pickpocketing and other scams. My father will be on a completely different case."

"Ah, but no," Ruggiero replied. "Even before we received the family's request, we assign you, for reasons that I will share with you in due time, to work also on these two cases. For some reason that we do not know, the superrich of your country are coming to Venice to kill themselves. So what we are asking is if the two of you can work with one another. Can you do that?"

The question twisting in Allyson's mind was different. Can my father work with me?

Chapter Three

On Tuesday, four days into her internship, Allyson met Father Fortis, Nick to her, on *La Giudecca*, an island in the lagoon so close to Venice proper that it is treated as a distinct *sestiere*, or neighborhood. The word "mainland" has no meaning for Venice, as the city is a series of islands off the true mainland of the Veneto. Automobiles can reach the most western *sestiere* of Venice, Cannaregio, thanks to a bridge that runs from Mestre, a rundown and industrial city of the Veneto region. From Cannaregio, Venetians and tourists move either by foot, by water buses called *vaporetto*, other watercraft, or by gondolas.

Allyson could see Father Fortis waiting at the *vaporetto* landing on the *Giudecca*. As he waved, she laughed as she realized once again that it would be very hard to miss him, his height and massive frame, along with his heavy black beard, setting him apart from most of the Venetian men.

Coming off the vaporetto, Allyson was engulfed in Father Fortis' massive arms and lifted off the ground.

"Yikes, put me down, Nick," she gasped.

He obeyed and stood looking at her. "You've changed, my dear. I would recognize you anywhere, but you've definitely changed. Your hair is much shorter, for one, and, can I say this as a priest, you are more womanly? Has it really been an entire year?"

"A little more than a year and a half. I'm in my sophomore year of college. But my haircut is new. My roommate took me to her *parrucchiere*—that's Italian for hairdresser. Like it?"

"Well, of course. The young men of Venice better watch out. Allyson is in town!"

"Then you are blind, Nick. The women of Venice are out of my league. I swear this city seems like a movie set."

Father Fortis took her arm and led her from the pier to the sidewalk. As he did so, Allyson noticed that he looked over his shoulder, as if to see who else departed the *vaporetto* with her. "Our restaurant is near, but I thought that we'd walk a bit."

"I knew you were coming, Nick, but I didn't know that you knew Venice. *La Giudecca* is a bit out of the way."

"Ah, so that's how you pronounce it. Actually, my dear, you've been in Venice longer than I have. But 'out of the way' was what I wanted, so I checked a map, a *vaporetto* timetable, and a restaurant guide. This area seemed perfect."

"That's a bit mysterious, Nick."

Instead of clarifying, Father Fortis asked about Allyson's internship and her living arrangements.

When she described where she lived and worked, she saw Father Fortis' eyebrows jump. "That's very close to where I am staying. That's not good."

"And now you're even more mysterious. I expect you to explain sometime tonight why we're not meeting in our own neighborhood," she said.

With another glance over his shoulder, Father Fortis nodded. "While nothing would please me more than to run into you in our neighborhood, if that happens, Allyson, I must ask you to pretend that we don't know one another. And yes, I will explain more tonight, but there will be plenty of time for that. Tell me how you like Venice."

They turned right at the next narrow lane and walked toward the center of the island. At the end of the walkway, Allyson could see the lagoon.

"Do you have a dream place, Nick?" she asked in reply. "I mean, is there some place that you go in your imagination when you're feeling... I don't know, maybe when you're feeling totally happy or totally bummed out?"

As they came to the end of the walkway, Father Fortis again took her arm and steered her to the right. "There's where we're eating tonight. It's famous for its seafood, but then all the Venetian restaurants seem to make that claim. But about my dream place, well, I'll probably surprise you. Two weeks ago, I would have described my favorite spot as Santorini, a Greek island where my family is from."

Allyson remembered why she loved this man. Nick never questioned her thoughts, but always seemed to think along with her. No wonder he's a good priest, she thought.

"So what happened in the past two weeks that changed your mind?" she asked.

"Rome is what happened, my dear. Or I should be more specific, I fell in love with the Abbey of the Three Fountains."

"I've never heard of it."

He stopped and with her looked out over the water. On the island and off on the mainland, the lights of the evening were blinking on. "Nor had I, Allyson. But when I was at this conference, I made friends with some Catholic monks. They took me there."

Who wouldn't befriend Nick, she thought. "So what is so special about these three fountains?"

"Absolutely nothing. But it's a Trappist monastery now, with three churches. Tradition says that the churches are built on the site of Roman barracks, the very place where St. Paul was imprisoned and ultimately martyred by being beheaded. Of course, this is a legend, but they say the blessed saint's head bounced three times, and from each place it bounced, a spring arose."

"That sounds awful, Nick."

Father Fortis laughed. "For some reason, that is, by far, the most peaceful place I've ever been. You enter a gate off a noisy Roman street and walk down this avenue lined with eucalyptus trees to an old medieval gate. Beyond the gate sit these three very old churches. And it was not just quiet, but still. I felt I was entering another world, a place where faith—St. Paul's, not mine—forever found some divine peace. I could have stayed there for only God knows how long."

Allyson nodded. "That's what Venice is for me, Nick. I've always dreamed about coming here. And yes, I know that I just got here, but Venice is more beautiful and haunting than I could ever imagine."

Father Fortis patted her arm. "How lucky for me, then, to be with you in your earthly paradise."

"Yes, except for one small development, life is perfect here."

"And what is this new development, my dear?" Father Fortis asked, as they strolled toward the lights of the restaurant.

"That's my mystery, Nick. I'll explain mine after you explain yours."

Christopher Worthy leaned back and felt the soft leather pillow behind him. I could get used to flying first-class, he thought. He could not remember the last time that he stretched out his six-foot-three-inch frame on a plane without jamming his knees into the seat in front of him. And he didn't even have to ask himself when was the last time that someone offered him a glass of champagne.

If he could not manage to fall asleep on the flight to Amsterdam, he would at least close his eyes and make some sense of the last three dizzying days. His superior, Captain Betts, asked to see him after his shift on the previous Monday. There was nothing particularly unusual about that, and he certainly felt none of the dread as he might have in the past. The truth was that his days of avoiding a superior who needed to go over every fine detail of his cases seemed over. With Captain Betts, Worthy was having the happier task of getting used to someone who trusted him and his rather unorthodox ways.

When he entered Betts' office, he found waiting for him an obviously grieving middle-aged woman, a young man with a stoic face, and an even younger woman who had also been crying. He was introduced to the Kuiper family: Georgina, the mother; Lance, the college senior; and Darcy, a high school-age junior.

Once he heard the Kuiper name, he knew why the family was grieving. According to the morning's newspaper, the body of James Kuiper, noted Detroit auto magnate, was found in Venice, Italy, with all the evidence pointing to suicide. Worthy would likely have skipped over the story, had the mention of Venice not brought to mind his daughter Allyson's internship with the Venice police.

With handkerchief at the ready, Georgina Kuiper asked her son to speak for her.

"My father was dying of cancer, Lt. Worthy. He was given no more than six months to live, and so we were as thankful as a family could be, under the circumstances, when he said he wasn't going to spend the little good time he had left sitting around pitying himself."

Darcy, the daughter, drew closer to her mother and held her hand. Mrs. Kuiper tried to cover a sob with a cough.

"Dad and Mom took a lot of trips after the diagnosis. They went back to Seattle where they lived when they were first married, and then to Machu Picchu. Dad always wanted to see that."

The son gave his mother a glance before continuing. "About three weeks ago, he said that he wanted to visit where his family was from in the Netherlands one last time. That's where we thought he was; I mean, that's where he said he was when he talked to us on his phone. We had no idea that he was in Italy, in Venice, until the police notified us last night."

Worthy turned his attention on the wife. "Why did he go alone on this trip, Mrs. Kuiper?"

Georgina Kuiper shrugged. "It was what he wanted. He said that I didn't know his Dutch relatives that well, and it would be easier for them to put him up if he visited alone. 'Less bother,' he said."

"Did he talk to any of you about returning home?" Worthy asked.

Once again, Lance took charge of the interview. "The Venice police asked us the same thing. Yes, he'd already ordered tickets for all of us to go on a cruise to the Caribbean."

Captain Betts remained silent, letting the family speak directly to Worthy.

So somehow, this has something to do with me, he thought. But his world was homicides, not suicides. As far as he could tell from the newspaper article, the evidence of an empty sedative bottle next to the body made the verdict pretty obvious.

"Did he ever show up at his relatives' in the Netherlands?" Worthy asked.

"He never told them he was coming," Lance replied.

Captain Betts added, "We checked with the airline. He was only in the Netherlands, in Amsterdam, for an hour to change flights for Venice."

Then at least we know he wasn't kidnapped or coerced to end up in Italy, Worthy thought.

"How about you?" he'd asked, looking at the high-school daughter. "As you think back, did your father say anything at all that would suggest why he was in Venice and why he …why he died there?"

The girl shook her head. "Daddy and Mommy took us all to Italy about four years ago, before he got sick. I remember Daddy hated Venice. He said the canals stunk with garbage, and the food wasn't as good as in Florence."

Georgina Kuiper looked up at her daughter. "I forgot about that, but you're right. Jim did hate that city. So why …?" her voice trailed off.

"And before he left, did Mr. Kuiper seem different—in lower spirits about his diagnosis?"

"No, no, not at all," Mrs. Kuiper insisted. "That's what's so terrible. Jim was a fighter, ever since he sold cars in Seattle. Jim never just gave up on anything. When we got the diagnosis, I remember him sitting quietly for a few moments. Then he turned to me and said, "I have some living to do, love, don't I?"

"That's why we need your help, Lieutenant," Lance offered as his mother began to cry softly. "Dad wouldn't have … you know, gone out this way."

"Lance, I know that it seems that way now…" Worthy said.

"I know other people can say the same thing in this situation, but there's something more. The Italian police said that Dad had a fresh scar on his back, by one of his kidneys. They asked what we knew about that. Lieutenant Worthy, that's complete news to us. We know nothing about that, and neither do Dad's doctors."

"What about the doctors in Venice?"

"The Venice police say there are no records of any procedure being done there either," Lance explained. "They especially checked the cancer specialists."

"There is just too much wrong with this whole picture, Mr. Worthy," the daughter added. "Will you help?"

"What do you think that I can do?" he'd asked, glancing up at Captain Betts as well as the family.

"Would you please go to Venice and find out what happened to my husband?" Georgina Kuiper pleaded.

Go to Venice? He heard a NO so loud in his head that he wondered if the others in the room could sense it. But how could he tell this family that he couldn't go because his daughter was in Venice and working as an intern with the same police? How could he explain that his daughter wouldn't want him there, would resent him coming, and would be right to do so?

Instead, he brought up the ever-present boundary issue. "Police departments don't like outsiders butting in. Captain Betts will back me up on that."

"But you did that in New Mexico, when you found that serial killer," Lance interjected.

"And I have to tell you that they weren't crazy about my being there. And that would be even more so with a foreign police department."

"Will you at least let Captain Betts find out about that?" Georgina pleaded. "Would you go if the Venice police agreed?"

WORTHY LOOKED OUT THE WINDOW OF the plane onto a vast Canadian forest below. The Venice police agreed and, from what Captain Betts shared, did so willingly. As she discovered in the phone exchange with an Inspector Ruggiero, James Kuiper was the second mysterious suicide of a wealthy American in the last month. The Venice police were eager to find out why rich Americans were coming to their city to kill themselves.

But Worthy still did not agree. He wanted to know Allyson's reaction. Would she not hate his coming to the very city and department within which she was working? Yes, he told himself that she was working on minor crimes of the cities involving English-speaking tourists, but certainly they would see each other. The question was, would they see each other more than Allyson could stand? She ran away once. Was he tempting fate to suddenly arrive in Venice?

He wished that he could have touched base with his friend, Father Fortis, who he knew was in Venice to see Allyson for a couple of days before returning home. But he had no way of contacting his friend, and there was no guarantee that Allyson would have told Nick of the new situation.

He settled for leaving two voice mail messages for Allyson. When he opened his phone yesterday, he saw that she had left him a voicemail.

"Dad, I know you are wondering where I stand on all this. Do I want you to come? I honestly don't know. Should you come? Yes, you should. Now the big question. Will you come knowing that I have also been assigned to the cases?"

He tried to call her back, but again she wasn't picking up his calls. He would therefore have to wait to ask her in person the one question that her voicemail left him with.

And that question would not be an easy question to ask. If he learned one thing about his daughter, it was that she would certainly be offended if he in any way doubted her qualifications. But assigning a college intern from America to work on the suicide investigation of a millionaire—really?

Chapter Four

"Oh, my Lord, that's wonderful!" Father Fortis said, after he heard the news about Christopher Worthy coming to Venice.

Allyson tried to smile, but she suspected that even Father Fortis could see that the effort was half-hearted.

"Of course, I'm being selfish when I say that," Father Fortis added, crossing himself. "I forget that your father's presence anywhere means that a family is grieving the loss of a loved one."

Allyson said nothing but looked out over the lagoon.

"Ah," he said, "I see. It took me a moment to realize what you meant before when you said that your life in Venice is perfect except for a new development. I'm sorry, I thought you and your father were on better terms."

Allyson speared the last of her shrimp and ate it. "That's probably a fair statement, but remember, Nick, I've been away at college for almost a year. Dad and I have done better since we're not seeing each other all that much. And just because I'm interested in criminology doesn't mean that we're all that alike." After a moment, she added, "Or maybe we're too much alike."

"And now it seems that your father is breaking into your personal paradise. Is that it?"

She nodded. "He's not just coming to Venice, remember. He'll be there every day at the *Questura*."

Father Fortis looked puzzled, so she quickly translated the word as "police station."

"My supervisor even has us working together on this important case." She looked out again toward the softly lapping tide.

"I think I understand," he said. "He's breaking back into your life. But you have to admit that this isn't exactly his choice, Allyson."

She nodded and took another sip of the wine. "It's just the unknowing that has me confused."

"What do you mean, my dear?"

"As you said, things are somewhat better between Dad and me. But this new arrangement, us seeing each other, working together—I see only old problems coming up."

"But you're not the same girl who ran away, are you? "

Allyson stared down at her empty plate. What if I am that same girl, she thought. What if my Dad does something, says something, and I just have to take off?

"And your father is not the same person he was then, either," Father Fortis added. "The last thing he would want to do is push you away again."

Allyson tried to force a smile. "Okay, Nick, I'll give him a chance."

"Now tell me what you can about these suspicious deaths."

Allyson shared what she was told was common knowledge: the names of the victims, the similarity of their being in Venice surreptitiously, and of their similar diagnoses of terminal cancer.

"My, my. Lorraine LaPurcell," Father Fortis mused with a chuckle. "I think she was the first movie star that I fell in love with. My Marilyn Monroe, I guess. But certainly Lorraine LaPurcell can't have been her real name."

"You're right. Her real name is Linda Johnson, not nearly as sexy. But the media know her only as Lorraine LaPurcell."

"And what will be your part in the cases, Allyson?"

"You mean, what crumbs will my Dad leave me?" She shook her head. "I'm sorry. I had no call to say that."

Father Fortis patted her hand. "Might as well get that out now, before your Dad arrives, don't you think?"

"Thanks, Nick. I have this tendency to see a problem where there may not be one. I wish I could change that about myself."

"You're human, my dear, and let's face it; your Dad's coming is a bit of a shock. Now, without talking about your father, tell me what you'll be doing."

"What the newspapers don't know about the two deaths is that both Lorraine LaPurcell and James Kuiper had recent surgeries. Both had scars with intact sutures."

Father Fortis frowned. "What kind of surgery?"

"That's just it, Nick. The wounds don't lead to anything. They're not even near the location of their cancers. They are just these slices cut into their bodies, and then the stitches."

"That is odd," Father Fortis said. "And what are you supposed to find out?"

Allyson laughed softly. "No one outside the police department here is to know anything about me but that I'm an intern whose job it is to interview American and British tourists who've been pickpocketed or swindled. And I will still be doing that. But that's now not just my cover. But they also want me to hang out with my roommate in clubs in the city, to meet locals my own age."

"Is that who they suspect?"

"My roommate is a nurse at the hospital. From what I'm told, a lot of young people work there. So they want me to be an innocent American intern whose knows hardly any Italian and is here in Venice on kind of a lark. Apparently, that's about par for how most college students from the States act."

"I saw some of that behavior in Rome," Father Fortis said with a frown.

"Only my roommate and the police have to know that I've been studying Italian for the past year and that I have a pretty good ear for the language. If I act dizzy enough—hey, don't smile that way. I can act dizzy. Anyway, they're hoping I might pick up something."

"Because the sutures suggest something medical, is that what they're thinking?" Father Fortis asked.

Allyson nodded and saw her assignment in a new light. The cloud that hung over her since she first talked with *Ispettore* Ruggiero began to lift. Someone with some medical training made those incisions or knows someone who could be involved. Going clubbing with Sylvia, pretending to be a bit flaky, and improving my Italian while keeping my ears open—yes, I can do that. And my father can't, she realized.

She smiled with renewed happiness and thought, this is not the first time talking with Nick has settled me. Is this what confession would be like, at least with him?

"Now it's your turn, Nick," she said. "Why are we hiding out like spies out here *on La Giudecca*? What's your mystery?"

WHILE ALLYSON AND FATHER FORTIS WERE ordering an after-dinner sweet and coffee, *Ispettore* Ruggiero was having his own dinner with his wife interrupted by a phone call.

"*Pronto*," he said into his *telefonino*. On the other end was the coroner, which puzzled the *Ispettore*, as the coroner already issued his preliminary and seemingly very thorough report on James Kuiper. Why would he be calling at this hour?

Ruggiero's wife was married to a policeman long enough to know that any objection on her part to these intrusions was wasted effort. An inspector was considered always on duty.

The coroner's message was more than an addendum to his earlier report. In fact, Ruggiero quickly understood that the investigations into the two American suicides had just taken yet another surprising turn. An assistant at the local morgue, a recent medical school graduate eager for recognition and early promotion, took, with the coroner's approval, samples of the skin around the two mysterious incisions.

The assistant's report, delivered just minutes before to the coroner, made even less sense than the puzzling initial report. The dermatological analysis of the skin cell samples revealed that the incisions were both made over recent scar tissue. In other words, the coroner stated, both of the incisions and sutures noted in the autopsy were in fact cuttings on skin still bearing the marks of an earlier and very recent incision.

Even though *Ispettore* Ruggiero knew the answer to the question, he posed it nonetheless. "And you are sure that these incisions suggest surgical procedures in both cases? They couldn't be stab wounds, for example?"

"*Non è possibile*," the coroner assured him. "The cuts are too shallow and too uniform."

"But this makes even less sense," Ruggiero observed.

"My duty is to report what we find, *Ispettore*..."

"Yes, I know," Ruggiero interrupted. "And my job is to explain what you find."

"*Sì, sì, precisamente,*" the coroner agreed before hanging up.

Ruggiero shook his head slowly and pushed his plate away, his appetite gone. What would compel anyone, especially American millionaires, to come to Venice, check in secretly to two of Venice's cheapest hotels, and allow cuts to be made on their bodies, only to have the same site on their bodies violated again?

For the first time since James Kuiper's body was found, Ruggiero began to wonder if the two suspicious deaths could be more than suicides. But almost as quickly, his logical mind concluded that the coroner's report supported neither murder nor suicide.

Father Fortis sat back from the tiramisu and exhaled deeply. "On that fateful day, when I stand before St. Peter, he is going to ask how I, a monk, ended up so fat."

"You'll have to remind him about all the time you've spent playing detective, and how much people open up to you over food," Allyson said.

"I don't expect St. Peter to be convinced," he replied. "He'll have a perfect right to ask why I didn't stay put at the monastery instead of trying to figure out who steals relics."

He was not sure before he met Allyson at the *vaporetto* pier how much of his own mystery he would tell her. The one demand that he knew that he had to make of her was that she should never tell anyone his true reason for staying in Venice and under no circumstances should she let on about their friendship should they meet by accident.

But when she shared so openly the cases that she was working on and then the news of her father's imminent arrival, he realized that he had to tell her much more, given that she, not he, would be the one to relay his situation to Worthy.

And if, as he sensed, it was good for Allyson to share her concerns about her cases and her father's coming, he also felt that certain aspects of his situation became clearer as he told her of his mission in Venice and of his subsequent first encounter with the three Russian monks.

His initial impressions of the Russians told him little. Brother Nilus seemed to have little knowledge of English or Greek, so Father Fortis knew him only as the quiet one of the three thin monks.

For it was their unhealthy thinness that first struck Father Fortis. They all looked like monks who fasted not as the exception, but as the rule. Yet, when he observed them at meal time at the center, they all ate ravenously. Perhaps, he thought, their large appetites only proved his point, that the three experienced malnourishment for most of their lives.

The second monk, Brother Alexei, had a better command of English, but much of it was in the form of American slang. Maybe from watching B-movies, Father Fortis thought. While Brother Nilus looked beaten down by life, Brother Alexei's Slavic cheekbones and dark eyes struck Father Fortis as furtive. He also had a slight limp, caused by what seemed a shorter left leg, so that he bobbed as he walked.

While none of the three seemed capable of smiling, Brother Sergius displayed a constant scowl. Brother Sergius was the tallest of the three and always seemed to walk a step or two ahead of the others. His English was the best, and his grammar suggested academic work based on British rather than American speech.

Father Fortis made a point of waiting until his second day at the Center to introduce himself to the three monks. Immediately, Brother Sergius assumed the role of speaking for the three. Father Fortis was surprised to learn that Brother Sergius already knew of his attendance at the conference in Rome. He also sensed from the fair-haired Russian a whiff of disapproval when Father Fortis explained that the conference brought together Catholic and Orthodox monks.

During the short conversation, Father Fortis noted that Brother Alexei studied him from head to foot, while Brother Nilus stared at the floor. Are these three capable of robbery, he wondered. Father Fortis met other Orthodox, parish priests as well as monks and nuns, who thought of the 12th-century fifth crusade as a recent crime, the wound still open and festering. Would that memory, along with the anti-Catholic feeling that was attached to it, have led these three to consider it an act of faith to steal relics from Venice's Catholic churches?

But if the three stole the relics, what had they done with them? Where could three very Russian-looking monks in black robes hide relics in Venice?

When he voiced that same question to Allyson, she surprised him with a suggestion. "Then they must have an accomplice in Venice, someone local who can move around and not be noticed."

Of course, he thought. If the three stole the relics and could probably assume that they might be suspected, would they not pass the relics as quickly as possible into the hands of someone else? And that meant that he needed to not just keep an eye on the three monks but also observe whom they would meet.

And if there was an accomplice, that would mean that there could be more than the three Russians interested in his own presence in the city. "When we leave tonight," he said to Allyson, "I'm not going to take the same water taxi as you."

"I get it, but how will you meet my Dad?" Allyson asked. "You do plan to see him, don't you?"

"Of course, but we need to work something out, don't we?" he answered. "Can we agree to meet here at this restaurant?"

"It's sure out of the way," Allyson agreed. "But we'll still have to devise some coded message when we want to do that."

"Like what, my dear? I have a cell phone, but I won't always be sure that someone isn't overhearing our conversation."

"Let's try this," Allyson said. "When Dad or I want to see you, I'll call and leave a message that the book you wanted is in."

"Good. Given my research, that should work. And if I want to meet with the two of you?"

Allyson dictated her cell phone number. "Why don't you leave a message saying you have another chapter of your research for me to read?"

"That's brilliant," Father Fortis said, as the two left the restaurant. "Now I feel like a real spy, my dear."

Chapter Five

Grateful for her short haircut, Allyson sat outside next to the pilot of the high-speed police launch. Behind her, in a small cabin area below deck, sat Inspector Ruggiero. Ruggiero insisted on coming to the airport personally to transport their guest to the apartment rented by the *Questura*.

That morning, Inspector Ruggiero shared the coroner's new report. Almost immediately, she felt some pressure, from where she wasn't sure, to sift through the evidence before her father arrived. But what kind of sense did an incision on top of another incision make? The only idea that came to her was from a newspaper story that described the addiction of some people to surgery. Some addicts, she read, had undergone more than twenty unnecessary operations.

But the more she thought about the account, the more she had to admit that such an obsession hardly fit these two cases. There were no other recent scars on the two bodies, and these two millionaires, she reminded herself, killed themselves soon after those incisions were made.

As Inspector Ruggiero boarded the launch, he waved a folder at Allyson. "Your father has a very impressive resume. Excellent record of solving complicated cases. Your family must be very proud of him."

Allyson bit her tongue. Their family broke apart under the strain of her Dad's obsessive way of working cases and forgetting everything else. "We paid, we paid," she whispered to herself.

But as the boat moved away from the quay, she resolved to hold on to what Father Fortis told her, that her Dad had changed since the divorce, as had she. Why couldn't her father's arrival in Venice, and their work together, be the start of something better between them?

The boat hit the wake of a ferry boat, its bow lifting out of the water before slapping down with a thud. Who am I kidding, she thought. I'm a lowly intern and my Dad is a famous detective. If I were just another American student working at the station and not his daughter, would the great Lieutenant Christopher Worthy even pay attention to me?

As they rounded a final bend and approached the airport's boat landing area, Allyson saw her father standing at the end of the dock. She took the time it was taking for the boat to approach through the slower "no wake" area to appraise her father. How would I describe him, if I never saw him before, she thought. Well, he was tall compared to Italian men, although not much taller than Inspector Ruggiero. And like me, he never seems to gain any weight, she continued, repeating a line her mother used to say in envy. His ears are too big for his face, she thought with a smile, but he still has a thick head of sandy hair. When the phrase from some cheap novel came to mind, that her father had a "strong jawline," she laughed. I don't think a person can ever really say what her own parents look like, she concluded.

But he does look older, she added as the boat nosed to the edge of the dock.

Before she could move, Inspector Ruggiero moved deftly around her and jumped up onto the dock. She could hear him introduce himself and then apologize for making him wait. Did his plane arrive early, he asked.

Christopher Worthy was giving his full attention to Ruggiero, Allyson noticed. But just as the inspector picked up her father's suitcase to hand it to the police pilot, her father turned his attention to her. For a moment, he didn't say anything as if he were waiting for her permission to step onto the boat.

"Hi, Dad," she offered. She stepped aside and pointed down to the hatch. "You can sit down there with *Ispettore* Ruggiero. I know you two have a lot to talk about."

As Christopher Worthy jumped down to the deck, he gave the boat a once-over. "She looks a bit faster than our old speedboat at the lake."

Good move, she thought. Their family's life at the lake was a safe place to start. The old place was the one thing to survive the divorce intact. Neither her mother nor her father wanted to sell it, and so they established a sharing arrangement of the place. Of course, they wouldn't be at the cabin at the same time, but Allyson found it maddening that neither parent took down even one of the family pictures. Why either of them wanted to be reminded of happier days was only one of the mysteries of the divorce that Allyson thought she would never solve.

As her father edged past her on the boat, he stopped to give her a hug that lingered. Seeing Ruggiero's eyes on her, she hugged him back and immediately wondered when that last happened.

"You like it here, don't you, Ally?" he asked as he took a seat next to Ruggiero. As the pilot began to slowly back the boat away from the dock, her father added, "I remember that book you had on Italy. You took it everywhere."

"I didn't know you noticed the book," she replied, and then immediately regretted how much the comment sounded like an accusation.

Her father looked out the side window at the lagoon. "Oh, I noticed," he said. "The pictures of Venice were all dog-eared, right?"

As the boat accelerated noisily into the open water, she nodded in acknowledgement.

Although she would be happy with their initial meeting being short, she knew that she had to honor Father Fortis' request, to tell her father of Nick's remaining in Venice, his strong desire to see her father, but also why that meeting had to be carefully arranged.

She could overhear a few words of the conversation between Ruggiero and her father. She heard the words "coroner's report" and could deduce the rest.

She looked back to see her father's set face, his left eyebrow raised as it did when he was in deep thought.

Here it comes, she thought. Here comes one of Detective Worthy's famous flashes of lightning, some new angle on the puzzle so amazing that Ruggiero, from that moment on, would never notice her.

But instead, the unexpected thought came to her. Again it was a memory, this time from her high school advanced biology class. The boy she secretly admired from a distance was in a hurry and botched the dissection of his fetal pig. Mr. Ebbeson, the teacher, demanded that he close the incision and redo it from the beginning.

Hmm, she wondered, could that explain the odd scars on the two millionaires? Was the first incision into both victims a mistake, with the second one a correction? If so, then it was possible that they were focusing, with the medical personnel of the city, on the wrong suspects. Whoever took a scalpel to Lorraine LaPurcell and James Kuiper had some medical experience, enough to explain the standard sutures, but not enough experience to properly perform the procedure.

If I am right, she thought with a thrill, we should be looking for an amateur, a bungler.

In the library of the Center, Father Fortis looked up from his notebook to check his watch. Assuming Worthy's plane landed, he uttered a prayer of thanksgiving for his friend's safe travel.

He thought back on their friendship, one begun by chance and then forged through two murder investigations. Father Fortis first met Christopher Worthy because of the murder of a novice at his monastery in Ohio.

Father Fortis' first assessment of the man who was to become his closest friend was that Worthy was a man in trouble. Even before his marriage began to dissolve, Worthy was clearly a man who was spiritually if not morally damaged by the horrors of his job. The son of a Baptist minister, Worthy was a man of faith until he solved two cases, homicides of children, that brought him notoriety in Detroit even as they took him over some cliff.

As a priest, Father Fortis could feel the vacuum of belief in Worthy. But as a friend and homicide detective, Worthy was in a class of his own for being able to enter the minds of killers.

In their first case together, they tracked down a killer in New Mexico who targeted nuns and monks. In the second case, the two of them had to contend with the murder of an old and beloved priest of Detroit. While Father Fortis admitted that his own contribution in each case was not insignificant, his appreciation for Worthy's unorthodox methods of tracking and pursuit grew through both experiences.

He thought of Allyson's trepidation at her father's coming. Yes, she knew as well as he did that Worthy commanded both frustration and ultimately awe from anyone who worked with him. In his own department in Detroit, he was accused of being a "headline hunter" whose preference to work alone won him few friends.

But Father Fortis knew that Worthy could, and did, count him as a friend. Although Worthy's faith did not survive his experiences as a detective, he had an impressive knack, from his childhood, for understanding religious communities and clergy. While Father Fortis knew instinctively that his friend would be immune to any clergyperson's attempts to reignite his moribund faith, he also knew that he spent more time, in their two cases together, discussing religious life and the inner workings of religious communities than he had with even his fellow monks. And whereas he once chastised himself, as a Christian monk, for his difficulty explaining the mysterious ways of God to others, he sensed with Christopher Worthy that this failure was part of the secret of their close bond.

And if Father Fortis sometimes worried that Worthy's exposure to the sordid side of religion would erode his friend's faith even more, he now took solace in the fact that what brought Worthy to Venice, the strange death of James Kuiper, had no apparent religious dimension. That puzzling death, along with the actress', seemed linked to the medical, not the religious, community.

Of course, he couldn't say the same about the mystery that brought him to Venice. The stealing of relics had religion stamped all over it. The relics would have no monetary value in the modern world, but their symbolic value in certain sects and religious circles was undeniable. He hated to think that the case would go cold until the relics turned up, if they ever did, in some reactionary group in Russia or some other Eastern European country.

He gazed down at his notebook and its entries about Byzantine chant. Secreted below that notebook was a second notebook to which he now turned. The pages here contained jottings in Greek under the headings of S, N, and A, the first initials of the three Russian monks. Although he could not be sure that Brother Sergius was ignorant of Greek, he thought it unlikely that any of the three could make much sense of his jottings.

To this point, the few entries in this notebook registered the times when the three monks appeared at the Center for meals or Divine Liturgy. Now that he detected the monks' quite consistent pattern of coming and going, he was able to plan his next step. He would position himself in a *taverna* across the narrow canal from the Orthodox church and follow the three monks to their lodgings.

And why does that matter, he asked himself as he looked at his watch again. He closed his notebooks and rose from the library table. Because the three monks, he said, answering his own question, were unlikely to have money of their own. Someone was paying their rent, and while their benefactor might be back in Russia, their Venetian landlord could also be a benefactor, or at least a person of interest.

He was indebted to Allyson for helping him make this connection. The Russians must have a contact outside the Center. And tonight he would take his first steps to bring that hidden person into the light of day.

Chapter Six

Christopher Worthy awoke at four in the morning, Venice time, and tried to orient himself to his new surroundings. The Venice police had put him up at an apartment near the *Questura*. With the exception of one or two of the bathroom fixtures, the apartment was not unlike what Detroit P.D. would provide for an out-of-town case consultant.

But Worthy had learned the hard way that the important cultural differences are not those on the surface. When he was sent to New Mexico to work on the disappearance of a Detroit college student, he found it all too easy to step on toes and offend the Hispanic and Native American cultures. And although Worthy sensed from his two meetings with Ruggiero that the inspector held no resentment for his presence, he also understood that Italy would present a far greater cultural adjustment than New Mexico had.

And there was the additional issue of working with his daughter. True, the chasm between them was lessened by his daughter's decision to pursue a career in law enforcement, but now, he worried, their working on the same case might reopen the old wounds. He could sense Allyson's guardedness at the airport, and he felt a hint of aggressiveness when she offered, at their last briefing with Ruggiero, her theory that the oddly layered scars pointed toward a far less accomplished suspect. It was hard for him not to feel that her aggressiveness was meant for him more than Ruggiero.

So, what do I do, he asked, as he got out of bed and gave up on the idea of falling back to sleep. It would be nearly eighteen hours before he accompanied Allyson to meet Father Fortis for dinner. What can I do in the meantime to contribute to this case without offending my Italian counterparts on the one hand and alienating my own daughter on the other?

The safest place to begin, he reckoned, was to study the photos of two hotel rooms, the ones where the two American millionaires died. While the scene of Lorraine LaPurcell's, or now Linda Johnson's, death four weeks earlier was cleared and turned back over to the landlord, the room used by James Kuiper was still controlled by the police and open, if necessary, to his personal inspection.

While brewing a cup of coffee, Worthy sat at a table in the kitchen area and opened the first of the two files that Ruggiero gave him. Flipping through English translations of the reports of the first responders, the doctor on duty in the emergency room of the hospital, and the coroner, he brought out the police photos of Kuiper and his hotel room.

While there are no standard guidelines for how the room of a suicide is different from the room of a homicide, Worthy knew that the way a person lived could, in some cases, relate to how that person died. On the most obvious level, a suicide note next to a body—there was none in Kuiper's case—held roughly the same credence that a ravaged room with multiple blood stains did for a homicide. Certainty, of course, was not possible, as a killer could forge a suicide note, even as a suicide could have been the subsequent result of a bloody confrontation with someone hours earlier.

And as he looked down at the photos from James Kuiper's room, Worthy knew that the family back in Detroit sent him to Venice because they wanted certainty, even as he knew that probability would be all that he could ever establish. So what did these photos suggest? What "probably" happened in this room?

Spotting the phone on the bedside table, Worthy first checked the records in the report of calls that Kuiper sent out or received in the room. None. But given that Kuiper used a cellphone, that could mean nothing. And his cellphone records, Worthy noted, listed only calls to his family in Detroit.

Worthy turned his attention to the photos and to two items that Worthy knew could be suggestive—Kuiper's glasses, if he wore them, and his shoes. If all the shoes were neatly stored in rows in a closet, and if Kuiper's glasses were folded neatly on the side table, such orderliness might suggest finality. That would indicate that the person was addicted to control or that the person wanted to leave this world with everything neatly in its place.

James Kuiper, it seemed from the list of personal effects, wore contacts, not glasses. Worthy circled the line of the police report that indicated that Kuiper's contacts were found in solution on the bedside table. Was that important? Did that suggest a man of habit or a man who intended to wake and look out on another day?

The meaning of Kuiper's shoes was harder to decipher. Slippers were sloppily left in the bathroom. Two pair of shoes were in the closet, but thrown there more than placed carefully. And there was one pair under the side of the bed with socks crammed into them.

Worthy next looked for Kuiper's wallet and keys. Both were on the bedside table, along with Kuiper's passport and what looked to be a Bible. Worthy flipped back through the reports to find that Kuiper's wallet contained over two hundred euros along with credit cards and photos of the family. If a photo was propped up on the bedside table or if it was lying down with the bottle of pills on top of it, that would tell a clearer story for Worthy. But there seemed nothing suggestive about what the police found in Kuiper's case.

The closet, too, revealed little. Based on what was hanging in the closet and what was stuffed into the laundry bag, Worthy estimated that the American brought enough shirts and pants for two or three weeks. Of possible interest was the fact that no piece of clothing bore European sizing. All seemed well-used and brought from the States.

The fatal dose, as well, came from medication brought from the States. The bottle of sedatives was empty, and that, along with the coroner's report on stomach content and blood analysis, pointed toward a no-fooling stab at suicide.

Worthy sat back and took several sips of his cooling coffee. The Kuipers want me to find something suspicious, something that would point toward homicide or at least misadventure. Do these photos show anything in support of their hope?

While nothing in the room screamed out for attention, Worthy did have to admit that the room itself seemed odd, at least for an American millionaire. The room was not simply basic, but clearly the worse for wear. The padding on one of the two chairs was coming loose at the side, and the carpet had several stains that suggested pets accompanied previous occupants. A broken piece on the headboard looked old, while the room's narrow windows faced neither canal nor lagoon, but rather the corroded downspouts on an adjacent building. While Kuiper could have seen little looking out, it was equally true that no one, from outside, could even have known that the room was occupied.

Worthy realized that he needed to see the room for himself, not because he thought the local police missed something, but to check out an impression that the photos left him. The room, Worthy realized, had all the telltale signs of being a hideout. But from what or whom was Kuiper hiding? Why did he lie to his family about the trip? Why did he come to Venice, a city that he clearly hated? And why did he have two incisions, one on top of the other, near his left kidney?

Turning his attention to the second case file, that of Lorraine LaPurcell or Linda Johnson, Worthy began by studying the photos of the corpse. Only with careful inspection could he link the publicity photo of the actress from a Venice film festival, a mere year before, with the pale and drawn face, sans make-up, her hair as tangled and matted as seaweed. The woman looked ten years older than in the photos, and Worthy sensed that that effect could not solely be attributed to the brackish water of the canal.

From a map of the twisting and turning city, Worthy was able to identify the location of LaPurcell's hotel. In an area on the other side of the city from James Kuiper's, the actress's hotel room in other ways was similarly sleazy. And while her window opened out to a narrow canal, into which she plunged or was pushed, Lorraine LaPurcell's view was to the gritty factories and shipyards.

He studied these photos as intensely as Kuiper's, based on the uselessness of personally visiting a room that was since occupied by who-knows-how-many guests, those keen on staying in the room of a famous American film star. The photos would have to establish to what extent the rooms of the victims were similar.

Worthy's first impression of the room in the photos was that the occupant stepped out for just a moment. The unmade bed and piled-up pillows still held the imprint of one body, undoubtedly the victim's. To the side of the bed, her puffy slippers sat askew on the floor.

Paper bags with opened food cartons covered a side table and spilled onto the floor. He flipped back to read the coroner's report of the stomach contents: calamari and seafood salad and cola were ingested in the victim's last three hours. So the food was most likely consumed at about nine p.m., given that the coroner estimated her death to have been near midnight. Her body was discovered in the canal at six the next morning by a city employee. Is someone intent on suicide likely to eat a full meal just three hours before, he wondered.

In the bathroom were more make-up bottles, a hairbrush, and a glass with a toothbrush inside. Towels lay crumpled upon the cracked linoleum floor, as if the woman recently showered.

Based on the photos, Worthy could establish little. If Lorraine LaPurcell killed herself, the state of the room suggested that she did so on an impulse. If she jumped to her death, something obviously became clear to her with crashing finality. Worthy searched the photos of the bed inch by inch. Off to the side of where she lay was a crumpled newspaper. Did she read something that sent her to her death? Worthy made a note to investigate that piece of evidence later. And in comparing the photos of the two different beds, he noted that in James Kuiper's room, there was what looked to be a Bible on the bedside table. In Lorraine LaPurcell's room, however, there was no Bible visible.

He looked at the photos of the actress' room a second time with the murder angle in mind. Did the state of the room support the possibility that Lorraine LaPurcell was pushed from the window? Certainly, the room offered no sign of struggle. Could someone she knew perhaps have lured her to the window and surprised her from behind? Again he checked the coroner's report. No sign of recent intercourse, which matched the single body imprint on the bed. So, if she had a lover, sex was not the prelude to her death.

Worthy leaned back and yawned. Yes, now that the sun was starting to rise, he was sufficiently tired to return to bed. To push away that urge, he stood and placed the photos of the two rooms side by side on the table.

Beginning with similarities of the two rooms, he noted that they were both cheap, especially for millionaires. Both rooms also shared a similar sense of being hideouts of sorts, both hotels located away from any major sightseeing attraction.

He turned to the differences between the two rooms based on the photos and what was listed in the file. James Kuiper registered as J. Kuiper with the hotel, while the actress registered as Linda Johnson. The rooms themselves suggested few other differences beyond the obvious, that a man lived and died in the one and a woman lived and jumped or was pushed from the other.

Closing the files, Worthy retreated to his own bed. As he waited for sleep to settle in, he thought of what else the two files had in common. Both victims were Americans, both wealthy, both dying of cancer, and both bearing odd scars on their bodies. The bags and food boxes suggested that both primarily ate by themselves in their rooms. And the coroner's reports indicated that both victims still had low concentrations of anesthesia in their bloodstreams, which was consistent with the more recent incisions occurring sometime in the last four days in each of their lives.

Worthy felt almost too tired to sleep as other questions arose in his mind. The files indicated that the two victims overlapped in Venice for two days before Lorraine LaPurcell died, but was there any evidence that the two knew each other in the States or in Venice, that they flew on the same airlines, that they knew any locals in common, or that they frequented the same restaurants or bars of the city? No.

But this Worthy sensed was inescapable—something or someone connected the two in Venice and in death.

Chapter Seven

Father Fortis smiled as he recognized his friend Christopher Worthy standing on the bow of the *vaporetto* next to Allyson. He wondered if either of them knew how much they looked alike. Both were tall, with fair complexions and sandy hair. Both looked like they stepped out of an L.L. Bean catalog. Americans, without a doubt. And Allyson—the perfect specimen of the tall blond young woman who tended to attract the attention of Italian men. So Father Fortis noticed in his time in Rome.

It was only three days since he had met Allyson at the same *vaporetto* stop, but those intervening days were full and more than a bit puzzling. It would be good to talk out with Worthy and Allyson the fragments of new information that he had gathered.

For his own sense of security, he looked carefully at the faces of others departing the *vaporetto* on *La Giudecca*. None seemed familiar to him, but to be safe, he toned down his customary bear hug of Worthy and settled for a warm handshake. He also led the two of them by a different route to the restaurant. Only when they were seated at one of the outside tables somewhat hidden in a corner of the building did he relax.

"You haven't changed a fig, my friend," he said to Worthy. "I keep getting larger and you just stay as thin as ever. And it looks like you inherited that from your father, Allyson."

Immediately, he wished he could take back the intended compliment. From his previous time with Allyson, he knew the last thing she wanted was to be treated as an appendage to her father.

Allyson, however, did not react with a grimace or pout as he feared but continued instead to smile faintly as she looked out at the water.

"She loves it here, Christopher," he added. "I hope you know she may not want to come home at the end of all this business."

Worthy stole a glance at his daughter. "Yes, I'm well aware of that. And you, Nick, how do you like Venice?"

"In some ways, if Venice were in Greece, the city would fit right in," he replied. "It's very Byzantine in so many ways. But, of course, if Venice were in Greece, the beauty of the place would make it the capital. How could Athens compete with a city that seems to float on water?"

"The shifting foundations of Venice are what give that impression, Nick," Allyson said, her eyes still on the lagoon in front of them. "Go into St. Mark's and look down at the marble floors. They're as wavy as this water."

"And I suppose, my dear, that also explains why so many of the bell towers are off-kilter," Father Fortis added. "Speaking of things off-kilter, Christopher, did Allyson tell you why I'm still in Venice?"

Worthy nodded as he studied the menu. "You're on the lookout for stolen relics. Sounds like an Indiana Jones movie."

Father Fortis sighed. "I want your opinion—I want both of your opinions—once we order. The Vatican sent me here to do what I could behind the scenes to find whoever is behind the thefts. But the Catholic Patriarchate of Venice seems to think that I'm only going to get in the way. I hope you both were given a better welcome."

Before Allyson or her father could answer, the waiter arrived at the table with a basket of bread and to take orders. Father Fortis chose a salad and pasta with cuttlefish, while Allyson ordered risotto with seafood as well as a salad. After some coaching from Allyson, Worthy ordered spaghetti with clams, the dish that both she and Father Fortis enjoyed three nights before.

"I thought 'patriarch' was an Orthodox title, Nick," Worthy said after the waiter departed.

"Ah, it is, my friend. But that just proves how influenced Venice was by Byzantium. So there is a Catholic patriarch of Venice and a small Orthodox community with a metropolitan, not a patriarch. Confusing? Yes, and, as it turns out, I'm not particularly loved by either."

Allyson sat forward in her chair and turned her attention to Father Fortis. "So, the Vatican wants you here, but the local Catholic authorities don't."

Father Fortis frowned. "Smell that foul odor?" he asked. "That's not the smell of this salty lagoon; that's the smell of church politics."

"But why would the Orthodox community give you a hard time, Nick?" Allyson continued.

"Well, it seems, because I came here from the wicked Catholic city of Rome and actually spoke at a conference with wicked Catholic monks, that I'm not to be trusted. You see, for at least the Russian monks whom I'm to watch, 'wicked' and 'Catholic' go hand in hand. The Venetian Orthodox aren't as prejudiced, but they know that the theft of those relics, all from Catholic churches of the city, has made their community suspect. And they blame the Catholics for that suspicion. Old animosities surfacing again, my dear. And I mean 'old.' Some of the tension goes back to the twelfth century."

"So, for the Orthodox of Venice, you have too many friendly ties with Catholics, and for the Catholics of the city, you are Orthodox and therefore part of the suspected group," Worthy summed up.

Father Fortis gave a short laugh. "How ironic; the place where I've been treated best is in Rome, in Vatican City, of all places."

"And the relics? What are you thinking so far?" Worthy asked.

Father Fortis explained his impressions of the three Russian monks, their less than polite treatment of him, and of his shadowing them the previous night. "Thanks to something you said, Allyson, I'm determined to find out whom the Russians know in Venice. So, I followed them last night to find out where they're staying. As I suspected, they're all staying together. I waited for about a half-hour to be on the safe side, but eventually I was able to walk by and note the number on the wall of the building." He took out a piece of paper from his clerical jacket and passed it over to Allyson. "Can you use your contacts at the police station to find out who owns the building?"

With a big smile, Allyson snapped up the piece of paper and put it into her backpack. "That should be easy," she said.

"I'm glad something seems easy. This morning, I assisted at the altar for Divine Liturgy. When I came out to distribute communion, I noticed that Brother Sergius wasn't with the other two monks. The more I see him, or don't see him in this case, the more he has subterfuge written all over his face. So where was he? Was he in the city somewhere meeting his mysterious contact? And how in the world am I going to be able to tail even one of them, much less keep track of the three of them, if they start splitting up?"

Father Fortis's face brightened considerably as the waiter placed the plates in front of them. "No more of that kind of talk while we feast on this," he said. After pausing for a moment to offer a silent grace and then to cross himself, he added, "But when we've polished off this amazing meal, it's your turn—both of you—to bring me up to date on your case. My problem is small potatoes—or maybe Italians say 'small pasta'—next to yours."

WHILE THEY ATE, THE THREE OOHED and aahed about their meals and did not return to their business in Venice until they ordered grappa and after-dinner sweets.

Father Fortis sat back and exhaled with obvious pleasure. "Perhaps it's for the best that I eat most of my meals at the Center. Eating at places like this would be my undoing. And now for my dessert, my friends. Tell me about your case, or is it cases?"

Allyson looked at her father, but Worthy seemed to be waiting for her. "The last two nights, Sylvia and I have gone clubbing with some of her friends from the hospital. Everyone I've met so far is bright and very friendly. I play dumb, and only Sylvia knows that my Italian is better than they expect."

"So you've had to take Sylvia into your confidence, then," Father Fortis concluded. "How much about the deaths of the two Americans does she know?"

"No more or less than anyone else we've talked to. She says that most of the nurses and aides who work at the hospital have noticed the police around more than usual. And a few of them, including Sylvia, have been interviewed about the deaths, both by the media and the police. So, at both clubs, I didn't do anything to get them talking about the deaths. It's a bit of excitement for Venice, I guess."

"I imagine they have their own ideas about the deaths," Worthy said. "The death of a movie star breeds a kind of frenzy in a hurry."

Allyson took a sip of grappa and winced. "Whoa. That's strong." She broke off a piece of bread and ate it. After taking a moment to recover, she added, "Let's see, what theories have I heard? First of all, you have to understand that James Kuiper would be of no interest at all if his death weren't like Lorraine LaPurcell's. Everything I've heard is about her. Like you said, it's the movie star business."

She paused a moment and took another sip of the grappa. "Some of the nurses who take the suicide angle say she must have had a secret lover here in Venice. So they think she died of a broken heart. When they said that, all I could think of is that they were confusing her death with one of her movies. More interesting to me is one of the aides interviewed by the police and then the media. He's sure that he saw LaPurcell two nights before she died. He said that he saw her walking in the San Polo area. He swears the woman he saw was Lorraine LaPurcell and that she looked like she'd been crying."

"Do you believe him?" Father Fortis asked.

"He's a bit of a show-off, Nick, but I don't know him well enough to know if it's all smoke. I'll ask Sylvia. They've known each other for years. But I do know that Lorraine LaPurcell's hotel was in Dursodoro, which is the *sestiere* next to San Polo. So it's possible."

"And does anyone think she was murdered?" Worthy asked.

"Several of them are sure that her death has something to do with the scars. They think that some doctor blew a procedure and killed her to cover up the mistake. But they are positive—with no basis, in my opinion, other than prejudice—that it couldn't have been a doctor in Venice. They seem to think every bad doctor in the area works over in Mestre."

Worthy tapped the table with his fingers. "Was there anyone in the group who wasn't saying anything? Maybe, like this person was listening in a way that didn't seem right?" he asked.

Allyson thought for a moment, having to concede that it was a perceptive question. "Yes, there was one person," she said. "Me. The others seemed typically Italian, if there is such a person. They were all fighting to get their own opinion into the conversation or having fun ridiculing someone else's theory. Yes, that's the one thing that struck me. They're having fun with her death."

"I've known more than one person who works in a hospital to have a very dark sense of humor," Father Fortis said.

Worthy took a final sip of the grappa. "Maybe I should be glad that the movie star's death is hogging everyone's attention. I've been focusing on James Kuiper and trying to figure out why he came here."

"Dad, am I right in remembering that both incisions weren't very deep? I mean, what kind of medical procedure would make such a superficial cut?"

Worthy nodded. "Yes, that's what the coroner's report questions as well. The area of the incisions was inflamed on both victims and showed some separation from the subcutaneous layer, but nothing that would be considered invasive surgery."

"A real puzzle," Father Fortis commiserated.

"So far, I've been focusing on James Kuiper's room. Inspector Ruggiero assigned one of the younger officers to work with me, a guy named Castelucci. He opened the room for me this morning."

"Did you have better luck?" Father Fortis asked.

"I'd already gone through the police photos of the room, so I didn't see much that was new. It was the room of a recluse; that was clear. But the feel of the room, just the way everything looked, suggested that Kuiper lived there. It just didn't seem the room of someone who decided to kill himself. But feelings are not evidence," he said.

Father Fortis raised his hand in mild protest. "Ah, but strong feelings can sometimes arise out of good, although buried, reasons, even as they can lead us astray. So I will ask you something that you would ask me, if I were in your place. If you think back over everything you found in his room, what gives you the greatest sense that Mr. Kuiper was intent on living, not dying?"

Allyson smiled. That was exactly like something her father would say.

Worthy only nodded, as if agreeing that the question was the right one. He explained the position of the shoes, the food containers on the table, and the toiletries laid out helter-skelter in the bathroom.

"I see what you mean. That seems like the behavior of someone going to sleep, not intent on going to sleep permanently," Father Fortis agreed. "Anything else?"

Worthy sat in silence, his finger making seemingly random designs on the table. After a few moments, his finger stopped. "There was something else, something that I noticed that was different from the photos of Lorraine LaPurcell's room. Kuiper's had a Bible on his bedside table."

"In English or Italian?" Allyson asked.

"What a good question, my dear," Father Fortis said. Allyson blushed, knowing she couldn't hide from Father Fortis that she enjoyed the praise.

"Huh, well, I moved the Bible to see if there was anything underneath," Worthy replied. "I just assumed it was like a Gideon Bible, one that comes with the room. But I'm pretty sure that this Bible was in English."

"Well, that didn't come with the room," Allyson added. "He must have brought it with him."

Worthy sat in silence again for a moment. "Tell me as a priest, Nick, would someone intent on killing himself have a Bible nearby, next to his bed?"

Father Fortis took a sip of his own grappa. "And there was no Bible in Lorraine LaPurcell's room?"

Worthy shook his head. "Not that I could tell from the photos."

"It's possible, Christopher, say if the person was ending his life to get back at God for something. But I think I see what you mean. When I visit someone in the hospital, or in a nursing home, or even at home, and I see a Bible by the bedside, I tend to think that they have been using it for solace, for some comfort."

"Would the family know if the Bible was his?" Allyson offered.

Worthy nodded. "I can check. So, if James Kuiper was using an English Bible, either something so terrible happened that he lost all hope, or he didn't kill himself at all."

"So someone forced the pills down him? Did it look like he'd struggled?" Allyson asked.

"No, not at all. In the photos, he looked like a man who just dropped off to sleep."

Worthy looked tentatively at Allyson, and then at Father Fortis. "Thanks, both of you." After a moment, he added, "I guess I need to find out if it's possible that he wasn't alone that night. Which means I need to find out how easy it'd be for someone to come to a guest's room at that hotel—it's a pretty shabby one—without being seen by someone at the desk."

Chapter Eight

As Father Fortis walked back from his *vaporetto* stop to his lodgings at the Orthodox Center, he reflected back on the evening with Worthy and Allyson. What most astonished him was how clear it was that the two of them, despite ostensibly working together, hadn't talked with each other about the case. What Allyson shared about her visit to the clubs was as new to Worthy as it was to him, and the same was true of what Worthy shared with both of them about James Kuiper's room.

Should I be discouraged by that, he asked himself. As he turned down a narrow causeway along one of the side canals, he decided he shouldn't. More important than what they didn't know about each other's side of the case was their willingness to hear what the other person shared.

While Father Fortis didn't take any personal credit for what transpired between father and daughter out on *La Giudecca*, he could accept that his affection for both of them may have contributed to the favorable outcome. If so, then he would be happy to bring the two of them together again.

It was at that moment that he first wondered if he strayed off from the route to the Center with which he was familiar. Even in the daytime, he found his map insufficient for all the twists and turns of the maze that made up Venice. But at night the challenge quadrupled, as the lighting of the walkways and bridges was minimal.

He decided to take the small bridge to his right, and as he did so, he thought he heard a crunching sound behind him. He looked back into blackness, but could see nothing.

He stopped on the bridge to listen. The gentle movement of the tide in the canal below caused a moored flatbed boat to kiss the side of the causeway.

Was that what he heard?

Walking again in the direction that he hoped would take him to the Center, he concentrated on what he was hearing. Thirty yards ahead, the way was blocked by another canal, forcing him to make a sharp turn to the right. He stopped at the dark corner to listen, and again thought he heard what could have been a footfall behind him. Then, silence.

He conceded that there could be any number of Venetians walking that way for a host of valid reasons, given that it wasn't much past ten in the evening. Hearing nothing, however, he asked himself a different question. If someone else is coming my way, why would the person stop when I do?

Picking up his pace to almost a jog, his thoughts shifted from finding the safety of the Orthodox Center—he was no longer confident that he was even moving in the right direction—to finding someplace to duck into and hide. With luck, Father Fortis' quickened pace would cause whoever was following him to drop his caution and run to catch up. If Father Fortis could find some dark place to hide which opened out to a well-lit walkway, he might catch a brief glance at his pursuer.

Lumbering more than sprinting, he saw ahead a light attached to the wall of a house, its feeble glow offering Father Fortis what looked to be his best chance. Not used to running, he was out of breath when he passed through the light's glimmer and ducked into a small alleyway no more than ten yards beyond. With limited success, he tried to quiet his pounding heart and gain control of his breathing. He felt a wave of nausea as the memory of the pasta and cuttlefish flashed through his mind.

As he waited in his shelter, he wondered if he imagined everything, or if a little old Venetian woman would walk past him. For several moments, he heard nothing. It was possible, he admitted, if he was being followed, that his pursuer might also have stopped to wait him out.

Resisting the urge to peek around the corner, he decided to give the situation five more minutes to develop when he heard running steps from the direction he came. He pressed himself back into the darkness and crouched.

The shape was past his narrow vantage point before he could determine much of what he'd observed. The hooded runner was moving fast and far more gracefully than Father Fortis had. Without much basis, he concluded that it was a man, in a sweatshirt and running shoes, but that was about all. Again, in case the figure was pursuing him and realized his mistake and would retrace his steps, Father Fortis thought it best to remain where he was and not try to steal another look around the corner of the building.

Ten minutes passed, all of them quiet ones except for the gentle lapping of the water in the narrow canal. Father Fortis decided to come out of hiding and go back in the opposite direction, when he heard footsteps again, coming from the direction from where the pursuer disappeared.

But these footsteps seemed quite different, as if this person was walking with a cane. From their sound, Father Fortis estimated that this person would not pass him for nearly a minute. He peeked around the corner and stared into the darkness. Yes, there was a shape, lumbering a bit, coming toward him. He expected to see an old-age pensioner taking a late evening stroll when the man's face was illumined by a blinking streetlight. No, this is not an old-age pensioner, he realized. This is Brother Alexis.

The fear Father Fortis felt when he was being pursued transformed in a second into anger. As the Russian monk drew closer, his one leg dragging, Father Fortis stepped out of his hiding place and blocked the narrow walkway.

"What are you doing out here?" he demanded.

Brother Alexis stopped and stared at Father Fortis. "What you mean, 'what I do here?' I walk, same as you."

"Walking where?" Father Fortis asked, still blocking the way.

"My business where I walk. Where you walk?" Brother Alexis asked in challenge.

"I'm heading for the Center," Father Fortis replied.

"Good for you. Center is just this way," Brother Alexis said, pointing in the direction from where he came and toward where the pursuer sped off. "Forty meters, turn right."

"And you?" Father Fortis asked again.

"I come from Center. Now I go to apartment. But this my business. Please excuse."

Father Fortis stepped aside and watched as Brother Alexis clomped along the causeway. No, this was not the runner who had whizzed past him fifteen minutes before. But did the runner and Brother Alexis meet? Did they know each other? Could the runner have been one of the other two Russian monks? And why was it that Alexis didn't seem frightened when Father Fortis stepped out of the darkness?

Five minutes later, following Brother Alexis' directions, Father Fortis found his way to the Center. Turning the key to his room, he admitted to being shaken by the experience. What troubled him was not so much the possibility that his pursuer was one of the other Russian monks or even that the pursuer was in league with the monks. No, what nagged at his mind as he began to offer his evening prayers was this question: when had whoever was following him begun his pursuit? Was it possible that the person saw him on *La Giudecca*, eating with Worthy and Allyson?

He had tried unsuccessfully to follow the Russians to gain some sense of whom they might know in Venice. Had the Russians turned the tables and followed him? Did the Russian monks now know that Father Fortis had two

American friends in Venice? And if so, how long would it take them to find out that both Worthy and Allyson worked for the police?

Upon her return, Allyson found Sylvia still up and watching TV. Feeling keyed up from the dinner conversation, Allyson joined her roommate despite the fact that the TV personalities spoke Italian so rapidly that she could barely make sense of half of what she heard.

Sylvia had just rotated onto the second shift in the emergency room of the hospital. As she reached into a box of crackers, she described the evening as relatively uneventful and therefore disappointing. Besides the normal fare of colicky babies and children with stomach aches, the E.R. treated a fisherman with a hook imbedded in his palm. To use Sylvia's language, that was the only "entertainment" for the evening.

Allyson was not surprised to find Sylvia still up after her evening shift. Sylvia was a night owl, staying up later than Allyson even when Sylvia was on the morning shift. Despite that, and her love of clubbing, Sylvia never seemed tired or showed signs of fatigue. If Sylvia was a head taller instead of barely five feet tall, Allyson would consider her dark-haired roommate almost in the category of an Italian model.

But Allyson doubted if Sylvia, no matter how tall, could even pretend to be as aloof and unattainable as models looked in fashion magazines. What Allyson would have called Sylvia's "spunk" made Allyson realize that the models in magazines—and the women in Venice emulating that look—were posed to look as if they were half dead with boredom.

Not surprisingly, Sylvia was thrilled to have an American roommate, and was clearly delighted when Allyson confided in her what Allyson felt she could about her internship. While Allyson emphasized that her major responsibility was tracking the locations of tourist vulnerability to scam artists and pickpockets, she was, to a degree, forced to take Sylvia into her confidence about the two suspicious deaths. Not surprisingly, Sylvia was ecstatic at the new "entertainment" in her life.

With an episode of "Mad Men" with Italian talk-over in the background, Sylvia listed some suggestions for other clubs to try out on Friday evening. While each club pretended to present something unique for the young adults of Venice, Allyson accepted, with the exception of lighting and other changes of décor, that the clubs tended to be quite similar. And from Sylvia's plans for the weekend, it was clear as well as a bit disappointing to Allyson that they would be with the same basic circle of Sylvia's friends.

Allyson gave Sylvia only half her attention and ignored the TV program completely as she reviewed the evening on *La Giudecca*. She was aware not only of her own awkwardness around her father, but also her father's similar awkwardness around her. But some of that for her, and as far as she could tell from her father as well, evaporated over the dinner conversation with Father Fortis.

She felt a rush again as she remembered the moment that she'd raised the issue of the English Bible on the bed stand. Even if Nick didn't express his admiration for my insight, she thought, and even if my Dad didn't take my suggestion as seriously as he did, I knew as soon as that came out of my mouth that I offered something of real value. "I can do this," she whispered to herself.

"*Che*? What?" Sylvia asked. "What did you say?"

"Oh, nothing. I was just talking to myself. But let me ask you something, Sylvia. Do you remember last Sunday when we were at that one club over by the Rialto?"

"Of course. 'The Blue Diamond,' " she replied.

"I think it was your friend Enrico who told us that he saw Lorraine LaPurcell a couple of nights before she died?"

"Ah, Enrico's great, isn't he? He is such a *ragazzo*, such a big kid."

"So let me ask you this about him. Do you think that he fabricated that?"

"What do you mean 'fabricated?' " Sylvia asked. "Do you mean that he made it up?"

Allyson nodded.

Sylvia's face took on a sour expression. "Enrico doesn't lie, no."

"But could he be stretching the truth?" Allyson probed.

"Yes, of course, that's possible. We are at a club, we are enjoying our drinks, and we tell stories. True stories? Yes. But completely true? I don't know. Most completely true stories aren't much fun, no?"

And fun is why we go clubbing, Allyson thought.

Sylvia turned off the TV and faced Allyson on the sofa. "I read this in an American magazine. Let's try it. You say to me, 'on a scale of one to ten,' then ask me a question about Enrico.' "

Allyson laughed. "Okay, on a scale of one to ten, how big a crush do you have on Enrico?"

Sylvia threw a pillow at Allyson. "No, no, about his story, you… *merde*. No, that's French."

"Don't bother. I know what *merde* means. I'll be serious. Was Enrico in San Polo the night that he said he was?"

Sylvia slapped the couch. "Ten. Enrico is a jogger. Yes, I think he was there."

"Then how about this? On a scale of one to ten, did Enrico tell the truth when he bragged that he saw Lorraine LaPurcell that night?"

This time, Sylvia didn't slap the couch. After a moment, she said, "Seven, maybe eight. Yes, I think so."

"My last question, Sylvia. If he'd been jogging, could Enrico really have noticed that Lorraine LaPurcell was crying?"

Sylvia closed her eyes as if imagining the scene. "Sorry, Enrico, but only two. I think that was the Campari speaking."

While she learned nothing that she didn't already know about Enrico, Allyson gained a bit more respect for Sylvia's judgment. She yawned and rose from the couch. "I'm off to bed. Some of us have to work in the morning."

Sylvia remained where she was. "What, don't I get a turn?"

Allyson stopped at the door of her room. "Okay, one time."

"Ah, what should I ask? I know. On a scale of one to ten, how much of what you know have you told me?"

"About what?"

"About Lorraine LaPurcell's death. What else?"

"Eight to nine," Allyson replied.

Before she could close her door, she heard Sylvia ask another question. "On a scale of one to ten, was your saying 'eight to nine' just now the truth?"

"*Buona notte*," Allyson said. "Good night, Sylvia." In her room, she asked Sylvia's question of her again. No, it wasn't an "eight to nine;" it was a "four" at best. She hadn't told Sylvia about her father.

As she looked at her reflection in the mirror, she found herself facing other questions. On a scale of one to ten, how much would her father count on her to tell him the truth? Maybe a "two" would even be too high, given that she never divulged where she was when she ran away.

As she turned off the bathroom light, another question followed immediately. On a scale of one to ten, how much could she trust her father to tell her the truth? The answer that came immediately to mind troubled her.

"Ten," she admitted. The man can drive me crazy, but he always tells the truth.

CHAPTER NINE

"SO, YOU THINK MURDER, NOT SUICIDE?" Ruggiero asked after Worthy gave his update. "And that is based on what, the condition of the rooms and a book?"

"Not a book so much as a Bible," Worthy said, correcting him.

The two main highlights of his report twisted in such a fashion by Ruggiero reeked of skepticism. He wouldn't fault the trim and proper inspector if he concluded that Worthy jumped for murder as fast as they do on *Law and Order*.

"You must help me, Lieutenant," Ruggiero continued. "Italy is more Catholic than it is a country, if you know what I mean. But Venice is not, what should I say, particularly pious. Yes, we have beautiful churches, in my opinion, the most beautiful in all of Italy, including Rome, but without tourists they are empty. Now, you in the United States? A different story. I listen to what your candidates for being president say about God, and I see that religion matters much for you. So, me, I am not sure what the Bible in the room means."

"I can understand that," Worthy said. "And if these deaths occurred in my country, a Bible on a bedside table would not surprise me. In the States, they come with the room," Worthy said.

"How odd," Ruggiero interjected.

"And that's why finding a Bible in English in James Kuiper's room here in Venice is, as Allyson pointed out, a bit strange."

"Ah, Allyson," Ruggiero said, nodding. "And you think the Bible proves what, again?"

" 'Prove' is too strong a word. The Bible suggests to me a religious person, and such people, by statistics, are less likely to attempt suicide." Worthy hoped Ruggiero wouldn't ask for the data behind that claim. It was more a hunch than any certainty on his part.

"And you say the condition of the room, in the photos and when you visited Mr. Kuiper's room, also is only suggestive?"

Worthy once again heard the tone of skepticism in the question. In a measured tone, he replied, "Yes, the room seemed to be the room of someone who expected to get up the next day, a man ready to get on with whatever he was doing."

"Someone who expected to get up the next day," Ruggiero repeated Worthy's phrase. He paused for a moment before adding, "When the coroner first informed me about the incisions, I admit I myself wondered if we could be dealing with something strange, a ritualistic murder, perhaps, not a suicide. But then I ask myself this question, Lieutenant Worthy. If murder, what is the motive?"

Worthy realized that Ruggiero was not asking the question rhetorically. "We don't know the motive yet," he admitted.

"And then there is the question of method. There is no evidence of a struggle, yet one person, if we are talking about murder, was pushed to her death and the other was somehow given an overdose of sedatives."

Worthy understood by Ruggiero's pause that he was again expected to answer. Not having an answer, he waited.

"But with suicide, we have both the methods—jumping from a window and overdosing—and motive—in both cases, the cancer," Ruggiero offered.

"But why in Venice rather than back in the States?" Worthy said in return. "And why two suicides, just weeks apart, of Americans, both with, as you say, terminal cancer diagnoses?"

"Please understand me, Lieutenant. I agree, the similarities suggest some … some connection. And no one will be satisfied, especially our media, until we find that link. But are these not two connected suicides, not two connected murders?"

Worthy let silence build between the two of them. It was up to Ruggiero to make the next move. The inspector could end the meeting, which would mean that the two were committed to two very different conclusions. Or, Ruggiero could suggest something conciliatory.

Ruggiero seemed to sense the same potential impasse in their relationship and opted for being conciliatory. "But let us at least hypothetically view the deaths as suspicious. Some person or persons somehow entered the hotel and were not seen by the desk staff, no?"

"I looked into that this morning," Worthy said.

Ruggiero's raised eyebrows suggested that he was impressed. "And you found what?"

"As you know, both hotels are what might be described as 'inexpensive.' "

"You do not offend. They are both cheap lodgings, unworthy of our city," Ruggiero stated.

"I'm just thankful that those at the desks speak English," Worthy said.

"That they must if they are to survive, Lieutenant. Many of us think that Venice today exists not so much as a city, but as a destination for tourists. So we know Spanish, German, French, English, of course, and some are now learning Japanese and Chinese. Be that … how do you say, be that as it may, yes? What did you learn from your inquiries?"

"Both places assured me that there was a person on desk duty twenty-four hours a day. So I asked how many were on duty between eleven at night and six in the morning. They both admitted only one. So I asked what would happen if that person had to use the toilet, needed a snack, or was desperate for a short nap. In so many words, they both said that a person has to live. "

"So an outside person could have gotten by the desk and come to LaPurcell's and Kuiper's rooms," Ruggiero said. "And the lack of struggle?"

"Lorraine LaPurcell and James Kuiper must have let the person in. In other words, they knew the killer—again, assuming they were murdered."

Ruggiero sat in silence. "Possible, yes, possible. And this person, this man or woman known by the two victims, do you believe that this same person is somehow connected with these strange scars?"

"Yes, I do. When we find out what those scars mean, we're going to find out why these two millionaires came to Venice. But more than that, when we find out what the scars mean, I'm betting we'll find out why the two were killed."

FATHER FORTIS GLANCED DOWN IN PLEASURE at the 13th century manuscript. The Orthodox Center's museum as well as the city's ecclesiastical archives housed an important collection of Byzantine chant as performed in Venice in the late Middle Ages. If his thesis proved correct, he would have clear evidence that Venice's liturgical music for centuries continued to be influenced by Constantinople, despite the split between Eastern and Western Christianity in 1054. And while the 12th century crusade saw Venice, with papal blessing, sacking Constantinople and setting up a Latin patriarch, Father Fortis' research was clearly suggesting that Byzantine culture continued to shape Venetian worship until well into the Renaissance.

Father Fortis was pleased that his academic work was not a totally invented cover for his attempts to get to the bottom of the mystery of the relics. In his week in Venice, no other thefts of that nature were reported. While that was good news for the churches of Venice, it meant that Father Fortis found himself daily sifting through, over and over again, the evidence from the first robberies.

The corroding of Venice's buildings, his research into medieval Byzantine chant, and the missing relics all gave Father Fortis a sense of being transported back in time. Yes, there was a time when thefts of relics occurred all over Christendom. Relics were treated as bridges to Christ's throne and, consequently, added to the prestige of the churches that held them.

Venice's most famous church, the cathedral of San Marco, owed its name and fame to the theft, treated as a miraculous "transferal" at the time, of the remains of the apostle St. Mark from Islamic Egypt. Until that point, the patron saint of the city was St. Theodore, a nearly forgotten fact now buried in the guide books to the city.

Father Fortis could only guess how many of the other churches of Venice housed relics which came from other parts of ancient Christendom. During the heyday of the doges in the Middle Ages on through the Renaissance, Venice was not as much a city as the center of an extensive maritime empire. From the sacking of cities, especially in the East, Venice gained temporal wealth in the form of gold and silver and spiritual wealth in the form of relics.

Father Fortis put his pen down to ponder a question. Was there an official list somewhere of all the booty "absorbed" by Venice over the centuries?

He was at the point of considering another question—did the Russian monks possess such a list?—when Brother Sergius entered the museum library with Brothers Alexis and Nilus in tow. As usual, the two trailing monks avoided eye contact, but Brother Sergius wore his familiar scowl as he spotted Father Fortis and moved in his direction.

With no one else in the library, Brother Sergius made no effort to temper his opening words.

"Why you menace Brother Alexis?" he demanded.

"Menace?"

"Yes, menace. Why you make trouble for him?"

Although his right hamstring certainly knew what lay behind the accusations, Father Fortis decided to hear Brother Alexis' interpretation of the confrontation. With as convincing a look of bewilderment as he could muster, he said, "I'm afraid that I'm a bit confused, Brother Sergius."

"No, we confused," the monk retorted, poking a finger at his chest. "You menace. Alexis walk home last night, you stop him, treat him like criminal. Why?"

"Oh, that," Father Fortis replied vaguely, intrigued at the notion that Brother Alexis reported feeling treated as a criminal.

"Why you do that?" Brother Sergius repeated the question.

Father Fortis took a closer look at Brother Alexis who immediately glanced away as soon as Father Fortis caught his eye. Father Fortis noticed that the monk's left leg was indeed several inches shorter than the right. No, it was not this monk who pursued him. So what could Father Fortis say in his defense?

Deciding to use as a trap as much of the truth as he dared, he studied Brother Sergius' face as he said, "I was out for a walk right after doing some research in my room. On my way back here, I heard someone following me. When I stopped, this person stopped. When I walked fast, this person walked fast. So I hid. Someone ran by me. And then a few minutes later, Brother Alexis came from the same direction as whoever was chasing me went."

If Brother Sergius was Father Fortis' pursuer, his face showed no evidence of being caught. He turned toward Brother Alexis and spoke rapidly to him in Russian. After a few moments, Sergius turned back toward Father Fortis. His face was still red with anger.

"Alexis see no one. Just you. He fear you throw him in water."

Father Fortis shook his head, trying not to smile. In truth, he was angry enough to throw the monk into the canal.

"Why someone follow you? You some American big shot," Brother Sergius offered with a mocking laugh. When Sergius apparently translated his comment for his fellow Russians, Father Fortis could make out the letters "VIP" spoken in obvious derision.

"I have no idea why someone would follow me," he posed, keeping his attention on Brother Sergius. "Can you think of a reason?"

For a moment, the leader of the three Russians seemed confused by the question. Then the color of his face reddened even further. "How we know? We followed too."

There it is, Father Fortis thought, Sergius' first mistake. He decided to see what else the monk would tell him. "Yes, I'm sure that you've been followed in Russia. It couldn't have been easy for you before the Soviet Union was dissolved."

Sergius shook his head vigorously. "No, we followed *here*. Police follow us, we know. Police look through rooms too."

Father Fortis thought for a moment about where he could next direct the conversation. At some point, he knew that Sergius would realize that the tables were turned in the conversation, and it was he, not the American priest, who was answering the questions. Father Fortis had to press the Russian until that dawning occurred.

Again adopting the bewildered expression, he asked, "Why would the police follow you, Brother Sergius?"

For a moment, he thought the Russian tumbled to his predicament.

Brother Sergius crossed his arms and seemed to be weighing what else to say.

Finally, he answered, "Catholics have us followed. Catholics hate Russians." And then, as if to offer a final challenge, he leaned down over Father Fortis and said with a look of bitterness, "Catholics hate Orthodox."

Father Fortis let the comment hang in the air. How miserable these monks must be in Italy, in Venice, surrounded by churches of the perceived enemy, he thought.

He resisted the urge to challenge the absurd claim, to speak of his personal experience with Catholics both at the conference in Rome and in the States, and to remind the Russian monk that the Catholic and Orthodox Churches settled their ancient grievances in 1964, when Pope Paul VI and Ecumenical Patriarch Athenagorus embraced in Jerusalem and began dialogues promoting reconciliation.

Instead, he took the opportunity to ask a more vital question. "You know, Brother Sergius, I see the three of you here at the Center, at meals and at Divine Liturgy." Pointing a finger at the manuscript before him, he continued, "But I don't see any of you doing research. So tell me, Brother Sergius, why are the three of you here in Venice?"

CHAPTER TEN

WELL, WHY NOT, ALLYSON THOUGHT. As long as I keep my head about me, what's the harm in letting a cute Italian flirt with me?

The Italian in question was one of three friends of Enrico, and by far the cutest of the three, who asked her in basic English to dance. She loved the way he said her name. Al-ee-sown. And when the dance was over, Giovanni managed to corral his two friends to sit at the same table with Sylvia and Allyson.

Not for the first time, Allyson enjoyed the more intimate way that Italian men, teenagers, and boys enjoyed one another's company. She saw men, arms linked even as their wives' arms were linked behind or in front of them, taking the *passaggiata*, an evening walk, about the city. Yes, as the conversation before made clear, the young men at her table were competing for the attention of the women not unlike American teenagers and men. But Allyson sensed that not one of these boys, unlike their American counterparts, would try to seriously humiliate his male friends.

With the volume of the music and the number of conversations crossing one another at the table, Allyson had no trouble pretending to know little Italian. And it was from overhearing snatches of Giovanni's remarks to his two friends that Allyson realized that Giovanni agreed with Enrico's claim that the American girl, the intern at the police department, was cute.

Am I cute, she asked herself. No one ever called her a beauty, but attractive was a term she'd heard more than once applied to her. She was taller than the average Italian woman, and she guessed that her sandy-colored hair and fair complexion, like her father's, could make her look different, perhaps even exotic, in Italy.

Like Enrico, both Luigi and Paolo sported the current young male hair style of Venice that applied gel to send hair strands in all directions. And like Enrico, Giovanni's two companions worked in the medical field at the city hospital. Luigi was a respiratory therapist's aide while Paolo was a medical computer technician. The duo's command of English, as Giovanni's, was significantly less than Enrico's. At a point, a similar point noted anywhere in the world, the two realized that Giovanni and Allyson were connecting at a different level. They consequently gave up on talking with the American girl with very little Italian and concentrated their attentions on Sylvia.

The arrangement was perfect from Allyson's point of view. Sylvia agreed to raise in casual conversation the topic of Lorraine LaPurcell's death. This gave Allyson the opportunity to focus her attentions on Giovanni, who described his work as business-related but claimed his real passion and ultimate goal was eventually to own a club better than the one they were in. He described his plans to open a retro club out on Lido, the gold coast of Venice, that would bring back the glory that was once associated with the island beach of the lagoon.

In contrast to the others, Giovanni wore his hair long, forgoing current fashion, reminding Allyson of Andy Garcia. She could picture Giovanni remaining handsome even into middle age, his hair strikingly gray at the temples. What impressed her about Giovanni, besides his good looks, was his more serious expression. While the others at the table laughed loudly over their drinks, Giovanni seemed satisfied with a sideways grin.

Enrico, meanwhile, was competing with Luigi and Paolo for Sylvia's attention. But, as luck would have it, Allyson noted that Sylvia was stealing long glances at Giovanni. So Sylvia likes him, she thought. She was about to add the word "too" to her thought, but after a moment realized that she wasn't jealous. I may dream of falling in love with a Venetian, she admitted, but I can't see myself married to a club owner whose business demanded that he flirt with every young woman, especially every American woman, who came into his establishment. And she couldn't imagine an Italian club owner willing to be married to a police officer.

No, she didn't mind Sylvia's interest in Giovanni on a personal level. But Allyson specifically asked Sylvia to gingerly bring up with Enrico how he could be sure that he really saw Lorraine LaPurcell in San Polo two nights before her death. But Sylvia clearly forgot their agreement.

Giovanni leaned his head down to Allyson's ear and asked, "How long you stay in Venezia?"

"Just until December," Allyson answered, almost shouting to be heard.

"Ah, *Dicembre*. You here for *Natale*?"

Allyson pretended not to know the Italian term for Christmas. After

Giovanni asked Enrico to supply the English term for him, Allyson shook her head. "No, I leave a week before Christmas."

Giovanni made a sad face. "That is unfortunate. Christmas in Venezia is very, very special."

"I think everything in Venice is very special," Allyson said.

A beaming smile took possession of Giovanni's face. "Ah, you like my city? Yes, my Venezia is the most beautiful city in the world."

Allyson laughed. "Venice is your city? You must be very wealthy."

"No, no. Venezia is my city, it is Luigi's, it is Enrico's, it is Paolo's, it is your roommate's city. What is her name, please?"

"Sylvia," Allyson replied. At the sound of her name, Sylvia leaned toward the two of them. "I heard my name, yes?"

Knowing the effect that her answer would have on Sylvia, Allyson said, "Giovanni asked what your name is."

Sylvia's face glowed as she turned her complete attention to Giovanni. "And you are Giovanni?"

Giovanni smiled at Sylvia. "So, why are we talking English? We're both Italiani."

Sylvia laughed as if his comment was witty beyond belief. She then rattled off something in Italian, little of which Allyson caught except for Sylvia's comment that she usually went clubbing at the "Blue Diamond." Allyson concluded that she would learn little about the case this night.

Allyson felt herself favored when Giovanni continued the conversation in English. "Blue Diamond. Yes, over in San Polo, no? My opinion? Less noise, better food. What you think, Allyson?"

"What's the name of this place?" she asked, playing up the confused American role.

"La Casbah," Giovanni answered.

Before Allyson could give her evaluation, Sylvia asked Giovanni in Italian why she hadn't seen him at the clubs before.

Allyson understood enough of Sylvia's question to understand her roommate's real message. *I want to see you again.*

Giovanni replied, "Soon, I finish my degree at University of Padua."

I'm not just going to give him to Sylvia that easily, Allyson thought. "Does your university offer a degree in clubbing and flirting?" she asked.

Giovanni looked down for a moment at his drink and slowly shook his head. When he looked up, Allyson could see just the faintest evidence of a blush. "No, a degree in business management. My father thinks I will take over his business, but no, I will open a club on the Lido, the best club in Venezia." He waited a moment before adding with a smirk, "Maybe American men have to take a course of study in flirting. Not Italians. We are born flirting."

As a male peacock fans his glorious tail, Giovanni displayed his proficiency in flirting as well as his fairness by flashing his sardonic smile at both Allyson and Sylvia.

In her head, Allyson could hear her mother's teasing voice. "Don't let those Italian men charm your panties off."

Allyson gazed at her roommate's face, locked shamelessly onto Giovanni's. Sylvia better be careful, she thought. This charmer has already got her halfway into bed.

✝

The next morning, Worthy sat with an espresso by the window of a bar near his apartment, a folder open in front of him. Worthy knew that he was not alone in investigating the death of James Kuiper and secondarily the death of Lorraine LaPurcell. Inspector Ruggiero introduced him to two officers, Stefano Castelucci, whom he met before, and Lucca Basso. The two had been working the cases from the beginning, and approached them as suicides. As far as Worthy could tell from the folder, the two hadn't changed their minds about that.

Worthy could admit how such an approach, running parallel to Worthy's murder theory, made sense from Ruggiero's perspective. He also knew that he should be grateful, as their approach had the added advantage of keeping Worthy out of the media's glare.

This did not mean, of course, that the two approaches were being pursued in complete isolation. Evidence found through one approach could be of use and significance to the other angle, and that was why Worthy not only forwarded to both Castelucci and Basso a written version of what he shared with Ruggiero the day before, but also why he spent this morning studying the updated folder sent him from the two Italians.

What he was looking for was irregularities in two cases, a goal made more difficult by the fact that the cases already had irregularities that were similar in abundance. Two peculiar victims, both American millionaires, both battling terminal cancers, both for unknown reasons misleading their families, friends, or, in Lorraine LaPurcell's case, an agent, to come to Venice, both preferring sleazy lodgings to hotels commensurate with their wealth, and both having unexplained incisions on their bodies.

In hopes of new information, Worthy turned to the backs of the folders. In the Linda Johnson/Lorraine LaPurcell file, he found the final bank statements of the actress that came in from a bank account in Pasadena, California, and from another in Berne, Switzerland. The total assets in the first added up to over six million dollars, while the second held a little under four million.

Again, the impressive wealth of the woman made her reclusive stay in Venice all the more difficult to comprehend.

But when he turned over the two bank sheets, it was evidence of regularity that jumped out at him. From the California account, the actress withdrew thirty thousand dollars on the first day of every odd numbered month, while from the Swiss account the woman withdrew the same amount on the first day of every even numbered month. From the previous twelve months, Lorraine LaPurcell withdrew in total over three hundred and fifty thousand dollars. At that rate, Worthy figured, the actress would still not have emptied her accounts in more than three decades.

Except Lorraine LaPurcell knew, with her diagnosis, that she didn't have that much time left, Worthy thought. Her lodging and dining-in expenses in Venice for the three weeks previous to her death would have made hardly a dent in even one month's withdrawal. So what did she spend the money on?

Worthy turned to the James Kuiper file but, as he figured, the bank statements were not yet received. He made a note to email Captain Betts and have the Kuiper family find out all they could about the finances of their husband and father.

Even without that information, Worthy suspected that the Kuiper records would reveal something similar. As he already concluded, the irregularities of the cases were what the two victims had in common. Why wouldn't the odd withdrawal patterns be similar?

Worthy took out his pen and a blank sheet of paper from the folder. At the top, he wrote "Unanswered Questions." Without hesitation, he wrote below the heading all the questions that stemmed from the cases' irregularities. Cause of death. Reasons for coming to Venice. Cause of two incisions (one on top of the other). Choice of accommodations. And, reasons for hiding.

He paused a moment before continuing. He added "financial withdrawals" before asking himself other questions that logically belonged in that category. What would a terminally ill millionaire spend money on? Without knowing why he felt confident, he wrote in the margin, "Assume money spent in Venice." That changed the question to, what would a terminally ill millionaire spend money on in Venice?

Worthy thought of all the high-end jewelry shops and designer boutiques nestled near the Piazza San Marco. No such articles were found in the rooms, and Worthy realized that only a cancer victim completely submerged in denial would buy clothes and jewelry if she or he had just weeks or months to live. And neither Linda Johnson nor James Kuiper seemed to have been caught in any such self-delusion.

Was there a charity, foundation, or cause peculiar to Venice to which the two millionaires contributed? Since coming to Venice, he read of the various efforts centered on saving the sinking city, but he rejected this possibility as the "save Venice" projects were estimated to cost in the high billions. And James Kuiper, according to his family, didn't even like Venice.

For similar reasons, he dismissed as recipients the various efforts to save some of Venice's more famous *palazzi*, palaces, that were deteriorating due to air pollution and saltwater corrosion.

He thought again of the photos of the two rooms and Allyson's insight about the English Bible. Was James Kuiper conscience stricken? With death looming, did he opt to forsake his ego and think of the needs of others? Were there religious charities or foundations centered in Venice that not only appealed to the two millionaires but so touched them that they felt compelled to come to Venice?

But even as he pondered the point, his mind strongly resisted the possibility. A charity or foundation that was the fortunate recipient of such a gift would hardly have remained silent when the two deaths were reported. And why would two millionaires, if they contributed to such causes, have ended up dead, either by their own hand or the hands of others?

And, at bottom, he could not escape something so illogical that he found the question compelling. For what reason or cause would a cancer victim, nearing death, be the most likely to spend money?

He looked out the window of the bar and saw the tourists walking by the rank of gondolas. James Kuiper probably walked along this same causeway. Worthy picked out a man walking with guidebook in hand and pretended the man was Kuiper. Kuiper was a man known in Detroit for brassiness and ambition. He came to a city, Venice, that he was known to dislike, coming nonetheless and spending, if in fact his financial statements mimicked Lorraine LaPurcell's, over a third of a million dollars.

An answer came to Worthy in a flash. Although there was no corroborating evidence from the files, the idea felt stone-hard in Worthy's mind even as he instinctively knew that Ruggiero, Castelucci, and Basso would dismiss it without much thought.

Yet, if Worthy was right nonetheless, James Kuiper and Lorraine LaPurcell did not come to Venice out of some penance or compassion for the suffering in the world. Their egos were both too huge and well-fed for that. The millionaires came to Venice out of concern for themselves alone.

Despite all the testimony to the contrary from the doctors and medical personnel of the city, Worthy believed this: Lorraine LaPurcell and James Kuiper came to Venice for the only goal that mattered to them.

They came to Venice to battle cancer.

Chapter Eleven

THE SAME MORNING, ALLYSON STRUGGLED TO clear her head. Not only was Venice blanketed by fog, but the *vino* from the night before left her head in no better shape than the weather. When she came into the kitchen, she half expected to find Sylvia's clothes, purse, and shoes where her roommate left them on her way to bed. But seeing everything put away, Allyson realized that Sylvia had already left for work. That woman's stamina is amazing, Allyson thought.

She made a cup of tea and spread some marmalade on a slice of bread. Giovanni's smile came back to mind, and she wondered if he would, in fact, call her as he promised. "You need to see Lido, yes?" he said as he kissed both her cheeks in parting.

About the only thing in Venice that Allyson wanted to see that morning was her soft bed. She knew that she could make a case to *Ispettore* Ruggiero that she was on duty when clubbing last night and therefore owed more sleep, but she didn't want her excuse-making to get back to her father.

The other impetus to awaken fully was that she had somewhat neglected her official internship duties, that being to catalogue where tourists were being scammed or pickpocketed. What she discovered so far made the task truly daunting. Venice receives thirty million tourists a year, which averages out to nearly ninety thousand a day. Incredibly, the city, burdened or blessed, depending on one's point of view, by such massive tourism has a shrinking residential population of only sixty thousand.

For those Venetians alarmed by these statistics, Venice was becoming another Disneyland, with tourism being its only real business. And even the city's optimists did not deny that Venice was a massive shopping mall, but for them the city had to adapt in order to survive.

Tourism at a scale where more tourists, on average, were coming into the city every day than there were permanent residents meant that Venice was a tremendous place to take advantage of the gullibility of visitors. *Ispettore* Ruggiero already admitted in one of his briefings to her that the police department would need a thousand interns to handle the complaints of shop owners overcharging tourists, especially as they rang up credit card purchases. That was so expected, he stated, and the police treated that as normal business practice. Allyson was also to ignore the African street sellers, those who placed sheets on the sidewalks covered with knockoff purses and watches. The sight of police on foot sending them running was not unlike watching children spooking pigeons in Piazza San Marco.

Allyson's assigned focus was instead to be on the more egregious abuses against tourists. While muggings were rare in Venice, the inventiveness of the scam artists was truly impressive. Men in faux gondolier outfits would sit near unattended gondolas on some of the narrower canals and take reservations for rides later in the day. When the tourists arrived at the appointed time to enjoy their prepaid excursion, the fake gondoliers were nowhere to be found. Other respectable-looking men and even women loitered outside hotels—never the same places from one day to the next—to sell everything from false passes to museums to fake tickets for tours of the lagoon to discounts at *ristoranti* and casinos.

What made these practices even more difficult to prevent was the fact that the police suspected that most of the scam artists came into Venice every day from the mainland. Arriving on the same trains and buses as the tourists and the vast numbers of legitimate workers of the city, they plied their craft and returned to the mainland at night with their winnings. The permanent residents of Venice were legitimately angry that Venice was receiving a reputation for crime and pressured the city authorities for police screening at the mainland ports of Mestre and Correggio. Opposing that idea were the merchants who didn't want tourists to Venice being hassled in any way.

So, *Ispettore* Ruggiero explained, the trick was to create strategies to make it more difficult for scam artists while not obstructing the free flow of shopping by the tourists. As part of that goal, Allyson was to identify secondary tourist sites of the city where such crimes were becoming common. Allyson had no doubt that whatever ideas, however brilliant, that she would come up with in her three-month stay to thwart the criminal element would only spur those same people to find new and even more inventive ways to fleece gullible visitors.

And what did she estimate the chances were that her other assignment, to assist in discovering what caused the deaths of Lorraine LaPurcell and

James Kuiper, would be resolved by December? As Allyson walked to work through the fog, she admitted that the previous night was not a total waste. Despite Sylvia being distracted and then smitten by Giovanni, the roommate discovered one piece of information. Paolo, the friend of Enrico, had a friend in the hospital morgue who was the one to leak the news of James Kuiper's similar incision marks. Chatter in the hospital break room about Lorraine LaPurcell was consequently renewed, as now questions were being raised as to whether the two Americans knew one another.

Sylvia shared the information as if it would be big news to Allyson, and she therefore turned angry when she discovered that Allyson already knew about James Kuiper.

"Here you want my help, but you tell me little. And then you make a pass at Giovanni," she accused Allyson.

"What? I didn't make a pass at him. You did."

"How could I? You pigged him all to yourself, Allyson."

"I think you mean that I hogged him, Sylvia. Look, he came on to me."

Sylvia's face was pinched in a pout. "So you are not interested in Giovanni?"

Allyson realized that she had to answer the question carefully. Sylvia was her entre to the clubs of the city and Sylvia's cooperation was essential to picking up information from the hospital. She would not tell her that she planned to see Giovanni the next day for lunch.

"Okay, I think Giovanni is cute," she admitted. "I'm not blind. But I'll be gone in less than three months, and that means I have no desire to begin a serious relationship with anyone. So, if he wants to take me out to Lido—"

"He wants to take you to Lido?" Sylvia interrupted, another pout forming.

"He said he might. He said it was a mandatory part of my stay in Venice to visit Lido and see Venice from that perspective. He was surprised that I hadn't heard of it from reading Thomas Mann or someone else named Waugh. I told him that I hadn't even heard of those names before. He told me that the Lido is where he wants to have his retro club. But, who knows?"

She tried to minimize Sylvia's disappointment by offering what she was sure was a lie. "Maybe he was just bragging, like the other guys. But if we do go to the Lido, I promise we'll go together, okay? And then after I leave Italy, you can have him all to yourself."

Allyson shouldn't have been surprised when Sylvia did not refuse the offer or object to being cast as an unwanted third party. The smile on Sylvia's face suggested that she was thinking only of having Giovanni all to herself in December.

Nice to know I'll be missed, Allyson thought. "So what else did Paolo say about the scuttlebutt at the hospital?" she asked.

"What is this 'scuttle-thing?' " Sylvia asked.

"Sorry; that's an English expression, and I have no idea where it came from. Paolo said that people at the hospital were linking the deaths of Lorraine LaPurcell and James Kuiper. What else are people saying?"

Sylvia paused for a moment. "Nothing, really. Just that they wondered who will be the third body."

"The third body?" Allyson asked.

Sylvia kicked off her slacks and headed for her room. "Yes, of course. They expect another one. Don't the police?"

As Allyson walked up the stairs to the *Questura*, she looked overhead to see the sun beginning to break through the fog. Yes, that would be the question to ask *Ispettore* Ruggiero and her father. How do we know if there are other cancer-riddled millionaires hiding out in cheap hotels in Venice, soon to kill themselves or be killed?

Before entering the building, Allyson looked back at the walkways on either side of the narrow canal. The data that she was privy to indicated that the majority of those passing by were not Venetians, but tourists. How could she, her father, *Ispettore* Ruggiero, or even the entire police force of Venice find a reclusive millionaire in a city that welcomed nearly ninety thousand tourists a day?

HANDS RAISED AT THE ALTAR, FATHER Fortis invoked the Holy Spirit to come down and transform the ordinary gifts of bread and wine into the mystery of Christ's sacred body and blood. Metropolitan George Protasis, head of the Orthodox community in Venice, invited Father Fortis to serve at the altar for the Sunday Divine Liturgy and, as that is a gracious honor, Father Fortis accepted.

Ordinarily, the Metropolitan explained, the liturgy would be offered in liturgical Greek, the language of worship most familiar to the resident Orthodox community of Venice. But out of regard for the three Russian monks and the fact that none of clergy staff knew Russian, the Metropolitan asked that Father Fortis conduct some of the service, especially the homily, in English.

Ah yes, the Russians, Father Fortis thought. Allyson discovered that the apartment the Russians were occupying belonged to the Center. Was the Center also paying their living expenses, or did the three have a benefactor in Russia? Either way, limitless regard was exactly what the Orthodox Center was extending to the Russians. Why was the Center staff jumping to meet their needs?

Now as the chanter intoned his part of the service, Father Fortis could sense the eyes of the Russians burning into his back. During the homily, however, when he spoke on Jesus' prayer that His followers be one and on what was most promising in the current ecumenical efforts within Christianity, Father Fortis noticed that none of the three Russians would make eye-contact with him. I might as well have given the homily in Greek, Father Fortis thought at the time.

Certainly, in his recent confrontation with the three monks, Brother Sergius exhibited an arrogance that bordered on disdain. When Father Fortis baldly asked the leader of what he began to call the "unholy trinity" what they were doing in Venice, he first received the vague response that they were familiarizing themselves with the West.

"In America," Father Fortis stated, "we have an expression. We say, 'put your cards on the table.' That means, don't hold anything back. Be transparent. Do you understand? This," he said, again pointing to the open manuscript in front of him, "is why I'm here in this library. I'm doing research on Byzantine chant." Okay, Father Fortis admitted to himself at the time, that isn't showing all my cards, that isn't telling the entire truth, but it isn't a total lie.

"So, put your cards on the table, Brother Sergius. If you want to encounter the West, I can list ten cities closer to Russia that would offer a better opportunity. Why Venice?"

Brother Sergius crossed his arms and stared at Father Fortis. Good Lord, Father Fortis thought at the time, he looks like those old pictures of Khrushchev at the United Nations.

"Father Fortis, do you know Ravenna? No? Before you leave, you visit there. Ravenna, it is not far from here. Beautiful city. Special city. A train goes there easy. No problem. Walk around city and you observe carefully. Ravenna and Venice, both one time part of Byzantium. You must know this."

"Of course," Father Fortis replied. "That's why Venice is perfect for my research into Byzantine chant."

As if he hadn't heard Father Fortis' comment, Brother Sergius continued. "Italy only recent invention. Nineteenth century she become country," he said dismissively. "Before that, Venice was own empire. She go East to trade." He paused for a moment before adding, "Venice, Catholic place, yes?"

"Of course," Father Fortis admitted.

Brother Sergius' eyes widened, his face flushed once again. "No 'of course.' Mistake. Historical mistake. Big mistake. Venice, Ravenna, both Byzantine."

What is it about the Russian Orthodox, Father Fortis wondered, that they pretend the modern world can simply be brushed aside? No, he thought, that's an unworthy comment. He had only to look at the ever-present thinness of the monks and their ravenous appetites at mealtime to realize that they knew deprivation that he could not even imagine.

"So that is my cards on your table," Brother Sergius said in conclusion. "What is Venice? Venice is perfect place to study how West swallow East. Orthodox in Russia know West is hungry. West wants to swallow Russia."

As Father Fortis now turned from the altar and invited those present to come forward to receive the Eucharist from the chalice, he thought again about Brother Sergius' concluding comment. "Venice is perfect place to study how West swallow East." Was that xenophobic comment incriminating? Was that a justification for stealing back relics of ancient Eastern churches? Not necessarily, he admitted.

After serving communion, Father Fortis returned to the altar. It was when he was replacing the chalice on the altar that he realized something odd. The three Russians did not commune, and that omission struck him as so deliberate that he glanced back toward them. The look on the faces of the three Russians was one of contempt if not hatred.

And there, Father Fortis thought, we have all the cards on the table.

Chapter Twelve

At that afternoon's roundtable with Ruggiero, Allyson, Castelucci, and Basso, Worthy considered Allyson's report. The hospital speculation was that there would be more bodies, and the way that Allyson presented the possibility indicated that she agreed. Did he agree?

Worthy was never hesitant to disagree with a colleague or a superior. In fact, he was told repeatedly that his independent thinking bordered so closely on secrecy that few wanted to work with him.

Until now, that reputation was not something Worthy worried about. But the stakes were higher with Allyson. He felt trapped in an unspoken expectation to support her every comment, not so much out of courtesy for Allyson's standing with the Italians in the room but because of the fragility of their relationship. How could he keep every exchange, every non-verbal expression between them at a professional rather than personal level?

From his own experience, Worthy could guarantee that in most homicide investigations, one theory collided with another. He knew that, but he wasn't sure Allyson did. So it was not a question of *if* Allyson and he would disagree, but *when* that would happen. As Ruggiero waited to hear Worthy's reaction to Allyson's report, he had to decide if this was that time.

He looked across at the two Italians, Castelucci and Basso. They couldn't be that much older than Allyson, but still he wondered what they thought of two Americans, father and daughter, horning in on "their" case. The question made him feel protective of Allyson. If there was any resentment, the Italians would probably go at her, the intern, rather than a senior police officer from the States.

"What's positive about this theory," he began slowly, avoiding Allyson's name and eyes, "is that it forces us to think of the future and not just the past."

"Please explain," Ruggiero asked.

"We can't assume that these odd deaths will necessarily stop with our two known victims. There may be others in danger, and so we cannot focus solely on what has happened to this point. We also have to think how we can prevent other deaths, whether they be murders or suicides."

"Ah, yes. That is logical," Ruggiero agreed.

"But there is also a problem with this theory," Worthy continued, emphasizing the word "theory" in hopes that Allyson would understand that his comments were not personal.

Ruggiero let him off the hook by asking, "Am I right in thinking of your English expression, 'needle in a stack of hay?' "

"Yes, that's it exactly," Worthy said. "As you pointed out a couple of days ago, Inspector, Venice is flooded with tourists every day."

"We say that they wash in with the tide and wash out with the tide," Castelucci offered, the first contribution from that side of the room.

"But at least the tide in Venice is channeled into different canals," Ruggiero noted. "It is a pity, but we have no such system for tourists."

Allyson cleared her throat. "The question seems to be, how can we isolate in this tide of tourists those who fit the profile? Which are Americans, which are millionaires, and which are cancer victims."

"Right," Worthy said, relieved to find common ground with Allyson. "Passports only give us help with nationality. I mean, the hotel where the actress was hiding knew her from her passport as Linda Johnson, your average penny-pinching American. And the other hotel had no idea who James Kuiper was."

"Let us review what we say we know or believe we know," Ruggiero said. "We believe it is possible that Ms. LaPurcell and Mr. Kuiper came to Venezia because of cancer. We believe these strange incisions must have something to do with their diagnoses, despite what local doctors tell us. We know that both Americans died tragically and maybe suspiciously. Yes?"

All those in the room nodded in agreement.

"Sgt. Castelucci, have we ruled out any physician in Venice who might be associated with an experimental or unapproved treatment for cancer?"

"*Assolutemente, Ispettore*," Castelucci assured him.

"And Sgt. Basso, still no clue as to when and how the two Americans decided to come to Venezia?" he asked.

"No, *Ispettore*, we can find nothing on the Internet in Italian or English about Venezia, Venice, and *cancro* or cancer."

Something in the way that Basso phrased his answer struck Worthy as significant, but after waiting fruitlessly for the hunch to germinate into a thought, he asked, "So they met someone who gave them some hope, some false hope, obviously, that your city might hold a cure."

"And it seems pretty clear that the person who snagged them didn't do that here in Venice," Allyson added.

"Why you say such?" Castelucci asked. Once again, Worthy felt a wave of protectiveness for his daughter. Did this Italian resent Allyson's presence in the room because she was an American, a college student, or because she was a woman?

Allyson, however, didn't show any signs of being bothered by the question. "Because James Kuiper made it pretty clear to his family that he disliked Venice. For me, it's truly odd how anyone could say that. That's why I think it's important. So at least Mr. Kuiper became convinced that Venice was worth a return visit."

"And that would have happened in the States," Worthy said.

Allyson nodded. "As soon as he got to Amsterdam, Kuiper booked a flight for Venice. And his Dutch relatives never heard of any intended visit. The whole thing was obviously preplanned."

"Yes, I agree," Ruggiero said. "So, what do we have? Someone planted a … a seed of hope in Mr. Kuiper's mind, someone who knew that he had cancer and convinced him to come, but secretly, to Venezia. What else?"

Worthy waited for someone else to pick up the thread, but when no one did, he went ahead. "Someone else must have met him and probably Lorraine LaPurcell once they arrived. Maybe that contact happened at their hotels, or maybe they met on the sly somewhere in the city."

"In one of our five thousand bars," Basso added with a sigh.

"And since no one recognized Lorraine LaPurcell or James Kuiper, any meeting they had with a local contact wouldn't have raised an alarm," Worthy said.

"That's not exactly true," Allyson countered. "Enrico—he works at the hospital—claims he did recognize Lorraine LaPurcell a couple of days before her death."

"I forgot that," Worthy admitted. "Didn't this Enrico say she was alone?" Worthy asked.

"I don't think I asked him that. But I will now," she said.

"And perhaps it is time for us to put out a request to the public," Ruggiero said, "to find out if anyone else dealt with Ms. LaPurcell. Mr. Kuiper would be a nameless face, but the actress was no stranger to Venezia."

Get ready for the crazies, Worthy thought, those who'll claim that they were acquaintances, even friends, of the famous actress. But he kept that to himself.

Just as the meeting was ending, Castelucci raised his hand as if he were in class. A look of satisfaction beamed from his face. "*Ispettore*, Basso and I did find out something new, maybe *importante*, maybe no."

"Well, Stephano?" Ruggiero encouraged.

"We went back to hotels, talk with those at reception, yes? Ms. Purcell ask at desk for train timetable week before she jump … before she die."

"Did she say where she was going or when?" Ruggiero asked.

"No, no. But maybe she go somewhere. She not seen next day."

It was now Basso's turn. "We go to other hotel, yes? He too ask at desk for train schedule. They no know where he go."

"How many days before he died?" Worthy asked.

Basso looked in Worthy's direction with surprise, as if he forgot that the Americans were still there. "Two days maybe."

"So why'd they break their pattern of reclusiveness?" Allyson said. "I can't see either of them taking a train for pleasure. Maybe to visit a doctor elsewhere?"

"Very interesting," Ruggiero concluded, nodding at Castelucci and Basso. "Maybe someone recognize them on the trains and can tell us where the two of them got off."

After a moment, he added, "But it is doubtful, what you Americans call a 'long shot,' yes? Our train station is full of crowds, always. But Basso and Castelucci will ask. Maybe we get lucky."

Worthy lagged behind for a moment as the meeting ended and everyone left the conference room. Allyson was the first to leave and did not look at him, so he decided to give her space. As he stood up and looked out on the canal and walkway in front of the *Questera*, he felt old. I'm just emotionally tired, he reasoned. Or jet-lagged. He got through the conference with Allyson without a false step, their fragile bond still intact. She even corrected him, and that hadn't hurt a bit, he admitted.

But part of his fatigue came from the nagging feeling that he missed something. He replayed the part of the meeting where something struggled to break through, only to be pushed down. What was it about Basso's search on the Internet that gave him that feeling? Why did he sense that they were near a door that was yet to be opened? And who, he wondered, will be waiting on the other side of that door?

Allyson indeed bolted from the conference room, but more to create distance from Castelucci and Basso than her father. When Castelucci challenged her, she saw his foot poke Basso's under the table. And earlier that day, right after she returned from her lunch with Giovanni, Castelucci stopped by her desk to clumsily flirt. Talk about bad timing, she thought. Little did Castelucci know how boyish he seemed with his pungent aftershave in comparison with Giovanni.

If she had foreseen Castelucci's advance, she would have told Giovanni over lunch that he was wrong at their first meeting. Not all Italian men were natural-born flirts.

The hour for lunch with Giovanni did not disappoint her. He came to his personally selected *ristorante* dressed in a loose-fitting blue silk shirt atop tight jeans. Casual, yes, but also stunning, she thought.

It was clear to Allyson that the plan for lunch was for Giovanni to show interest in her. If this was his usual style in meeting women, he was very good at it. His follow-up questions showed a level of interest that she had not experienced to that point from men at Franklin College. Yes, Giovanni did end up asking her the stereotypical questions of the college freshman guy—where are you from, and what is your major? But the way that he asked those questions felt like honey dripping into her mouth.

When she described the data-collecting that she was doing for her internship, Giovanni shared that he once thought of becoming a policeman. But when he was told that his chances would be better with the *carbinieri*, he refused. The *carbinieri*, he explained with disgust, stood around in the piazzas and chatted up female tourists.

"Me? I have self-respect. *Carbinieri* not for me," he said.

He talked more about his plans for running a club on the Lido, something that he predicted would probably take him many years to realize. "Money, money. Venezia is dying, but she is still a very expensive woman to fall in love with," he added.

She involuntarily gasped when she realized the parallel of that comment with the death of Lorraine LaPurcell. When he asked what he said that was so surprising, she laughed it off and said that Venice did seem more like a woman. Inwardly, she reminded herself that she needed to chat up Enrico, the one who claimed to have seen Lorraine LaPurcell just days before she died. But how could she ask Enrico questions that demanded details without him getting suspicious? Or should she trust Sylvia with this assignment?

"Hello, hello," Giovanni said, laughing as he touched her arm.

"Sorry," she said. "We were agreeing that your Venice is like a woman."

"Not just a woman," he corrected, "*the* woman. The sublime woman. *La Serenessima*, that is what we call her. My own club, my dream. With money, it is possible. But Venezia may say no. She breaks hearts, from the very beginning, she always do this."

When they parted, Giovanni made the offer to take her the following evening to Lido. Once again when they parted, he kissed her lightly on both cheeks before whispering softly, "Ciao, bella."

So Giovanni two days in a row, she thought. I could get used to this. But then she remembered her promise to Sylvia. There was no way that her roommate would forgive her if she broke their agreement.

She thought of the outfits in her closet and realized that no matter what she chose to wear, Sylvia would outshine her. Sylvia's continued comments about Giovanni ("I love his hair, so classical," and "a business management degree; he must be brilliant") left Allyson with no doubt that Sylvia would have an agenda for the evening.

Do I also have an agenda, she asked herself. Am I fooling myself that I can't afford to start a relationship, given my responsibilities, public and covert, with the police department? She thought back on her third night in Venice, when she stood by the Grand Canal and watched the sun set over the lagoon. She thought of Venice as perfect. Would she still say that?

In one way, no. Having her father in Venice, also working with the police on the LaPurcell and Kuiper cases, still felt awkward. It seemed that they saw each other every day. Some of those days they talked naturally about the case or about the city. Her father was using her as his GPS, asking the best ways to get to certain addresses. But other days, especially when they were together with Ruggiero or Ruggiero along with Castelucci and Basso, she could feel the tension between them. Only when she was at her apartment or out with Sylvia at a club did she feel that she could let down her guard.

But if her father's presence detracted from her enjoyment of Venice, didn't meeting Giovanni compensate for that? If she knew two weeks ago, when she stood by the Grand Canal and declared her love for the city, that Giovanni would come into her life, would she not have concluded that now her time in Venice had become even more perfect?

So regardless of her duties with the police and regardless of how Sylvia will throw herself at Giovanni tomorrow night, she thought, she needn't dress and act like a nun. She dated enough in the States, especially in her first year of college, to know how to interpret the signs, and the signs that she picked up from Giovanni were that he was interested in her, not Sylvia. And while Enrico, Paolo, and Luigi tried to make an impression by being loud and brash, Giovanni's demeanor seemed more controlled, even introspective. Allyson smiled as she realized that Enrico and his friends were like Sylvia, while she was more like Giovanni.

The next night, when Sylvia and Allyson arrived at the boat dock, Allyson was surprised to find Enrico, Paolo, and Luigi also in the mahogany craft.

Giovanni seemed to see her stunned reaction, and asked if she didn't know that Sylvia called to say that she, Allyson, wanted the whole group to go.

Allyson glanced at her roommate who already managed, despite a blouse and jeans that she had to pour herself into, to jump onto the boat so that Giovanni had to catch and steady her. Sylvia turned toward Allyson with the look of "sorry, didn't I tell you?"

"The more the merrier," Allyson said, aiming the note of sarcasm at her roommate.

"Yes, is better with a group," Giovanni replied, although Allyson wondered if he didn't at that same moment realize what Sylvia pulled off.

"Giovanni's boat. You like boats?" Enrico asked over the sound of the engine, as Allyson took the only seat left after Sylvia bolted for the one in front with Giovanni. "You no get seasick."

"Not to fear," Allyson answered. "My family has a boat."

"Ah, a Chris Craft, wood like this, yes?" Luigi asked.

"No, I think it's fiberglass."

Luigi shrugged a bit with what seemed disappointment. "Fiberglass also good boat," he conceded.

The powerful craft made quick work of the short distance between the dock and Lido. Paolo tried to shout something to Allyson above the roar of the engines, but Allyson was happy to signal that she couldn't hear a thing.

As the boat slowed, Allyson scanned the long beach and boardwalk of Lido. An island of the lagoon not out of sight of Venice proper, Lido, despite a few automobiles, looked to her like a movie set from the early 20th century.

With the engines now only idling as Giovanni expertly nosed the boat to the dock, Enrico played the tour guide. "This is Grand Hotel des Bains," he explained, pointing to a stunning four-story building from a bygone era. "Very famous. And over there," pointing a few hundred yards down the beach with pride as if he were the owner, "this is Grand Hotel Excelsior. Also very famous, very expensive."

Despite being distracted by Sylvia playing the helpless female and asking Giovanni to help her step onto the dock, Allyson did have to admit that the buildings were impressive. "Who can afford to stay in these places?" she asked.

"Ah, many, many millionaires from all over the world once stay on Lido," Luigi added.

Allyson managed to exit the boat without needing the outstretched arms of the three men apparently assigned to her by Sylvia. As she walked to the causeway, she could see Sylvia ahead, linking her arm into Giovanni's. Giovanni stole a look back at Allyson in what she hoped was a sign of disappointment.

She remembered a platitude written on the chalkboard from her introduction to psychology class in her first year of college. Although she wasn't sure of the exact wording, the sentiment was that what life deals us is called fate; but how we respond to what we are dealt is free will.

Allyson wrote the phrase down and underlined it. At the time, the bit of wisdom helped her put to rest the nagging questions remaining from her parents' divorce. For too long, she ruminated on the unexpected split as something that she should have prevented. What had she missed? More than once, she wondered if her decision to run away was a fruitless attempt to force her mother and father back together.

Through that bit of wisdom from her psychology class, she was able to reframe the divorce. The divorce was something that life dealt her, and she would only be wasting time in trying to make sense of it. How she was going to respond to it was all that mattered.

As she watched Sylvia thwart her desire to be with Giovanni, and what she hoped was his desire to be with her, Allyson considered her situation in the light of that wisdom. Was her being stuck with Enrico, Luigi, and Paolo her "fate" for the evening, or did she have a choice?

She took a deep breath, as if to say goodbye to Giovanni for the evening, and turned her attention to Luigi, Paolo and Enrico. Hadn't she wondered earlier that day how she could maneuver a conversation with Enrico about Lorraine LaPurcell?

"You make it sound as if millionaires no longer come to Venice," she said to Luigi.

"Yes, but of course, they still come," he said, obviously pleased to be addressed by Allyson, "but not like the old days, the days of my grandfather. Lido was maybe like Monaco, like the Riviera. Very grand, like the names of the hotels," as if the thought just came to him.

Allyson slowed down to create a bigger gap between herself and Giovanni. I don't need to hear what Sylvia is chattering about. Well, look at me, she said to herself, I'm acting like an adult.

Paolo touched her arm and pointed in the beach's opposite direction: "The film festival is held there. Many movie stars come, many millionaires then. But not so many now."

Allyson gave her best impression of someone interested in Enrico. "Someone told me that Lorraine LaPurcell was here last year for the festival. And then I heard that she died here a few weeks ago."

Enrico swallowed the bait in a gulp. "Yes, and I saw her here in Venice. One day, maybe two days before she die."

"Are you sure? I mean, what did she look like?" Allyson said, continuing to focus on Enrico to the dismay of the other two.

"I big film fan, very big. I come to Lido every year. I see Madonna, Robert DeNiro, Kiefer Sutherland," he said, counting the names off on his hand.

"But Lorraine LaPurcell was an older actress from the seventies, right?"

As if he felt he was being tested, Enrico smiled confidently. "Old films, my favorites. She was in *Rest Assured*, 1984. Romantic comedy. She play a young widow. She left by husband to run an old people's home. She fall in love with Jeremy Irons. Jeremy Irons in Venezia maybe twenty, thirty years before to film *Brideshead Revisited*."

Enrico looked at Allyson as if to see if she was impressed. "Okay, film nut," she said to challenge him, "what did Lorraine LaPurcell look like? Did you talk with her? Did you ask for her autograph?"

Enrico sighed, as if he failed to complete an assignment. "No autograph, but I have good memory for faces. I spot Lorraine LaPurcell right away. Beautiful eyes. Still beautiful woman. Not like Sophia Loren or Anna Magnani, but very beautiful. American beauty, you know? I make no mistake, I swear."

"Wow, you really saw a movie star," Allyson said, playing up her admiration for Enrico. "What was she doing?"

"She had shopping bags, both hands."

"I mean, was she wearing makeup? Was she having to fight off the crowds?"

"No, others pass by her, don't see who she is. Not film fans. No makeup, and wearing a beret. Long raincoat. Burberry, I think. Yes, Burberry."

As nonchalantly as she could, she asked the question that she was saving. "So was she alone?"

Enrico looked puzzled. "I tell you, people all around. Me too."

"But was someone with her?" she clarified, and then looked into an antique shop window as if she barely cared about the answer.

Enrico paused and Allyson wondered if she was too obvious in her interest. To emphasize her apparent casualness, she pointed to a piece of jewelry and asked Paolo how old he guessed it was.

Enrico seemed to realize that he could lose Allyson's attention. "Lorraine LaPurcell, her face look like she was crying. Maybe someone else with her, maybe they have a fight." Enrico hardly waited half a beat before adding, "Yes, I remember. Man with her holding an umbrella, yes? Holding it over her head."

"I suppose another American, maybe her manager," Allyson suggested.

"Not American. No, not American."

Allyson looked at him and laughed easily. "Are we that easy to recognize?"

Enrico shook his head. "No, he a smoker. But he hold his cigarette like this," he said, pretending to hold a cigarette between his thumb and forefinger.

"And how do Americans hold their cigarettes?" she asked.

Enrico shifted the pretend cigarette between his first and second fingers. "Americans smoke like cowboys. This man maybe from Europe somewhere."

Allyson again asked herself the same questions. When could Enrico be believed, and when was he simply trying to impress? If he was jogging, did he see all that he claimed? The detail of how the cigarette was held by the man was certainly very specific. Would he describe the scene in the same way if questioned by the police?

Allyson dropped the subject and watched as Sylvia repeatedly asked Giovanni to dance, eventually got tipsy, and even tried to kiss Giovanni. To Allyson's delight, Giovanni turned away and laughed at her.

Allyson wanted to believe Enrico—that Lorraine LaPurcell was with someone in Venice. She wanted to believe Enrico—that the actress seemed to be crying. That might connect with her cancer and ultimately, two days later, with her suicide or murder. She wanted to believe Enrico—that the man was not an American, but a European. That might suggest that this same man was her contact in Venice. She wanted to believe that the man might even be the one who killed her and two weeks later killed James Kuiper.

But if there was one thing that she learned from watching her father over his career, it was this: never confuse what you want to be true in a case with what the evidence suggests.

CHAPTER THIRTEEN

THE NEXT DAY, AFTER A LESS than satisfying lunch at a stand-up pizza bar, Father Fortis found a note taped to his room door. *Please make yourself available for a meeting at the Metropolitan's office today at 1400 hours.*

Should I plan for another protest from the Russians about my encounter with Brother Alexis, he wondered. From the glances and whispering of the three monks at yesterday's meals at the Center, Father Fortis sensed that some new development might have occurred.

Or perhaps, he thought, the Metropolitan wants a progress report on the relic thefts. Progress? He had no proof that the Russians were involved, so he was no further than the police were weeks ago. And if the Russians were not involved, he would have to admit to the Metropolitan that he had no other idea who was behind the crimes.

He thought again of the phantom figure who pursued him three nights before. Given where he hid himself, he probably saw the figure for little more than a second. He closed his eyes and tried to remember details.

He was almost certain that the figure was a male, despite the figure being hooded. At least the long strides of the figure seemed those of a man, and a man fleet of foot. He seemed to fly by Father Fortis' hiding place, and Father Fortis didn't remember the man breathing heavily as he had in the alley. So the man was in good shape and probably thin.

He tried to recall the kind of shoes that the pursuer was wearing, but that was all a blur in his memory. A thin man in dark athletic clothes who could run like the wind.

He imagined trying to sell the Metropolitan on such a scant recollection of the pursuer and even on the idea that he was pursued. As Brother Sergius asked, why would anyone be following you?

If I was, in fact, being pursued, Father Fortis thought, I must be viewed as a threat in some way. But what have I done that could alarm the thieves, assuming they're the ones tailing me? Even if there'd been a leak somehow about my true reason for being in Venice, the thieves would surely know that I've made no progress.

At two in the afternoon, upon entering the Metropolitan's study, Father Fortis saw a room full of men and concluded that he'd guessed incorrectly as to the purpose of the meeting. He recognized the Catholic patriarch of the city along with what looked like two staff members, also priests, sitting next to him. On the other side of the room sat the Metropolitan and his chancellor. The room seems too quiet, Father Fortis thought. Why aren't they talking with one another?

The chancellor of the Center gestured toward a vacant chair, one positioned between the two groups and under an early icon of the Holy Trinity. What does that mean, Father Fortis asked himself. Do they see me as a bridge between them, or are both groups disowning me?

The Metropolitan fiddled with his bishop's staff with one hand while pulling down on his luxurious grey beard with the other.

"Father Fortis, you no speak Italian, yes?"

Father Fortis wasn't sure how to answer the question. Do I say yes, I don't speak Italian or no, I don't speak Italian?

"Your Eminence, I do not, unfortunately," he replied.

"And my English is weak," the Metropolitan said. "So please excuse. We have new problem, Father. Sometime, in last three maybe four days more, another relic has been stolen. Very serious."

Father Fortis sat in stunned silence. Was this what the three Russians were whispering about the day before? "What relics, your Eminence?"

The Metropolitan nodded toward his Catholic counterpart. The patriarch held out toward Father Fortis a sheet of paper, a police report in Italian, he realized as he took it.

"The report confirms that someone has broken into a church on Murano," the patriarch said.

Father Fortis looked puzzled. "Murano?"

One of the Catholic priests explained that Murano was one of the larger islands in the Venetian lagoon. "An old church, known for its marble floors, not its relics," the priest added.

"And no one is exactly sure when the theft occurred?" Father Fortis asked.

"No more than four days ago, but maybe only two," the priest continued to speak for the Catholic side.

Which means the theft could have overlapped with him being pursued three nights before. Was that just coincidence?

"And I assume the relics were from an Eastern saint," Father Fortis probed further.

The room returned to the uncomfortable silence that greeted Father Fortis when he entered. Finally, the chancellor confirmed that the relic taken was a finger bone of St. Eusebius of Antioch, a third-century church father.

"Where was the relic kept in the church?" Father Fortis asked. "In the altar or in a reliquary?"

"In a reliquary, locked, in the crypt. But not secured very well," the Catholic patriarch explained. "And the church is open during the daytime."

"No security cameras?"

Again, the room returned to tense silence. "People expect them to be open for prayer," the talkative priest shared.

Father Fortis paused for a moment. He could not ask the question that was uppermost in his mind and perhaps in the minds of others. *Do you suspect the Russians?*

When he looked up at the divided room, he felt all eyes upon him. Oh, I see, he realized. I'm supposed to know the answer to that question. They want me to tell them if they should turn the Russians in for questioning, if the police should ransack their rooms, if the authorities should grill the Russians until they find out all they knew.

But how sure is anyone that the Russians are involved, he asked himself again. If I argue they are and I'm wrong, I'll have lost whatever cooperation the Center could provide. If I argue they may not be and I'm wrong, I'll lose the cooperation of the Catholic side.

"I may learn nothing, but would you give me a few hours to talk with Brother Sergius and the other two Russians?" He was careful as he asked the question to make eye-contact with both sides of the room.

For a moment, he wondered if anyone would answer his question. Finally, the Metropolitan coughed and tapped his staff on the floor. "There, we have a problem," he said, not making eye contact with those on the other side of the room.

"Oh?" Father Fortis asked.

"Brother Sergius, he is gone."

"And the other two monks?"

Shrugging, the Metropolitan answered, "Yes, they are in Venezia, but they say they do not know where is Brother Sergius. He seems to have vanished. We are hoping that you will find him. Can you?"

✝

AT THE SAME TIME THAT FATHER Fortis was given the task of finding the elusive Russian monk, Ruggiero assembled Worthy, Allyson, Castelucci, and Basso in the morgue of the city hospital. On the slab in front of them was the bloated body of a man, an obvious drowning victim. On the man's right hand was a ring with a diamond insert.

The coroner, however, was more interested in an incision, puffy and red, under the armpit of the corpse.

"Like the others," Ruggiero translated for the coroner, "it looks like one incision on top of another. The one you see now is only days old."

Worthy bent down to take a close look at the incision. Yes, it did look identical to the other two in the photos. "Any identification found on the body?" he asked.

"Not on the body," Ruggiero replied. "But on shore, out on Lido, we found clothes. Inside wallet, a Ukrainian driver's license. Nicholai Monsinoff. No word on cancer until autopsy."

Worthy felt a bit sucker-punched by the news. He assumed the murders or suicides were confined to American cancer victims. Were they now dealing with something international?

Next to him, he heard Allyson gasp. "You said Lido?" she asked.

"Yes, it is very popular bathing spot," Castelucci replied with a tone of authority.

"I know what Lido is," she said curtly. And I also know that Venetians say "Lido," not "the Lido," she thought. "Where on Lido?" she added.

Ruggiero looked at Allyson with a puzzled expression. "Near one of the big hotels," he explained. "We are checking. Maybe he is guest there. Many Eastern Europeans come to Venezia. Much, much money since Soviets finished. They enjoy bathing on Lido."

"If so, then he breaks the pattern. The others were staying in cheap places here in Venice," she commented. "I've been told the hotels on Lido are very expensive."

"Si, si," Ruggiero agreed, adding in a mix of Italian and English, "*molto* money."

Good point, Allyson, Worthy thought. The differences of the cases may be as important as the similarities. "Was anything found in our victim's swimming trunks?" he asked.

For a moment, Ruggiero seemed confused by the question. Then, "Ah, bathing suit. You say trunks. No, he was found like this. Naked."

Basso said something to Castelucci in whispered Italian, bringing a slight sneer to the colleague's face.

Ruggiero gave them a cautionary look before saying, "Maybe he is a nudist. We have those on Lido."

Worthy asked Ruggiero to ask the coroner to open the victim's mouth. The coroner raised his eyebrows at Ruggiero, but complied. The jaw opened to the coroner's touch as if on a spring.

With a flashlight, Worthy bent over the victim's face. He peered into the Ukrainian's mouth. He could see sand and some vegetative matter on the lower teeth, but he was studying the dental work. Several of the teeth were capped and three of the teeth had gold inlays.

"You find something?" Ruggiero asked.

"I have no idea of the quality of dentistry in the Ukraine, but the dental work in his mouth could have been done in North America."

"So maybe he come to Venice from the States, like the others," Ruggiero concluded. "And if he has cancer, maybe he hear something in your country that brings him to Venezia, yes?"

"Maybe so," Worthy replied. "If we have his I.D., we should be able to check on his recent travels." Worthy stepped back and lifted the corpse's limp right arm.

Again, with the flashlight, he inspected the incision site. "And we have no idea what would cause this?" he asked as he looked around the room.

It was the coroner who, hearing the question translated, shook his head. Ruggiero translated his rapid reply for Worthy. "He say he never see cuttings like the three bodies. Very shallow, barely into muscle."

Ruggiero seemed to wait respectfully to see if Worthy was finished with his inspection of the body. When Worthy nodded, Ruggiero took control. "Basso and Castelucci, you check to see where Nicholai Monsinoff stay and how long he here in Venezia. Allyson, you please check on where he fly in from, yes? Good. We know more tomorrow when autopsy finished."

Worthy didn't mind being left out of the assignments. He knew exactly what he would do next, and he needed Allyson to set up a meeting with Father Fortis.

Chapter Fourteen

Allyson was used to Father Fortis responding to one of her coded requests for a meeting within hours, so his failure to do so puzzled her. As she waited for his response, she tried to concentrate on the complaint forms submitted over the past weekend from fleeced tourists. The standardized form in plain English, through which the affected tourist described both the appearance of the perpetrator and his or her techniques, was one of her first strategies to address the problem. The response to the forms was good and she guessed potentially helpful, even if the number of forms she now dealt with suggested that scamming was a thriving business in Venice.

But she found it hard to keep her mind on the forms. The body lying on the slab in the morgue made her feel that she was watching a TV forensic crime drama. She half-expected the body to sit up and complain of the cold in the room. But then when *Ispettore* Ruggiero informed them that the body was in the water for perhaps two days before being pulled out on Lido, she felt herself grow cold with the news. Had Giovanni's boat come near the body?

She watched her father inspect the victim's mouth and comment about the evidence suggested by the advanced dental care. And she observed her father studying the sutures and incision. If anything, he seemed curious—no, more than curious—energized, to be able to probe the recently deceased victim.

Allyson wondered if such casual professionalism would come to her after more experience. Would her father behave the same if the victim were a child? A young mother?

All Allyson knew at that moment was that she would not have been able to take one step closer to the drowned man. The body was bloated, and there were marks that suggested that sea creatures had already begun to feast on it. The smell also, a mix of human decay and salt water, nauseated her.

I could have passed this man out on Lido, she thought. And, assuming that this man stayed at one of the hotels on Lido, it seemed even more probable that Giovanni, who worked part-time on his school vacation at the club they frequented that night, could have seen this man.

So, part of the shiver that passed through her was caused by the eerie coincidence of her and her friends being so near to where this man was last seen alive.

A second disturbing thought was the realization that, if her father's theory was correct, this man did not die due to accidental drowning, but was somehow killed, stripped of his clothes, and made to look like a drowning victim.

But there was yet a third reason for that sudden chill she felt in the morgue. Was it really possible that the body that lay in front of her was so recently alive, as alive as she or anyone else in the room? Were death and life so close together?

She closed the folder with the tourist complaints and decided she needed some fresh air. She walked in the direction of the Grand Canal, realizing that her desire at that moment was completely opposite of what she usually felt. Now, instead of wanting to find a bit of solitude in tourist-crowded Venice, she wanted to be surrounded by people, people fully alive, people with no thoughts of death.

FATHER FORTIS DID NOT SEE THE coded note left by Allyson because he was searching, without success, for Brother Sergius. Brother Alexei and Brother Nilus were of little help, and Father Fortis wasn't sure that the two weren't using their lack of Italian or English as a smokescreen. A question as simple as "Did Brother Sergius leave the apartment at any time last evening?" would have to be rephrased three or four times in the most basic English before the two would shake their heads to indicate that they weren't sure.

Reluctantly, and not just because of their difficulty of understanding the request, the two finally gave Father Fortis permission to look through Brother Sergius' possessions. They first wanted to know why Father Fortis was involved, and they seemed dissatisfied when he told them that the Metropolitan requested that Father Fortis be the one to conduct the search.

The two consequently watched Father Fortis suspiciously as he looked through Brother Sergius' meager possessions. Are they afraid that I'll steal something, or are they afraid that I will find something, he wondered.

In order of significance, Father Fortis found Brother Sergius' passport, a packet of plane tickets, a wallet, and a circled map of Venice. The presence of the passport and the plane tickets, flights in a week for Moscow via Paris, suggested that Brother Sergius was still in Venice. Perhaps if Brother Sergius is at all connected with the latest theft of relics, Father Fortis thought, he's in hiding with his local contact.

When asked about Brother Sergius' plans for returning to Russia in a week, the two monks both claimed that they knew nothing of those plans. "We have no ticket for home," Brother Alexis was able to get out. Easy to check on that, Father Fortis thought. If they're telling the truth, then Brother Sergius has been keeping secrets from them.

By getting on his knees to search under the bed, Father Fortis managed to slip the monk's map into his pocket. The map was of interest to him for several reasons. One, he thought it significant that Brother Sergius did not need it for what called him away from the Center. And two, Father Fortis understood that his search for Brother Sergius in Venice might be expedited by such a map. He would begin with the marked locations nearest the Orthodox Center and work outwards.

But what did it mean that not one of the churches burgled by the relic thieves was circled on the map? And when was a circled location just a favorite eatery or bookstore of the monk, and when was it a place of rendezvous?

Was it significant that the official Russian representative's office was circled, or was that to be expected? And what did the word mean, written at the bottom of the map in Cyrillic, that Father Fortis, with the help of a dictionary from the center, had been able to translate as "Torcello?"

After stopping in at six of the closest circled locations on the map only to find himself in a stationary store, a watch repair store, and a small market, Father Fortis returned to the Center, bone-tired from the miles of walking. His first thought on finding Allyson's coded message was that he couldn't afford to take an evening off when finding Brother Sergius, and perhaps the relic as well, was so important.

But when he took his shoes off and eased himself onto his bed, he realized what he needed most was to sit, eat, rest, and share his new challenge with Worthy and Allyson.

Chapter Fifteen

The meeting at the familiar restaurant on *La Giudecca* was to take place at seven in the evening. Each was to come on his or her own to avoid any suspicions. Allyson arrived a bit early, followed twenty minutes later by her father. By ten after seven, Father Fortis had still not arrived.

Allyson sat across from her father and gazed out on the calm waters of the lagoon. A few fishing boats with nets draped over the bows sat next to a polished mahogany inboard, not unlike Giovanni's boat. This boat, however, bore the same name as the restaurant, *La Barca Bella*, the beautiful boat.

While they exchanged pleasantries of weather and Venetian anecdotes more typical of tourists who'd been thrown together than of a father and daughter, Allyson wondered what she would have said if someone told her a year earlier that she would have an internship in Venice and be working a case with her father. What would have been the bigger surprise to her, being in her beloved Venice or working a case with her father?

In a sense, it was true that the two of them were thrown together like fellow travelers. Certainly, she would never have asked her father to be part of her internship in Venice, and she guessed that her father would feel the same about working with her on this case. That similarity between them made her smile.

"What's so funny?" her father asked. The question didn't sound accusatory but rather simply curious.

Okay, she thought, let's see how telling the truth works for the two of us.

"I was just thinking that the way we are together can feel awkward—at least for me—well, it's kind of like we're two strangers who just happen to have been thrown together."

She waited to hear if her father understood. After a moment and a sip of water, he nodded slowly. "Anytime I have a new partner, whether in Detroit or on a case like this one, I always feel like I'm learning to dance all over again. No two cases are ever the same; new partners are that way too."

"Unless you work with them for a long time," Allyson said.

"I suppose so. When I was a kid, there was this cop show on TV called *Dragnet*. Anyway, these two cops in Los Angeles always worked together. Sometimes the one would finish a sentence begun by the other one. Looking back, they were more like brothers than partners, at least in my experience, which, come to think of it, probably isn't a fair example."

Not that long ago, Allyson viewed her father's difficulty in working with partners as providing some insight into her parents' failed marriage. No one would argue that her dad was a loner in his career. His successes in solving complex and frustrating cases often led to only him receiving the commendations from the mayor. When she hated and blamed him for the divorce, she pictured him as Sherlock Holmes without a Watson—and without a wife.

Seeing her father in a new light, maybe it would be fairer to say a faint glimmer of light, was the result of getting to know him through Father Fortis. The two men worked together brilliantly, solving a serial killing spree in New Mexico and a puzzling homicide of an old priest in Detroit.

And now that she saw the two of them together, she saw that her father wasn't the narcissist that she judged him to be. Father Fortis helped, responding to a letter she wrote him in her first semester of college. She asked the monk why he thought her father seemed such a loner. Father Fortis wrote back, asking that she try to imagine how lonely it might be to grow up a minister's son in a small town in Kentucky.

"I gathered from the meeting this morning that you'd already been out to that island," Worthy said, interrupting her thoughts.

"Yes, Sylvia and I went with some of her friends the other night to a club," she answered.

"Did you learn anything?"

"Maybe," she replied. "I think one of the guys from the hospital—that's Enrico, the guy I mentioned at the meeting—I think he really did see Lorraine LaPurcell in Venice."

"Were you able to ask him if she was alone?" Worthy asked.

"I didn't want to be too obvious, but I did get around to that. He described a man holding an umbrella for her."

Worthy leaned forward. "Really? Any details?"

Allyson was relieved that they were talking about the case, like two professionals, not like a father probing into his daughter's life. She felt that her father would be asking the same questions of Father Fortis or any other partner.

"Enrico thinks the umbrella was a Burberry, which is a pretty expensive English brand." She thought for a moment before adding, "I suppose it could have been a knock-off, though. I've seen a lot of those being sold on the streets. He also thought that the man was European from the way he was smoking."

"What did he mean?" Worthy asked.

Allyson held her spoon between her thumb and forefinger, as Enrico demonstrated. "Like this."

"That's interesting. People smoke a lot here in Italy, at least as compared to the States. Even in restaurants like this one." He nodded in the direction of another table.

Allyson glanced over to see a couple with cocktails and lit cigarettes. They hold the cigarettes as Americans do, she realized.

"I haven't made a study of Italians on smoking, but I bet most of them smoke like those two, like Americans. Like the Marlboro man, I guess," he said.

She shifted the spoon between her thumb and forefinger. "So what would this other way of holding cigarettes mean?" she asked.

"I'd say it was somebody who grew up where they didn't show a lot of our TV programs and films."

"Like in the Ukraine?" she asked.

Worthy shrugged. "No harm in checking out Monsinoff's hands for tobacco stains. And if that shows a match, then I think we need to have your friend Enrico look at a picture of our latest victim."

Allyson grimaced at the plan. "Here's the problem with that. There's still a big chance that there's no connection between Vladimir Monsinoff and Lorraine LaPurcell. If that's the case, I won't be of much use to the investigation if Enrico finds out about my part in all this."

"No, I understand that. And he shouldn't know that we're related. I hope you can trust me, that I won't blow your cover."

Allyson glanced up at her father and realized that she did trust him. Whatever their issues in the past, she knew her father to be straightforward, a man of his word.

Panting, Father Fortis entered the restaurant, apologizing profusely for a nap that lasted too long. Allyson realized that her panicky need twenty minutes earlier for Father Fortis to save her from having to talk one-on-one with her father dissipated as the two of them focused on the case. She felt that her father was open with her, and she with him, not guarded as usual.

So I trust him, yet I didn't tell him about Giovanni, she confessed. And why should I, she asked herself. That's personal, not part of the case. The fact that Lido is Giovanni's playground as well as where the Ukrainian's body was found is simply a coincidence.

✝

"Allyson, I thought I shared your love of Venice," Father Fortis said, having still not quite caught his breath, "but this has to be the easiest city in the world to get lost in. If it weren't for the fact that you'll eventually run into the lagoon, I think in about a week someone would find my withered body halfway to Albania."

He slapped the map on the table. "And they should call these Benedict Arnolds. They don't guide you; they betray you."

He asked for a glass of water and, when it came, downed it with hardly a pause. "Yes, I admit it. I'm cranky, I'm frustrated, and I'm tired of feeling that I know less and less every day. You won't believe what has just happened."

"From the looks of the map and your beet-red face," Worthy commented, "I would say that this is one mouse who hasn't found the cheese."

Father Fortis threw up his hands. "Exactly. I'm a mouse caught in a maze. And even when I find a place I'm searching for with this blasted thing," he said, pointing to the dog-eared map, "there is not even a hint of cheese."

"All right, now you've lost me," Allyson said. "What's the cheese, the missing relics or the thieves?"

"Ha," Father Fortis exclaimed. "It's both! Can you beat that? Another relic was stolen in the past three or four days, and, God help me, now Brother Sergius has disappeared."

Worthy whistled. "That can't be a coincidence."

When the waiter approached the table to take their orders, Father Fortis quickly scanned the menu while Allyson ordered *insalata misti*, a mixed salad, and *spaghetti alla bolognese*. Worthy quickly asked for the same thing.

"First things first," Father Fortis said to the waiter. "We'll have a bottle of Valpolocello and another bottle of Pinot Grigio. And I will have chicken alfredo and a side order of calamari." When the waiter left, he looked at his two friends and said, "They may find my body halfway to Albania, but they will not find it withered." After another long gulp of water, he continued. "But I'm being selfish. It always good to see both of you, but one of you, not I, asked for this meeting."

Father Fortis watched as father and daughter made eye contact before Worthy nodded in Allyson's direction. Very gracious, Father Fortis thought. But would Allyson read the look as condescending?

"A third body was found, Nick," she began. "Similar scarring, some major differences, and quite a bit yet unknown."

Father Fortis crossed himself. If he was frustrated with not being able to find Brother Sergius, how much more burdened must Allyson, and especially Worthy, feel at not being able to end these deaths?

"Did this person die due to another fall or an overdose?" he asked.

"Neither. A man, in this case, apparently drowned, whether by suicide or by someone's design we can't say," she replied and looked at her father. "You still think this drowning wasn't accidental?"

Worthy nodded. "Not unless Lorraine LaPurcell just happened to fall out of her window and James Kuiper took twenty-two sedatives by accident."

"Where was the body found?" Father Fortis asked.

"Off of Lido. That's the beach island of Venice," Allyson explained.

"Lido? Where have I heard that before?"

Allyson remembered what Giovanni told her about Lido. "Apparently it was once one of the posher spots in Europe. Back in the twentieth century. Have you read Thomas Mann or someone named Waugh, Nick?"

The first course arrived, letting Father Fortis off the literary hook. His calamari was lightly deep-fried, just as he liked it. At least the food and wine are turning out well, he thought.

Just as he was squeezing lemon onto his last calamari, he stopped and reached for Brother Sergius' dog-eared map. "Lido, Lido," he murmured. "Would that be on this map?"

Allyson reached for it and folded out the proper section. "Here it is," she said, pointing to the narrow spit of sand in the Venetian lagoon.

"Has the island been circled or marked, my dear?" Father Fortis asked.

Allyson studied the map for a moment. "No, nothing there."

Father Fortis shrugged. "Just a wild shot, off-target, I guess," he said.

"And let's remember that we're not sure our last victim had any connection with this island. That's just where his body and clothes were found," Worthy added. "If he was killed, his clothes and body could have been dumped there. By the way, Nick, it turns out this victim is Ukrainian."

Father Fortis sat back, a look of surprise on his face. "Not an American?"

"From his dental records, we can't rule out that he's spent some time in the States. But he had a Ukrainian driver's license. We're still finding out where he stayed, how long he's been in Venice, and if anyone knows if he took a similar daytrip out on the train. We can't even rule out that he knew Lorraine LaPurcell."

"But you're wondering something else, aren't you, my friend?"

"Yes, I think you can guess. I know it's a long shot, but do you think a Ukrainian in Venice would know Russian monks?"

"Whoa," Allyson said. "Really?"

"Like I said, another long shot," Worthy admitted.

Father Fortis thought for a moment. "I can't say that there's any love lost between Ukrainians and Russians since Russia invaded Crimea. And even if your victim were a Russian millionaire, one of many who I'm told are coming more than ever to Venice and Italy to spend their ill-gotten fortunes, I wouldn't think that the monks would have anything besides language in common with a Ukrainian."

"Might they know him at the Orthodox Center?" Worthy asked.

"I can ask. What's your victim's name?"

"Vladimir Monsinoff," Allyson replied.

"Don't get your hopes too high. Mr. Monsinoff is just as likely to be Catholic as Orthodox. The Ukraine is split almost fifty-fifty."

Worthy pointed to the ring finger on his right hand. "Vladimir Monsinoff's wedding ring was on his right hand. I thought you told me once that this was an Orthodox custom."

"Actually, it is an Eastern Christian custom."

"What's the difference?" Allyson asked.

"Ukrainian Catholics are Eastern Christians. Yes, they are officially linked with Rome, but they worship like we Orthodox."

"So they wear their wedding rings on the right hand. Oh, well, I guess I was just hoping he might be Orthodox and know the monks from the Center," Worthy explained.

"I can't see how he could," Father Fortis replied. "As I said, Ukrainians and Russians are not on good speaking terms. Is being in a foreign city enough to draw them together? Maybe, but it is just as probable that they would have avoided one another."

As he started to fold up the map, Worthy stopped him. "What's that word at the bottom of the map?"

"I used a dictionary to translate it as 'Torcello.' "

Allyson leaned in again toward the map. "Torcello? Okay, that's an island out in the lagoon. I remember something about it from art history. Ah, here it is," she said, pointing to an island at almost the edge of the map. "Well, it's not circled, anyway."

"Could it be the name of a restaurant?" Worthy asked.

"Ah, that's a possibility. Or, I suppose it could be the name of a store," Father Fortis agreed. Pointing to the map, he asked, "Are we done with this?"

Worthy nodded, but as Father Fortis removed the map to make room for their main courses, he noticed Worthy's lingering eye. He'd seen that look before. His friend noted something new, something no one else had even considered.

CHAPTER SIXTEEN

"I HATE TO ADMIT IT," FATHER FORTIS said, "but I wish Brother Sergius or whoever's stealing the relics would target icons instead."

Their plates were removed as were the wine bottles. The three were now sharing coffee and watching as the lights twinkled on over on the mainland.

"Why icons?" Allyson asked.

"Well, my dear, a stolen icon is more than likely to turn up someday in an art collection or, God forbid, in a church somewhere in the world. And that means if some nosy and knowledgeable dealer of antiquities happens to see it, all she or he has to do then is type the name of the saint and the icon's probable date into the Internet for the icon to show up as stolen."

Allyson put down her coffee. "But wouldn't a relic be even rarer?"

"Rarer? Yes, Easier to spot? No. You see, a relic, in the case of the most recent theft from Murano, is a toe bone. Now, granted, that relic is undoubtedly tagged with the name of the saint. But what happens if the tag is removed?"

"Then all you have is a toe bone," Worthy answered.

"Precisely. Someone could easily glue on a new tag, and just that quickly our relic isn't a bone of St. John the Damascene, but rather St. Theodore the General or Saint Simeon, or Saint anybody," Father Fortis explained. "And where would be the safest place to hide that renamed relic? Wherever other purported relics of Saint Theodore the General or Saint Simeon are kept."

"But Nick, how can a person, say an historian, know if any relic is genuine?" Allyson asked.

"In all honesty, with most relics, we're talking in terms of probability at best, not certainty." Father Fortis admitted. "For example, I visited this small church in Rome that purports to have the head of St. John the Baptist. And what did I see? I saw a skull, with the saint's name tagged to it. In studying the skull even superficially through the glass, I could see that this was likely the skull of someone who was beheaded. That would match the story of St. John the Baptist, but not just him. Many other early Christians suffered that fate, not to mention others the Romans considered criminals. So other than the marks indicating decapitation, what else is the relic's claim of authenticity? Almost always we rely on an accompanying story, in this case of the skull's journey from 1st century Galilee to some Christian area in the early Church to eventually ending up in Rome."

Allyson nodded in understanding. "So that story could be a legend."

"A pious legend, to be fair. And some of those stories are undoubtedly true," Father Fortis said. "I would put the accounts of how St. Peter's bones ended up beneath St. Peter's basilica in Rome in the category of near certainty. But a skull that ends up in a minor church in Rome? All I know for certain is that for two hundred or five hundred or a thousand years, Christians have been venerating this skull in this church as the skull of St. John the Baptist."

"How common was it for relics to be moved around like that?" Worthy asked.

Father Fortis motioned to the waiter for more coffee for the three of them.

"How common? So common that we have a considerable number of days on our Church calendar on which we do not celebrate the saint at all, but rather what the Church calls the 'translation of the relics' of the saint. In some of those cases, what we're celebrating might well be the theft of a relic from one location and its appearance in another more approved site."

"So those who are stealing the relics of Venice, could they be thinking that they are 'translating' relics rather than stealing them?" Allyson posed.

"Don't think that irony has not crossed my mind, my dear. Especially when now a third relic goes missing and Brother Sergius disappears at the same time. Whoever is doing this, hard as it is to believe, seems to have a medieval mind. At least then, stolen or 'translated' relics had some monetary value. But now, in the modern age, what value would they have?"

Again, Father Fortis noticed a faraway look in Worthy's eye. When Father Fortis saw that look before, he knew that his friend would withdraw, maybe for a few hours, but maybe for a few days. And when Worthy resurfaced, he would offer an unexpected new approach to the puzzle. Sometimes the new approach would wash out almost as soon as Worthy raised it. But more than likely, Worthy would have opened a door that others hadn't even seen.

Father Fortis hoped that Allyson also understood the look and could accept that her father would now cut her and everyone else off until he felt it was the right time to share whatever has bubbled up. If she understands that distancing of her father, he thought, she will know not to say a word. If she doesn't understand it, she could very likely find herself as angry as most of Worthy's partners who felt that Worthy, without any provocation, stopped trusting them. And, for all Father Fortis knew, Allyson might find herself discovering her mother's main reason for divorcing the man.

WORTHY HAD A HARD TIME GETTING to sleep that night, and he knew his restlessness was more than coffee-induced. Eventually he stopped trying and, getting dressed, opted for a walk. Within ten minutes, he was walking through the piazza in front of the Basilica of San Marco, now completely deserted. He came out of the piazza by the bell tower and onto the promenade by the Grand Canal, stopping by the bobbing gondolas tied up like horses in front of a saloon.

The wind rose, and Worthy recognized the smell of rain in the breeze. Perhaps a storm was coming, he thought. Faint lights from the church of San Giorgio Maggiore across the canal danced on the choppy waves.

He was not thinking of Vladimir Monsitoff, their latest victim, but of Brother Sergius, Father Fortis' puzzle. For some reason, he could not get the runaway monk out of his mind.

Worthy looked back onto the Doge's Palace, its gothic recesses now in shadows. What is this city, he thought, but a million different hiding places? Somewhere in this maze, as Father Fortis appropriately described it, was hiding someone who cut into the skin of millionaires, not once but twice. Somewhere in this twisty-turny city was a killer or killers who specialized in cancer victims. Somewhere all over this city slept Allyson's nemeses, scam artists ready for another day of fleecing the tourists. Somewhere in this city was a Russian monk hiding for some reason, maybe with stolen relics.

And in this same phantasm of a city was a detective from Detroit, restless at three in the morning with a sense that puzzle pieces were just waiting for someone to put them together and reveal a picture. Why, he wondered, did he think that the puzzle, once solved, would have as its centerpiece the runaway Russian monk?

He felt a chill as the wind picked up. The gondolas were now banging against one another and the bumpers along the causeway. He wondered if storms in Venice came, as they did in Detroit, with lightning and thunder, or if they just arrived with the wind.

He thought back on the intuition that struggled to surface over the past few days. The first tremor occurred in the meeting with Ruggiero and the others, when Basso reported on his fruitless Internet search for any connection between Venice and cancer. And tonight he felt a second tremor when Father

Fortis and Allyson were huddled together over the map.

As he turned to stroll back toward his apartment, he wondered about the connection between the two experiences. Both caused that odd, yet familiar, feeling to pass through him again.

But this island, Lido, he reminded himself, was not circled on Brother Sergius' map. So that puzzle piece did not fit. So why the feeling of a balloon about to burst or of a gunshot about to go off?

Then an image slowly formed, and he realized that he was seeing only what Father Fortis and Allyson unconsciously acted out in front of him. Up until the moment of Father Fortis and Allyson studying the map together, Father Fortis was obsessed with his puzzle of missing relics, while Allyson and he were absorbed in the more deadly puzzle of the cancer-riddled millionaires who came to Venice for a cure, only to die.

The two cases were two puzzles, and what is the first priority when two people are in one room working on separate puzzles? You have to keep the puzzle pieces apart. And wasn't that what the three of them were so careful to do whenever they were together? Either Father Fortis would bring out his puzzle for the three of them to consider, or Allyson and he would describe recent progress on their own puzzle.

But in that moment when Allyson and Father Fortis' heads nearly touched over Brother Sergius' map, he felt the dividing line between the two puzzles begin to dissolve. After nearly two weeks of on-again, off-again frustration, something in that image seemed absolutely right. Wasn't the assurance pulsing through his brain at that moment the conviction that the puzzles would never be solved separately?

Once again he recalled the first tremor he felt, when Basso reported in the conference that nothing of significance came up when "Venice" and "cancer" were typed in together on the Internet. What he understood now, but not then, was that the wrong terms were entered for the Internet search. Hadn't he been on the verge of suggesting that Basso type in two other terms—"Venice" and "relics"?

No, that still wasn't right, he realized. The first wave of a cold rain hit his back, and he ducked under a shop overhang. And yes, in the distance, he could hear the rumble of thunder.

If not "Venice" and "relics," he wondered, what's left? Another wave, this one of relief, now engulfed him.

Yes, somehow in a way that he still could not fully understand, the answer lay in this truth—Basso should have typed in three terms, not two. And those terms were "Venice," "cancer" and "relics."

Chapter Seventeen

By their own choice, Castelucci and Basso sat directly across from Allyson in the conference room. As the three waited for *Ispettore* Ruggiero, who called the meeting, the two local police carried on a conversation in what Allyson could only assume was the local Venetian dialect. Knowing that she was being deliberately snubbed, Allyson looked down at her folder and studied the latest results of her survey.

On the rise in the city were either one or two teams of men who positioned themselves near mid-priced hotels and flashed phony police badges as they asked to investigate tourists' currency. When the gullible tourists handed over their Euros, the men studied the notes and declared them to be counterfeit. The men then confiscated the Euros, leaving the tourists with a printed telephone number to be called to arrange a pickup of genuine currency. And when the tourists called that number? They heard a recording of the local weather report.

By plotting the estimated times and locations of the scams, Allyson was able to establish two facts. On the one hand, it seemed impossible that one team of men was responsible for all the crimes. But on the other hand, two teams in different *sestieri* of Venice were employing the identical approach and leaving the same printed telephone number.

Somewhere in Venice or more likely on the mainland, Allyson realized, there was a training school for scam artists. Those posing as policemen were not self-taught. They were working for someone in the shadows, someone too smart to put himself in danger of being caught.

And similar training seemed even more so in the case of the murdered millionaires. Someone lured the victims to Venice with a hope for a cure.

Someone else was the contact person in Venice. The man holding the umbrella and the cigarette in the unusual way could be such a person. Someone else made the incisions, incisions somehow connected with each victim's cancer and hope for a cure. And finally, if her father's theory was correct, someone or some group killed the victims in such a way that suicide was first suspected.

An elaborate scheme, she concluded, elaborate in design and elaborate in scope.

Ispettore Ruggiero entered the room, a sheath of papers in his hand. He glanced at the three, separated on opposite sides of the conference table, and frowned.

He took off his glasses and cleaned the lens with a handkerchief. "We know much more about Vladimir Monsitoff. He was not staying on Lido. He stay in Venezia, in a small hotel on *La Giudecca*."

Allyson inhaled involuntarily. Could that be important, that the victim was staying on the Giudecca, where she and her father met Father Fortis?

Ruggiero continued. "From the autopsy, yes, he drowned. Why on Lido, we don't know. But he has the same cuttings, incisions. And we have good news," he said, the frown however still remaining. "A train conductor has answered our request," he said. "She recognized Vladimir Monsitoff as a passenger last week on the mid-morning train to Milano."

"Milano?" Castelucci asked, following the question with a string of words that Allyson took to be curses. Milan was a massive city in the millions. If we've had trouble following clues in Venice, Allyson realized, Milan would be a hundred times worse.

"Si, si," Ruggiero replied. "But the conductor think that Monsitoff got off the train before Milano," Ruggiero replied. "She think maybe Padua, Verona, and Vicenza."

He passed out a sheet of paper to each of the three. Allyson's was in English and contained photos of the three victims. "You will retrace Mr. Monsitoff's steps the day he take train. One of you, you go to Padua, another go to Verona, and the third go to Vicenza. In the train station of your city, you show the photos. Ask if anyone see one of them. If no one in the station, move to taxi stands. Then nearby bus stops, yes?"

Before the other two could respond, Allyson offered, "I'll take Padua."

She saw Castelucci glance at Basso before shrugging. He offered to take Vicenza, which left Verona for Basso.

"*Eccellente*," Ruggiero said, stacking the remaining papers into a neat pile and standing up. "Tomorrow morning you go, early, yes? And return by evening. The next morning, we meet again."

Allyson left the room behind Ruggiero and before Castelucci and Basso. She wanted to create some distance from the three in case they asked her reason for choosing Padua. That would be hard to explain to the three Italians. She certainly couldn't tell the truth, the truth being that Giovanni was a university student in that city—someone who'd given Allyson his cellphone number.

Such an admission would give the opposite impression than she wanted to give Ruggiero, Castelucci, Basso, or anyone else—that she was an American college girl infatuated with an Italian. She would not deny that she would like to see Giovanni without Sylvia, and Allyson had the clear impression that Giovanni felt the same.

But there was another reason, one Allyson considered completely legitimate, for seizing the opportunity to see Giovanni. Ever since Sylvia and Allyson met Giovanni, Sylvia's obsession with the good-looking Italian clearly diminished her interest in helping Allyson. Recently, whenever Allyson sat down with Sylvia, the roommate seemed quickly bored with talk about the hospital and shifted the conversation to Giovanni.

I need another ally in Venice, someone more stable and mature, she reasoned. Why not the quiet and thoughtful Giovanni? While he might not have daily contact with hospital personnel, he could easily use his friendship with Enrico, Luigi, and Paolo to uncover the latest gossip. And a confidential visit to Giovanni at the university would offer the perfect opportunity to determine his interest in this proposal as well as in her. Of course, just as Ruggiero asked, she would dutifully question those at the train station, taxi stands, and bus stops and do that first. But then, in whatever time remained, she would head for the university to meet with Giovanni.

She felt a pang of guilt, knowing that Sylvia would see this as Allyson going behind her back. But Sylvia did not have to know, Allyson reasoned. And wasn't all this really Sylvia's fault in the first place?

As she gathered her files from her desk, she asked herself another question. Would she tell her father about her trip to Padua? She weighed the issue the entire way back to her apartment.

In the end, she decided not to tell him. If her father was not her father but simply another American who also happened to be assigned to the case, would she feel any obligation to tell that person about an assigned daytrip? Not likely. And then there was the possibility, although very unlikely, she admitted, that her father would ask her or, worse yet, ask Ruggiero if he could accompany her to Padua. Why even raise the possibility?

But there was a third reason. For the last part of the meal the night before with Father Fortis and her father, she felt her father pull back, as if he were hiding something. When he had walked with her to the *vaporetto* stop, her father said barely a word. The openness that she felt with him before Father Fortis arrived for dinner evaporated. The old barrier between them was back.

No, she didn't owe her father an explanation for the trip to Padua. If anyone should tell him about her assignment, that would be Ruggiero, not her. And he certainly didn't deserve to know about her plan to see Giovanni.

✝

Father Fortis exited the Center as soon as the Sunday Divine Liturgy concluded. He stood toward the rear, where he could observe the behavior of Brother Nilus and Brother Alexei.

Was it just his imagination, or did the two seem distracted at times during the service? No, there was nothing obvious, but as the two Russians stood throughout the service, as was common in Orthodox countries, he had an impression that Brother Nilus was jittery. Once, Brother Alexei even turned to look in Father Fortis' direction. Father Fortis held his gaze. Yes, I am watching you, that gaze said.

It was now forty-eight hours since the relic from Murano and Brother Sergius dropped out of sight. He knew that the Metropolitan's staff asked the local police to inform the Center if Brother Sergius for any reason came to their attention.

Father Fortis saw little value in tailing the two Russians. While he couldn't provide a bit of evidence to support the feeling, Father Fortis nevertheless felt that the two were genuinely bereft without their leader.

No, Father Fortis' plan for the day would take him temporarily out of the maze of Venice. After dinner on *La Giudecca* with Worthy and Allyson, he returned to his room to study Brother Sergius' map. It did not take him long to find the island of Murano. And then he found the island that Allyson pointed out to him, Torcello.

Consulting his *vaporetto* schedule the same evening, he realized that he could take a boat to Murano and then take another one from there to Torcello.

As he now proceeded toward the appropriate *vaporetto* stand on the Grand Canal, Father Fortis was careful to walk past the stand and duck into the nearest narrow *calle*, or alleyway. While he decided not to follow the two Russians, he couldn't be certain that the two of them weren't following him. If they knew where Brother Sergius was hiding, then by following Father Fortis they could warn their compatriot should Father Fortis come too close. And if they did not know where Brother Sergius was hiding, they might follow him in the hopes that he would find their leader.

Father Fortis waited fifteen minutes in the shadows of the narrow walkway before venturing out and proceeding to the *vaporetto*. The day offered bright sunlight, and the air seemed cleaner after the overnight storm. He would appear to others on the *vaporetto* to be a typical tourist, map in hand, as he stood at the rail and gazed out at the sights.

As the *vaporetto* left the immediate area of Venice, he saw a spit of land ahead. That would be Lido, he realized, the place where Vladimir Monsitoff's body was found. He asked at the Center, as Worthy requested, if the Ukrainian was known. The answer was no, although the Metropolitan suggested that he ask the two remaining Russian monks. He did not do that, as he found himself believing nothing that they might tell him.

Past Lido, the *vaporetto* chugged ahead, and Father Fortis saw that he was not alone in taking advantage of the beautiful weather to visit the islands of the lagoon. He knew from the schedule that the first stop would be Murano, his stop of interest and the Venetian island famous for glassworks. The city of Venice was full of tourists shops offering miniature horses and, for some reason, orchestra performers made from the blown glass of that island.

As expected, more than half of those on the *vaporetto* clambered off the boat at that first stop. Father Fortis took the opportunity to observe those who, like him, were walking toward the island's glass factories. There was a couple who looked German or Scandinavian, busy with their guidebook, as well as an elderly man carrying plastic bags.

Father Fortis spotted a bell tower that leaned at a precarious angle and walked in that direction. With its own canals and prominent church, Murano was a miniature version of Venice. It seemed likely to Father Fortis that the church directly across the canal from where he was walking was the only one on the island.

Murano was a sleepy place, one he suspected was not accustomed to thieves or to having their church burgled. As he crossed an old brick bridge to approach the apse end of the church, Father Fortis looked around at the neighboring homes and shops. No doubt every resident in the past few days was interviewed about strangers being seen in and around the church. As he made a final visual inspection of the neighborhood before entering the door of the church, he noticed an older man looking down at him from a window.

The horse has already left the barn, my friend, Father Fortis thought.

After his eyes adjusted to the darkness of the interior, Father Fortis tried to find evidence of security equipment. None was apparent. He walked carefully on the wavy marble floor, more evidence of the shifting reality of Venice and these islands. The intricate pattern of circles and woven strands of color in the marble was clearly the most notable feature of the church. The mosaic of the Theotokos, the Blessed Virgin Mary, in the apse was not as impressive and reminded Father Fortis of ones in Greece. Brother Sergius, if he was indeed the thief, would certainly have felt the Byzantine presence in this place.

In front of the altar, steps led down to the crypt, where all the relics besides those encased in the altar would be kept. The stairway was now blocked off with a wooden barricade and signs that Father Fortis assumed were left by the police. Glancing around to make sure that he was indeed alone, Father Fortis moved the barricade to one side and descended.

The darkness of the crypt was even deeper than in the nave above. Father Fortis was grateful for the small red light that hung at the far end of the passageway. He recognized it as a perpetual lamp of presence, God's presence. Its modern electric bulb replaced the candles once used.

The meager red glow illuminated a padlocked, glassed-in case within which he could see ornate reliquaries. Much as in Greece, the containers of the relics in this church were of gold or bronze, their shapes varying depending on the significance of the saint or the relic itself. Most of the reliquaries were pillar-shaped, upon which the relic, usually a bone, was on display. Each reliquary had an identifying plaque attached at the base.

The assortment of relics and reliquaries in this church was modest, at least by the standards of the larger churches of Venice. Studying the array carefully, Father Fortis thought he detected an empty space where another reliquary, perhaps the one that contained the missing relic, once stood.

He took a closer look at the padlock and realized that it, along with the accompanying latch, was new. Where both latch and padlock were attached, the wood looked distressed, but in the inadequate light, Father Fortis could not tell if those marks were also new or because of centuries of use.

Father Fortis ascended the stairs, replaced the barricade, and sat down in the nave. He wondered how he would have explained his actions if the police discovered him in the crypt. He could hardly say that the Orthodox Metropolitan of Venice gave permission to break the law. But he was not sorry that he took the risk. He needed to see the actual site of the crime.

As he faced the mosaic of the Theotokos in the apse, he offered a prayer for her protection and guidance. The irony of the moment did not escape him. If Brother Sergius was the thief, the Russian monk very likely did the same, asking the Blessed Virgin's blessing on his "repatriation" of the relic.

Using his own experience of the morning, he tried to recreate the actions of the thief, be that thief Brother Sergius or someone yet unknown. First of all, the thief traveled to this island. If the thief was bold enough to take a *vaporetto*, he would have done so within the scheduled hours of operation. If the thief had private transportation, he could have come whenever he thought best.

Did the thief come to the church during daylight hours? If so, he found the church open as Father Fortis did himself. But would a thief risk coming in the daytime when interruption was possible? Maybe so, especially if the thief had an accomplice, a lookout.

If, however, the thief chose evening hours, or even the middle of the night, he had to break into the church. Was there any evidence of that, he wondered.

Father Fortis thought also of the choice of object. A relic of an Eastern saint was taken, but numerous others were left, suggesting prior reconnaissance of the church. So the thief undoubtedly followed a plan, one that led him immediately to the crypt where he broke into the case containing the reliquaries. The entire operation could have been completed in three to five minutes, Father Fortis estimated.

Then what? If the crime was committed in the daytime, would the thief have then strolled around Murano, acting the part of a tourist until the returning *vaporetto* arrived? Given that the gaunt figure of Brother Sergius would have been unusual and therefore memorable on a small island like Murano, Father Fortis doubted this scenario.

But if Brother Sergius was involved, it seemed more likely by far that the heist was accomplished sometime during the night when few if any of the locals would even know of the thief's presence. A boat waiting at any of the numerous docks could quickly return the thief and the relic to Venice.

He took one final look around the church before exiting into the bright sunlight. Looking up at the houses nearby, he saw that the old man was still at his windowed sentry post. Re-crossing the bridge and walking in the direction of the shops, restaurants, and *vaporetto* stand, Father Fortis toyed with the other possibility. The private boat did not head back to Venice but continued on to Torcello.

With twenty minutes to wait before the *vaporetto* taking him to Burano and Torcello would arrive, Father Fortis bought a pastry and soft drink and sat down on a bench to study his guidebook. The attraction of the lesser-visited Torcello seemed to be the glimpse it offered the hearty tourist of Venice's origins. Yet another island of intersecting canals and bridges, Torcello was the first island occupied by those fleeing the invasions of the Goths and then Lombards in the sixth century. The two oldest churches of the lagoon were on Torcello, both described as retaining strong Byzantine elements. But beyond the churches and a few ruins in the same area, the island was described as nearly deserted, except for a few summer homes. Torcello might be a perfect location to store stolen relics, Father Fortis thought. And maybe from this out-of-the-way island, the relics could be more easily smuggled out of the country.

From information posted at the *vaporetto* stand, Father Fortis noted that only one boat every two hours journeyed on to Torcello. Father Fortis was consequently not surprised that only a few whom he'd been with earlier, the German couple and the foursome from Britain, boarded the *vaporetto* and remained on after the stop at Burano for Torcello. On board already were a group of long-haired backpackers and one young man who was sitting alone, reading a newspaper.

The sun was high overhead by the time that the *vaporetto* nosed into the dock on Torcello. He looked around the dock, without success, for a place to buy a sandwich and wished that he purchased something more substantial than a pastry on Murano.

The trek to the churches looked to be nearly a mile on the map supplied at the *vaporetto* stand. At least the breeze is cool, Father Fortis thought. The backpackers set out at a brisk pace, munching on sandwiches that looked very appetizing to Father Fortis, while the English tourists lagged behind. The young man from the boat walked in the opposite direction, leaving Father Fortis to follow the tourists.

The walkway to the churches followed a narrow canal almost devoid of boats. As he passed homes and one larger place that looked like a farm, Father Fortis heard none of the expected sounds of animals or family. Yet there were numerous very well-fed cats slinking around the outdoor tables and the bird feeders were filled with seed, indicating that some people must still live on the island or frequently visit it.

Ahead, Father Fortis could see the bell tower of one of the churches. For some reason, the straightness of the tower, not leaning as was characteristic of the churches of Venice and Murano, added to his feeling of melancholy. Broken only by the twitter of birds, the silence of Torcello was that of a place abandoned or evacuated.

To his surprise, Father Fortis found both ancient churches of the island sitting side by side. With the English tourists, Father Fortis entered the more modest one, Santa Fosca, which was a squatty round construction from the twelfth and thirteenth centuries. On the altar were candles and paraments, indicating that the Mass was celebrated there recently. The chairs indicated a very small community.

Santa Fosca made a sorry comparison with Santa Maria Assunta, the Romanesque church that was its neighbor. And the tourist board of the region must have agreed, as visitors to Santa Maria Assunta paid an entrance fee. The two young Italian women running the ticket booth and meager postcard stand, chatting easily with one another, abruptly broke the island's spell of melancholy.

He paid for his admission and approached a heavy and obviously ancient wooden door leading into the nave. He pulled on the door, but nothing happened. Turning to the two women, he saw one motion for him to push, not pull. Of course, he thought, remembering that in Italy, most of the doors had to be pushed open.

Nevertheless, the door didn't budge. The woman who'd motioned him to push, not pull, approached and rattled the door several times before it swung inward.

"The lock," she said, "she is old. Sometimes we think she is locked, but no, she is just sticking."

Father Fortis was not prepared for what awaited him inside the church. Very likely, the English couple and the backpackers would have found the interior unimpressive when compared with San Marco, Santa Maria Gloriosa dei Frari, or any of the other ornate churches of Venice.

But the effect on Father Fortis was so great that his knees went weak. Where am I, he wondered. His work on Byzantine chant and its effect on Roman music transported him back, through those ancient sounds, to a time when the Christian Church, East and West, was united. Yes, the branches of the Church always had their differences, and those differences would erupt in the 11th century into a tragic split, but for the entire first millennium, the Church experienced this diversity within overall unity.

And here, surrounding Father Fortis, was a church that, though simple, reflected that unity. The mosaic of the Theotokos in the apse was purely Byzantine. On the back wall was a massive mosaic of the Last Judgment, with a throng of humanity divided between those descending into hell and those ascending into heaven. The scene bore close similarities to others from Sicily and southern Italy, areas that Father Fortis knew were also heavily influenced by Byzantine culture. And bisecting the nave was a wooden partition with what Father Fortis could only describe as icons. Was the partition a true iconostasis, an icon screen, or was it an earlier version of the rood screen of the Western Church?

The answer to everything that Father Fortis was observing with such astonishment was "both." The church and all its elements were Eastern *and* Western, or, more properly, the church represented a time when Christianity was one, both East and West.

Father Fortis felt as if he were sitting within some answer for which he'd been searching for a long time. Even as a boy in Baltimore, he grew up surrounded by mainly Italians and Portuguese. He attended weddings and funerals at the nearby parish Catholic churches, and his friends reciprocated by coming to services at what was known by everyone as the "Greek church."

He was in grade school in 1964 when the pope of that time, Paul VI, embraced Ecumenical Patriarch Athenagorus in Jerusalem, leading to the dissolving of the anathemas that existed between the two branches of Christianity for over nine hundred years. But for Father Fortis and his friends, the gesture of forgiveness offered by the two leaders in Jerusalem seemed only natural.

In seminary, Father Fortis consequently found himself with others on one side of a great divide. For the conservatives, Orthodoxy still needed to protect itself from the wiles of Catholicism and especially the ongoing intrigues against the Orthodox Church that were orchestrated by the Vatican. For them, the past was not abrogated by the embrace in Jerusalem. Sitting in the pew in Santa Maria Assunta, Father Fortis thought how close that position was to what Brother Sergius and the other Russian monks believed.

For Father Fortis and some of his allies in seminary, this position was xenophobic and outdated. They challenged the conservatives to become, in fact, more conservative, to reflect back past the nine hundred years of conflict and recriminations to the previous thousand years of unity, when East and West were in communion.

And here in Santa Maria Assunta, Father Fortis felt that he was sitting in both that ancient past and in the only possible future for Orthodox and Catholics that made sense. He would have liked nothing more than to drag Brothers Sergius, Alexis, and Nilus into this church and to ask a simple question. Is this holy place Eastern or Western?

The thought of Brother Sergius reminded Father Fortis of his real reason for coming to Torcello. Did the monk come to Torcello? Did he sit where Father Fortis was now sitting?

Reluctantly, he left the peace of the church. Returning to the women at the ticket booth, he asked if either saw a tall Russian monk with full beard in the last month. It took him three tries in differently-worded English for his question to be understood, but both women eventually shook their heads. The one with better English told Father Fortis, however, that the two of them did not work on weekends, when others would monitor their stations.

"So, perhaps yes, perhaps no," the one said with a shrug.

Walking to where he was told that he could find drinking water, Father Fortis had just finished quenching his thirst when he looked up and across a field and canal leading to an abandoned warehouse. Coming up the canal at rapid speed was a police boat. And on the bridge of the boat, he saw the last person that he expected to see on Torcello—his friend, Christopher Worthy.

Chapter Eighteen

If Castelucci and Basso were on the same early morning train as she, Allyson couldn't see them. When she was getting her own ticket and then waiting by the proper train line in Venice's station, she half expected to look up and find Castelucci, wearing his cheap aftershave, hovering over her. Gratefully, she seemed to be traveling alone.

As the train crept along the first stretch of track crossing the lagoon to Mestre and the mainland, Allyson looked back on the skyline of Venice. Would this city of dreams still exist in fifty years? Would she tell her grandchildren how she spent three months in a magical place that no longer existed? She consoled herself that Venice made a living out of dying, the corrosion of salt water, the acid rain, and the rising tides caused by global warming being just the most recent threats to the city. The city survived the plague, bell towers collapsing, Napoleon's invasion, and, in the last century, the replacement of aristocratic visitors with middle-class tourists. Venice had a history of adjustment, most recently the takeover of some of the oldest and most prestigious palaces of the city by European and American corporations.

She was warned that Mestre was one long industrial zone of smokestacks, factories, and warehouses. With its belching trucks and metallic-tinged air, the city certainly seemed to symbolize all that Venice managed to keep at bay.

Twenty minutes later, as the train edged out of Mestre, Allyson was happy to see vineyards and vegetable farms. Here was lowland, where the ever-present water of the region was controlled by straight channels and ditches.

She gazed around in her train car and noted with pleasure that fellow passengers seemed to be Italians. Some were obviously in business, their briefcases in the overhead compartment and their newspapers opened to give them a bubble of semi-privacy. Would that be Giovanni in five years, she wondered.

There were also families chatting with their children and offering slices of fruit or other snacks when the kids became too boisterous. Allyson loved to be around Italian children. In pleading with their parents or vying with one another, the children spoke the most basic Italian, and they spoke it both slowly and loudly.

As the fields and vineyards passed outside her window with increasing speed, Allyson pulled out her guidebook and found the section on Padua. She read carefully, looking for anything that would interest three millionaires who happened to have cancer. The city's prominence in Shakespeare's *Taming of the Shrew* seemed to her to have little appeal to the victims. She dismissed as well a chapel near the train station whose frescoes were painted by Giotto. No, if the three millionaires journeyed to Padua, they didn't come to see the normal sites.

She spent longer on the guidebook's description of the basilica dedicated to St. Anthony of Padua. Once again, she read nothing that would have drawn the three to a church. There were plenty of stunning churches in Venice if the three felt an urge to pray.

In studying the map of Padua in the guidebook, she found without difficulty the location of the university. Now the question was, what would she say to Giovanni if she called him? She couldn't very well explain her real reason for being in the city. Would her sudden appearance come across as too bold? Would he think that she was not different from Sylvia?

She tried to think of another reason for being in Padua, one linked to her data-gathering for the police department, but everything that came to mind seemed forced.

She closed the guidebook, reminding herself that her questioning of personnel in the city's train station, nearby bus stops, and taxi stands might take up most of her time. What I'll do, she told herself, is walk over to the university and play the situation by ear. If I can think of a good excuse to call Giovanni, then I will. And if I can't think of a good excuse? she asked herself. Then, as I said, I'll play it by ear.

After three weeks in Venice, with only water traffic, Allyson found the sounds and smells of the trucks, cars, and buses of Padua assaultive. And she noted that the pedestrians walked faster in Padua, as if their pace was linked somehow to the cars and motor scooters that zipped through the narrow streets. Or perhaps, she realized, maybe the slower pace in Venice was because of the calming effect of the narrow canals.

The four hours that she spent showing photos of the three victims in and around the train station of Padua, its taxi stands and bus stops, were not particularly fruitful. Most of those whom she interviewed replied that they could not be sure. One taxi driver thought he recognized Lorraine LaPurcell's photo, but in pressing the matter further, Allyson concluded that he might have seen her in a movie. A woman at a tobacconist returned several times to the photo of Vladimir Monsitoff, but in the end said that she couldn't be sure.

The only positive part of the experience was that Allyson felt quite satisfied with her command of Italian. With each conversation, she found herself asking the person less and less to repeat something he said.

By two-thirty in the afternoon, she felt satisfied that she'd completed her task, fruitless though her efforts would seem to *Ispettore* Ruggiero. She bought a *panino* and a bottle of water at a stand-up café and checked the city map in the guidebook again. Estimating that the walk to the university would take only thirty minutes, Allyson realized that she would still have plenty to time to meet Giovanni and make it to the train station to take one of the evening trains back to Venice.

As she walked with purpose toward the university, she glanced at the shop windows. Maybe, she thought, I'll see something that I can use as an excuse for my visit. But there was nothing in the shop windows of the provision stores that she could not find in Venice.

As she looked around, she noticed the brown signs at intersections directing tourists with helpful logos to the various sites of Padua. By the time she passed the sign for the Scrovegni Chapel, she realized that her safest bet was to claim to come to Padua to see what drew most visitors. With each passing intersection, she realized that what she read in the guidebook was right. The main attraction of the city was the Basilica of St. Anthony, which just happened to be near the university.

Okay, she thought, I can say that I have come to Padua to visit this church. But to see what? As she rounded a corner and saw the massive domed basilica in front of her, she realized that any truly convincing answer to that question would have to be found inside.

Wouldn't Nick like this, she thought as she approached the front entrance of the church. Here I am, going into a church as an excuse to meet a man. Someday, if the time was ever right, she would share the joke with him.

The interior of the church seemed somehow even larger than the exterior. Estimating that the building could hold thousands, she asked herself the same question as before. What would visitors be most attracted to here?

She picked up a brief guide to the church that was printed in Italian, English, Spanish, French, and German. From that, she realized that visitors came to the basilica for a variety of reasons. There were, first of all, various masterpieces painted by some of Italy's most renowned artists in the church's numerous side chapels. There were also the paintings in the dome and in the church's apse. Visitors interested in sculpture would find the altar and pulpit to be of most interest. Musicians would want to admire the bank of pipes of the massive organ.

But most of all, she realized from the guide, people came to visit the crypt of St. Anthony. So, that is what I will do, she concluded. I have come to Padua to visit the gravesite of the city's most famous saint.

Not as she expected, the crypt of St. Anthony was not below ground, but raised above the main floor behind the altar. And, as she neared the altar, she realized that there was a line to visit the crypt. If the line moves fast enough, she concluded, I'll still have plenty of time to get to the university to see Giovanni.

As she waited with others, she read the signs telling the story of St. Anthony. As saints were never part of the spirituality of her mother and dad, both of whom stopped attending church in the year of the divorce, she read the signs with interest.

On one of the signs, she read that Anthony was already a monk when he experienced a call to join the movement of St. Francis. Through his persistence, Anthony eventually became a Franciscan friar and requested missionary service to the Muslim tribes of North Africa. On route to his mission assignment and what he assumed would be his martyrdom, Anthony became deathly ill and was forced to remain in Italy. There, his gifts of preaching so impressed St. Francis that he became a noted evangelist within Italy for the new movement. Toward the end of his life, Anthony became a hermit who lived near Padua in a tree and was known far and wide for his miracles. The basilica was built to house his remains.

So, I'll finally get to see some relics, Allyson thought, as she moved closer to the steps of the crypt. She observed, in waiting, the behavior of those who approached the crypt. Most put their hands on the marble side, said a prayer, and crossed themselves. Some even kissed the marble block. These aren't tourists, she thought. These are pilgrims.

When she arrived at the top of the stairs, she realized that there was nothing to see beyond some Latin words inscribed on the marble facing. She thought back on what she read on the last sign, that people mainly prayed to St. Anthony for lost items but also for young men in trouble. Apparently, she realized, saints are given different assignments in the afterlife.

Feeling that she was testing the limits of hypocrisy, she began nevertheless to construct a story for Giovanni. Yes, she would say, she came to Padua to visit the basilica. Why? Because, she would answer, she was concerned about the health of a college classmate who was in remission for leukemia. At least that was the truth, she consoled herself. And to either complete the charade or legitimize her visit, she thought to herself, okay, St. Anthony, please help

Kevin.

Someone behind her coughed, and she realized that she was still standing in front of the crypt. To her surprise, her hand was touching the marble facing exactly as the pilgrims before her. She hurried down the stairs and exited the basilica as quickly as possible. And to her further surprise, she felt a lightness, almost a slight weightlessness, a feeling that she normally associated with the immediate aftermath of solving some problem.

The University of Padua bore little resemblance to her own college, Franklin, back home. At Franklin, campus visitors would encounter dormitories, fraternities, and sororities long before they arrived at the ivy-covered main buildings.

The University of Padua, however, didn't seem to have a "campus" at all. Instead of green lawns and shade trees, there were massive buildings with the name of the discipline on the façade—*Economia, Filosofia, Scienza Medica*. Numerous bike stands and restricted areas for parking scooters between the buildings suggested that students in Padua lived somewhere else in the city or area.

After practicing her story one more time, she rummaged in her purse for Giovanni's cellphone number. Her phone was in her hand when she glanced up and saw Giovanni standing less than half a block away, smoking a cigarette in front of the building labeled *Scienza Medica*.

This is meant to be, she thought, as she began to walk toward him. But she got no more than ten steps before she saw the doors of the building open and a stream of students begin to pour out.

For some reason, she felt embarrassed as she slowed her gait to see whom Giovanni was waiting for. As she feared, a young woman, her arms filled with books, joined Giovanni. Giovanni kissed her on both cheeks and then offered her a cigarette.

Allyson moved to the side of the walkway and studied the woman as anyone would study a possible rival. The woman was thin with sleek black hair; perhaps, Allyson admitted, a beauty to some. But the woman looked worried, and she seemed to be arguing with Giovanni. He, too, looked upset, not the suave guy whom she lunched with just days before.

On occasion, the two turned to glance at the door, and in a few moments, another college student, this time a man, joined them. He, too, lit a cigarette and for a moment joined the two in their animated discussion.

When the three began walking away from her, Allyson considered her options. Calling Giovanni now seemed out of the question given the mood that seemed to emanate from the three. And yet, Allyson felt compelled to follow the three. What have I turned into, a stalker? she asked herself.

Yet, she followed at a safe distance. The man ahead gesturing in apparent frustration was not the Giovanni she knew. The three stopped, and suddenly the other man grabbed Giovanni by the arm. When Giovanni tried to break free, the other man held on more firmly and grabbed for Giovanni's throat. And Giovanni, at least a head taller that the other man, gave way to him. What hold does this guy have on Giovanni, she wondered.

It was the woman who came between the two men and then, once again, they moved off together. As they did so with Allyson continuing to follow, questions, unexpected and unwelcome, bombarded Allyson. Was she fooled by Giovanni? What does anyone notice when she is attracted to someone? And how much does anyone reveal when he wants to be found attractive?

Allyson felt that she had to be careful, as the third person in the group, the other man, now began to occasionally glance behind himself. Why would a college student worry about being followed? Yet, I'm following them, she had to admit.

The three turned into a café and took a table in the corner. Allyson walked by on the opposite side of the street, being careful to pull her hat down and look at the three only in the reflection of a shop window. Twenty yards farther down the block, she ducked into a narrow passageway and waited.

Why am I doing this, she asked herself. Is it simply that I want to learn more about a man I'm attracted to? No, that was no longer the reason. There was something in the way that the other man grabbed Giovanni's arm and then his throat that made her want to save Giovanni from something.

The meeting among the three lasted first a half-hour and then three-quarters of an hour. Allyson was beginning to fear that her watching the café from the shadows made her look suspicious. She resolved that if Giovanni didn't emerge in the next fifteen minutes, she would circle the block and head back toward the train station.

But it was only five minutes later that the three emerged from the café and stood to talk. With a big smile, the other man initiated a hug with Giovanni which Giovanni seemed to return half-heartedly. The woman exchanged kisses with both men before walking away on her own. For several more minutes, the other man continued to talk to Giovanni as if he were trying to convince him of something.

When the two men parted and began to walk in opposite directions, Allyson decided to follow Giovanni. He lit a cigarette and proceeded more slowly than before. He seemed preoccupied, bumping into an old man at one point.

When Giovanni arrived back at the university, he walked down the row of buildings until he stood looking up at the *Scienza Medica* facility, the same place where he'd been waiting earlier, Allyson recalled. Why would a business student stop at this particular building?

With a quicker step, Giovanni proceeded to walk in the direction of the train station. If he is headed back to Venice by train, she decided, she would have to wait for a later train. Now it was imperative that he not know Allyson followed him.

But just when Allyson was sure that Giovanni was hurrying for a train, he took a jog to the right and approached, to Allyson's surprise, the Basilica of St. Anthony. At the door, he hesitated and looked at his watch before entering.

Allyson waited for several moments, and then reentered the church. She remained in the back, fumbling with the paper guide as she tried to determine where Giovanni was in the massive building. Maybe he sensed that someone was tailing him, she thought, and ducked into the church, leaving by one of the other exits.

But then she saw Giovanni at the end of the line to approach the crypt. Why come into the church for this, she wondered. From her safe vantage point behind the pillar, she watched him as he waited. He looked neither at the explanatory signs nor elsewhere in the church. And it was clear that he chose to speak to no one. Perhaps, she thought, he came here many times before.

Checking her own watch and seeing that it was already six-thirty, she realized that to be on the safe side she could not afford to stay more than thirty minutes. The line moved slowly, agonizingly so for Allyson, but Giovanni seemed almost frozen. His arms hung limply to his sides, his head facing forward as the line gradually shortened.

Fate seemed to dictate that Allyson would need to leave at almost the same time that Giovanni would have his turn at the crypt. She found herself urging, under her breath, the line to move faster. At one point, she pictured herself having to walk fast to make the station on time. And then she pictured herself having to run. Should she leave?

No, she told herself, this is somehow important, and then immediately doubted if there was a basis for that conclusion. She felt her legs tingling with expectancy as two things dawned on her at nearly the same instant. One, she could wait until Giovanni left the basilica and still make the train if she took a taxi to the station. But it was the second, an observation more than a plan, that rooted her in the spot. As Giovanni mounted the steps and placed his hand on the crypt, she saw his face in profile. It was tortured, and tears were running down his face.

An hour later, as the train slowly departed from the Padua station, Allyson closed her eyes and thought about all that she observed that afternoon. Yes, I saw it all, but what does it mean, she asked. Did I learn anything about Giovanni, or did I just unlearn what I thought I knew?

The man who stood tearfully at the crypt was a far cry from the one who piloted the sleek craft to Lido. Whatever burden he tried to leave with St. Anthony, Allyson felt certain that it must have something to do with the two others that he met and argued with in Padua.

She gave herself permission to let the puzzle go as she felt close to sleep. There was no need to stay awake, she reminded herself, as Venice is the end of the line. As she was drifting off, the image of Giovanni leaning dejectedly against the crypt returned. One thing seemed clear to her: he was not feeling any of the lightness that she felt at the same spot.

As the train clacked rhythmically, Allyson returned to that delicious feeling of lightness and felt herself falling into it. Her father once told her that he more than once solved some puzzle while he was falling into or coming out of sleep. She remembered him saying something about the human mind being able to see matters more clearly when it lets go of other distractions.

The sleepier she became, the more she felt encased in that feeling of lightness. Now it was not Giovanni who she saw at the crypt, nor even herself. In what could have been the beginning of a dream, she saw Father Fortis pulling her father up those stairs and pointing at the crypt while saying, "The answer is right here, Christopher. Can't you see it?"

She awoke with a start as if she surfaced from being underwater. She gasped for several breaths, oblivious of the surprised look on the faces of those sitting across from her. Of more importance than anything was the realization that the words of Father Fortis in her dream held the key to *everything*. Yes, the answer was right there.

Chapter Nineteen

The rub with being a consultant, Worthy knew from experience, is that wherever you are sent, you start with only a vague reputation and therefore little credibility. Reputations in law enforcement are made in towns, counties, cities, but sometimes only in certain regions of a major city. Worthy's renown in Detroit was enough for the Kuipers to send him to Venice, but that reputation simply didn't translate.

And so he was reluctant to even try to explain to Inspector Ruggiero his growing conviction that the missing relics played some part in the deaths of the three millionaires. He had no hard evidence and no real circumstantial evidence either. All he had was one of his hunches. Even Captain Betts back home, with whom he had some credibility in the trust bank, would have warned him against overreaching.

Inspector Ruggiero would be perfectly in his rights to demand to know how Worthy became so knowledgeable about the relics cases. And while there was certainly nothing illegal or unethical about his conversations with Father Fortis—after all, the assumption was that the two cases were unrelated—Ruggiero might feel that Worthy, and Allyson with him, went behind his back. Yet, if his hunch was right, Worthy knew that it was only a matter of time until his relationship with Father Fortis would need to be revealed.

Worthy had a history of angering those supervising his cases, so he didn't worry for himself about Inspector Ruggiero's reaction. But Allyson as an intern could be a different matter. Would Ruggiero try to punish Worthy by sending her home? Worthy had no doubt that his fragile relationship with his daughter would not survive such an outcome.

If he could have leveled with the inspector, Worthy would have asked to be kept up to date on any developments related to a Russian monk, Brother Sergius, who went missing along with another relic. His hope was that the monk would be detained at some airport or train station in Italy.

It was when he was finishing his third cup of coffee of the morning at his desk that he noted a buzz going through the roomful of police personnel. Without a command of even basic Italian, Worthy had to depend on his own experience to know that something happened.

Inspector Ruggiero hastened into the room, his face somber as he approached Worthy's desk.

"Come with me, please. Another body."

Worthy threw on his sport coat and followed the inspector along with two uniformed police out of the building and to the department's loading point on the narrow canal. The engine of the blue boat marked with *Polizia* on the side was already revving. When all jumped aboard, the boat shot forward out toward the Grand Canal, forcing Worthy to hang on to a side railing. Just as suddenly, the boat slowed for a moment at the intersection of the two canals before speeding away from Venice and into the lagoon.

Worthy tapped Ruggiero on the arm and shouted over the motor. "Where are we going?"

In staccato bits, the inspector shouted back. "Torcello. An island. Not far."

Father Fortis estimated that he was less than a half mile from where the police boat with Christopher Worthy aboard cut its speed and was now only edging forward. With the map of Torcello in his guidebook listing only the walkways approved for visitors, he was at a loss as to how to make his way over to the boat.

Father Fortis retreated into the entryway of the church and asked the woman at the ticket booth if she would please come outside. The woman looked suspicious at the request, but Father Fortis sensed that his clerical collar once again performed its calming magic.

He pointed across the fields to the boat, now stopped, its lights still flashing. "How can I get over there?" he asked.

"*Dove*? Where?" she replied.

"I need to get to that boat, that *barca*."

"Oh, *sì, sì*," she replied, but shook her head and pointed back toward the walkway leading to the *vaporetto* stand. "Your boat, this way."

"No, no, I need to go there. The boat of *polizia*, yes?"

"*Perché*?" she asked.

"*Perché*?"

"Why?" she translated.

"I can't explain. But I need to go there," he said, making his fingers pretend to walk in that direction, "to the *polizia* boat."

Shaking her head at him as if he were crazy, the woman turned and headed back into the church.

Father Fortis saw no other choice but to go cross-country and hope that there were bridges across the canals that stretched between the churches and the police boat. He straddled the first stone wall and stepped into a field of some water-soaked crop unknown to him. His foot began to sink into muck as soon as it hit the first row between the crops. He managed to move more quickly by jumping from one raised row of crops to the next. Ten sweaty minutes later, he crossed another stone wall and found, to his relief, that this field was weed-covered and drier.

Halfway to the police boat, he found himself cut off by a narrow canal, no more than five feet across. He looked up both directions of the canal, but saw no bridge. And turning back was not an option, he told himself. He had to find out for himself if what he feared, and maybe feared since he stepped on Murano that morning, had happened.

"Joshua walked through the Jordan River," he said, "so I guess I can walk through this." He stepped into the water and began to wade across. Fortunately, the water was only a foot deep, though the canal bottom seemed to suck his feet down another foot.

He flopped down for a moment on the other side to catch his breath and wipe his face with his handkerchief. "No more canals, I beg you," he prayed as he rose and moved into the next field.

There were no more canals, but there was a final field of brambles and thorns, so by the time he got to the near side of the canal that held the police boat, his hands and one cheek were bloody, his hair disheveled. No wonder the police, one by one, turned around when they heard him approach and stared at this unexpected and ludicrous sight.

One of the uniform policemen began yelling something in Italian and with vigorous gestures motioned for Father Fortis to leave the scene.

"But I am a priest," he said. "You need me, don't you?"

Ruggiero came over to the side of the boat nearest Father Fortis. "Why you think we need you?"

Wiping blood from his cheek, Father Fortis asked, "You found a body, didn't you?" When the inspector continued to stare at him, he added, "Lieutenant Worthy will vouch for me."

Ruggiero turned to Worthy and said something. Worthy nodded slowly.

"He say you are American. Also Orthodox. Is this true?" Ruggiero asked Father Fortis.

Father Fortis made eye contact with Worthy. Had he inadvertently betrayed his friend? Worthy's face gave no hint as to the answer to that, but he nodded in Father Fortis' direction.

"Yes, I am an Orthodox priest, and yes, I know Lieutenant Worthy."

Ruggiero looked from Father Fortis to Worthy and back again. "And we need you, Father, why?" he asked the priest.

Father Fortis looked up at the sky for a moment. How crazy he would look if what he said next was completely wrong. "Because I think you found the body of a Russian monk," he said in a quieter tone.

Ruggiero did not have to confirm that Father Fortis was right. Confirmation was given by one of the uniformed officers on board, who knew enough English to cross himself and stare at Father Fortis as if he were possessed, or maybe the killer himself.

CHAPTER TWENTY

ALLYSON KNEW THAT SHE WOULD HAVE a fitful night of sleep in any case after Padua, but Sylvia's explosion when she found out where Allyson had been kept them both up until two in the morning. Trying to explain without giving any details how she saw Giovanni but not actually met him only infuriated Sylvia all the more. Over and over again, Sylvia yelled, in Italian no less, that their friendship was finished. And then, when that did not seem to crush Allyson, she made it clear that her helping Allyson was over.

The end result was that Allyson did not enter sleep until five in the morning and consequently did not awaken until ten. She felt groggy as the memories of the day and night before flooded back. Allyson would have felt worse about Sylvia's reaction if her mind was not consumed with what seemed far more important matters.

Giovanni was clearly in distress, and she felt sure that his pain had something to do with the other man and woman. Allyson felt a need to speak with Giovanni as soon as possible, as Sylvia had everything to gain by contacting Giovanni and describing Allyson's trip to Padua as a case of stalking.

But even Giovanni's torment could not trump her main preoccupation as she entered the *Questura* at half-past eleven. What came come clear to her on the train was building slowly all day, maybe even longer, she thought. In her recollection of tearful Giovanni at the crypt of St. Anthony, she thought of her own prayer at that same site earlier that day for Kevin, her fellow college student who was battling leukemia.

The pieces were still arranging themselves in her mind, but most of the picture was coming into focus. Piece one: the crypt of St. Anthony. Piece two:

St. Anthony, a saint known for helping find the lost, especially young men in trouble. For a moment, piece three seemed to be Giovanni as one of those young men in trouble. No, she thought, that doesn't fit, at least not yet.

She backed up in her mind. What is piece three? she asked. There it was: piece three is Kevin, not Giovanni. Now pieces of the puzzle, pieces she didn't even know were part of the solution, began to scream for attention in her mind.

Piece four: leukemia is a form of cancer. Piece five: Lorraine LaPurcell, James Kuiper, and Vladimir Monsitoff, all cancer victims. Piece six: wouldn't cancer victims who were losing the battle with the disease be more likely to seek a miracle? Piece seven: Lorraine LaPurcell, James Kuiper, and Vladimir Monsitoff, all in Venice at nearly the same time and undoubtedly for the same reason.

And piece eight? Was it not the missing monk, Brother Sergius, and the missing relics, relics of saints who might be thought to, to do what? she thought. What is the word? Yes, she thought, saints might be thought to "intercede" for people in trouble.

The rest of the pieces were still unclear in her mind, but she knew she would have felt the exhilaration of being so close to solving the entire puzzle if Giovanni's face did not keep coming back to her. Did he fit into the puzzle somehow, and, if so, where? And did the other man and woman from Padua, who seemed to have such a hold on Giovanni, also fit?

To her surprise, she felt a strong desire to lay this all out to her father. But immediately, a warning surfaced in her mind. No, she realized, I won't tell him about Giovanni, not yet. And that meant that she couldn't talk about the two others in Padua. She reminded herself that she had no basis for linking Giovanni's distress, whatever its cause, with the three victims and the missing relics. Is it not possible, she asked herself, that Giovanni's face keeps coming to mind for one simple reason: that her revelation about both cases began while she was observing him at the crypt in Padua?

With that decision to share only part of what she discovered with her father, she looked for him at his desk in the *Questura*. To her disappointment, he wasn't there, and when she asked, she heard the news of the morning, that another body was found.

"*Dove*? Where?" she asked Basso who was sitting at his desk, reading the sports page.

"*Dove*?" he repeated. "*No ho capito*, I no understand."

"The body," she answered. "*Corpo*. Where was the body found? *Dove e corpo*?" She was sure that her Italian was very flawed, but was glad to see Basso's face light up.

"*Sì, sì*," he nodded. "*Torcello. Isola Torcello*, the island Torcello. *Un ragazzo*, a young man, found in the water."

Allyson felt her breath stick in her throat. A young man? On an island that could only be reached by boat? Frozen in her mind was the troubled face of Giovanni.

Ispettore Ruggiero paced behind the head of the conference table. Almost every seat in the room was taken. He felt the tension in the room and decided to do nothing about that until everyone arrived. He was thinking especially of Allyson, who came to work late that morning but yet was reported to have gone to lunch at one in the afternoon. She would owe him an explanation, but not for coming back late from lunch. No, she and the other two Americans, Lieutenant Worthy, her father, and this priest, Father Fortis, had far more than that to explain.

As he cleaned his glasses, he noted the seating arrangement. On one side of the table were the two Americans; on the other were the two Italians, Castelucci and Basso, the coroner, and the other inspector who'd been assigned to the stolen relics investigation. Despite occasional murmuring in the room, no words were being exchanged across the divide. We look like a NATO meeting about to turn nasty, he thought.

From what he gleaned from Lieutenant Worthy out on Torcello, the room was likely divided in a more important way than by nationality. Worthy explained the odd presence and then the seeming psychic abilities of the rotund and bloodied priest by saying that Father Fortis had been sent to Venice by the Vatican to look into the thefts of the relics.

Ruggiero found that Worthy's explanation only made the situation more confusing. Of course, he was apprised of the problem of the missing relics by his colleague, and he was not surprised that the Vatican, with its connections, would have a vested interest. But his counterpart shared that the Church authorities of Venice suspected someone or ones within the Orthodox community. So why would the Vatican send an Orthodox monk from America to meddle in that problem?

"*Ingerenza*," the Italian for "meddling," seemed to be precisely what these American guests specialized in. An American Orthodox monk comes to Venice to hunt relic robbers, yet the culprits are suspected to be none other than Orthodox monks. An American detective comes to Venice to investigate the death of an American auto magnate, but uses, no, exploits, the similarities of that death to those of Lorraine LaPurcell and Vladimir Monsitoff to meddle with those cases. And now he learns that this same detective, since coming to Venice, has met repeatedly with this American Orthodox monk and has come to the incredible conclusion that the death of the millionaires and the disappearance of the relics are somehow linked. And then there is my American college intern, who just happens to be the daughter of the American detective, who has done an admirable job at collecting data on *uomini de fiducia*, con-artists, but has also been meeting with this priest-monk and her father to work on the relics case.

He didn't know whether to scream at the Americans or laugh at them. From everything that they knew, the body of the Russian monk found on Torcello was likely not even Ruggiero's concern, but rather the latest development, albeit an escalation, in the other investigation—the missing relics. He could see no connection whatsoever between the strangled body on Torcello and the three dead millionaires, especially if those deaths were, as still seemed probable to him, suicides.

Perhaps, he thought, this mixing facts with imaginings was a characteristic of American police work. That combination made for good headlines and popular TV crime shows, especially those from the United States, but that approach violated all of Ruggiero's own training and disposition.

He always believed that his earlier academic interest in chemistry provided him an appropriately cautious foundation for police work. And central to scientific methodology was this tenet: don't ever tell the data what they show. Let the data talk to you.

And wasn't that what these Americans did—sharing pieces of two investigations with one another, night after night for all he knew, the bottles of wine flowing, until a mirage formed in the bleary haze? Forensic work is a science, not a cheap mystery novel.

He consulted the aviator chronometer given to him on his promotion to *ispettore* the year before as Allyson Worthy entered the room. He watched as she assessed the room and then took an empty chair on the other side of the priest. Interesting, he thought, that she didn't take the only other unoccupied chair, the one next to her father. As far as Ruggiero could tell, she didn't even glance at her father as she passed him.

He introduced Father Fortis to Castelucci and Basso without explaining why the priest was in the room, and then set forth his plan for the meeting.

"Much, much has happened in Venezia in the past days," he began. "What is necessary now is to be clear on what we know, yes? I mean, what we know with certainty about the deaths of the three foreigners." Before anyone could question why "three" deaths and not "four," he continued. "We know that Ms. LaPurcell, Mr. Kuiper, and Mr. Monsitoff take day trains to a city or cities not far from Venezia only days before their bodies are found, yes? So, we start with what was discovered yesterday by these three," he said, nodding in the direction of Castelucci and Basso and then in the direction of Allyson.

Basso began, giving his report concerning Verona in Italian and leaving the English translation to Ruggiero. He showed the passport photos of Vladimir Monsitoff, James Kuiper, and Lorraine LaPurcell in the train station, the taxi ranks, and the bus stops. Most of those whom he asked said they didn't recognize any of the three, though most added that they could not be sure. What Basso was confident about was that none of the three, if one or all traveled to Verona, took a taxi.

"But maybe different drivers on that day?" Ruggiero asked.

Basso looked sheepish as he admitted that possibility.

Castelucci learned from his colleague's gaffe. He avoided expressing confidence in what he learned in Vicenza, but in the end reported the same results. No one in the city of the Vicenza recalled any of the three.

Again, it was Ruggiero who asked at the end of the report, "No one recognize even the actress?"

"No, *Ispettore*," Castelucci assured the room.

"Verona, no. Vicenza, no," Ruggiero summarized. He turned his attention to the other side of the room. "So, Allyson, Padua?"

He was surprised that the American intern, normally so quick to respond to any question, now seemed to have failed to hear him. The room grew quiet, and it was the priest who touched Allyson's arm and seemed to jar her out of her revelry.

"Excuse me, *Ispettore*, but I don't think that I'm up to date. I heard this morning that another body, a young man's, was found on Torcello."

Ruggiero thought he heard a tremor in her voice as she asked, "Do we know who this person is?"

Ruggiero frowned at her as the room resumed its tense silence. He planned to leave the discussion of the Russian monk's body until the end of the meeting, as his way of emphasizing the likely irrelevance of the morning's discovery. But now his intern was ruining his plan.

"It is the body of a Russian, a monk," he said brusquely. "He has been staying here in Venice for several months. A known suspect in the robberies. His body would have been washed out with the tides, but his robe was caught on a drain pipe. The initial report suggests that his arms were bound before he died. I believe no connection ..." he added before the expression on his intern's face caused him to pause.

Allyson had a tissue to her eyes, where tears were flowing freely. All she said was "Oh," and Ruggiero had the odd feeling that she was relieved at the news.

I will never understand these Americans, he thought.

Chapter Twenty-One

Allyson's voice indeed broke when she asked about the identity of the body found on Torcello. Ever since Basso told her the news, she felt a terrible foreboding. Unable to sit patiently, she consequently spent her lunch hour walking through the Castello *sestiere* that included the *Questura*. Choosing side walkways, she sought to avoid the parade of tourists, for whom Venice was still a dreamy oasis of tranquility. The afternoon autumn shade already gave the narrow walkway a sense of gloom that matched her fears.

Okay, I admit it, she thought. I was only trying to fool myself by denying a connection between Giovanni and one or both of the mysteries. That was proven so clearly by the question that came to mind as soon as Basso told her the news. What if the body is Giovanni's?

She could not walk fast enough to outrun two images that kept alternating in her mind. One was of the last time she saw Giovanni, his tortured face as he grasped the edge of the crypt of St. Anthony. The other was her standing before the bloated body of Vladimir Monsitoff, only now the face was Giovanni's.

Somehow despite her preoccupied thoughts, Allyson began to have a queasy feeling that she was being watched. She slowed her pace and blamed the sensation on having followed Giovanni and the two others in Padua the day before. But the feeling persisted. She stopped to use a shop window to view the reflection from the opposite walkway. Without her knowing why, her eye followed someone in a dark green sweater for several seconds before she realized that the figure was a lot like the man in Padua who grabbed at Giovanni's throat.

She could feel her heart pounding in her chest as she entered the next shop, a fountain pen store, and moved to the back of the shop. She positioned herself near the end of a counter where she could observe the other side of the causeway. Pretending to be interested in different colors of ink, she waited and watched.

Yes, the figure returned, walking briskly into her line of vision and then out of it. It was the same man. Suddenly clear to her was the mistake that she made in Padua. When the three separated outside the restaurant, she watched the unknown woman and man walk in one direction before she followed Giovanni in the other.

She never considered what must have happened next. As she followed Giovanni, one of the other two apparently turned back and followed her.

As she exited the pen shop and hurried toward the *Questura*, she felt a wave of fear. She knew that she was being followed, but at that moment she was not afraid for herself. True, she could no longer be sure that the two she saw with Giovanni in Padua were not linked somehow with the two cases, the missing relics and even the deaths.

But the core of her the terror lay elsewhere. Whichever of the two followed Giovanni and then her into the basilica saw Giovanni weeping at the crypt. Did she inadvertently put Giovanni in danger by luring one of them to witness his obvious agony? Would Giovanni's emotion suggest to that other watcher that he might betray them? Had they already moved against him?

So as she entered the conference room, the dread she felt could not be hidden any longer. She hardly noticed who was in attendance and took the first unoccupied seat that she saw. The reports by Basso and Castelucci concerning Verona and Vicenza were just noise to her, and she feared that she would throw up if she did not hear learn the identity of the body on Torcello.

And yet, when she heard that the latest victim was Brother Sergius, she felt only the slightest breeze of relief. Giovanni was still alive, but would he be next to die?

If Ruggiero was confused by Allyson's tearfulness at the news of Brother Sergius' body being discovered, Worthy was just as lost. Allyson hadn't met the Russian monk, had she?

Once again, he was reminded that there was much his daughter did not choose to share. Take the trip to Padua, for example. Why had she not told him about that assignment? Then again, if Ruggiero assigned that trip to him, would he have felt obligated to tell her?

His problem, he realized, was that he was still struggling to see Allyson as a colleague and not simply as his wayward daughter. Ruggiero, not he, was her supervisor on her internship, and she owed only the inspector an explanation. And yet it was clear to everyone in the room that her display of emotion also caught Ruggiero by complete surprise. Was she keeping aspects of the case from him?

The rest of the briefing was a clear display of Ruggiero's own perspective on the case. Allyson remained mute as the new victim, Brother Sergius, was discussed in the context of the missing relics, not the deaths of the millionaires. Worthy considered interrupting Inspector Ruggiero, but what was the point? Ruggiero already knew how Worthy saw recent events, from the relics on Murano being stolen, to the hunt for Brother Sergius, and now the discovery of the monk's body, in a completely different light. If Ruggiero was not even going to raise the alternative possibility—that the two cases were linked—then that was his decision.

The truth was that the discovery of Brother Sergius' body did not necessarily clarify anything. Even his close friend Father Fortis, as well as Allyson, probably saw the situation no differently than Ruggiero. From their point of view, Brother Sergius' disappearance at nearly the same time that the Murano relic was stolen pointed clearly to the Russian monk's involvement. Father Fortis went to Torcello because that island's name was written on the bottom of the Russian's map. Father Fortis undoubtedly hoped to find Brother Sergius on the island, and maybe even the missing relics. That the trail ended with a corpse would mean to Father Fortis that those behind the thefts were more dangerous than anyone first assumed. If the Vatican thought that a murder would accompany the thefts, they would never have asked Father Fortis to look into the matter.

But for Worthy, the new development on Torcello underscored his conviction: Brother Sergius not only was involved in the deaths of the millionaires but was also involved in the thefts of the relics. Ruggiero placed great stock in the fact that the Russian's body bore none of the telltale scars. Worthy didn't even try to explain to the inspector that he would never have expected that. Brother Sergius did not come to Venice as a cancer victim, but Worthy was still convinced that the coincidence in time between the deaths and the thefts could not be ignored. To Worthy, the Russian's death signified that there was some falling out between the monk and the others involved, even as the death complicated the case even further. Brother Sergius, Worthy was convinced, died with the knowledge of how the entire puzzle fit together. But with that death, where could Worthy now pick up the trail?

With Ruggiero's agenda controlling the outcome of the briefing, Worthy turned his attention to planning the evening. He could think of nothing more important that another dinner meeting with Father Fortis and Allyson. It was time to clue in the other two on his conviction and solicit their help.

And, he knew, it was time for Allyson to explain her reaction to the news of the morning. What had she held back from Ruggiero? What was she holding back from him?

Coming first to the restaurant on *La Giudecca*, Allyson looked out over the lagoon, the same scene that she'd enjoyed before with her father and Father Fortis. Yet, the scene now seemed menacing. Out there was Lido, where Giovanni hoped to start his club, but now associated for her with the bloated body of Vladimir Monsitoff. Past that island was Torcello, where Brother Sergius' body was found. And now, Giovanni was somewhere out there.

In thinking back on her time in Padua, she couldn't help but conclude that the normally suave Giovanni was being led, maybe even being controlled, by the other two.

And now Giovanni communicated. The text message came after the conference and its tagline was simple. "I need your help." The rest of the message asked her to meet him at ten that evening at the same dock where, only days before, they'd met for the trip to Lido.

She thought back on that evening, when Sylvia tried so hard to corral Giovanni's attention. Even despite that, she remembered the laughter and flirting as if it were a lifetime ago, when all of them seemed so much younger.

She pondered again the last sentence in Giovanni's text message, which begged her to keep their meeting confidential. Could she do that? When she remembered his face as he stood before the crypt in Padua, she realized that she had no other choice but to help him. And to do that, she had to accept his terms.

Not that keeping Giovanni out of the dinner conversation with Father Fortis and her father would be easy. She had no fear that she could keep her father's curiosity at bay. She had long known how to put him on the defensive. But she had no such confidence about bluffing Father Fortis. The man seemed to see right through her.

Chapter Twenty-Two

Father Fortis exited the *vaporetto* and headed for the rendezvous with Worthy and Allyson. In the afternoon meeting, he was puzzled by the tension that he felt from both of them. Sitting between Worthy and his daughter Allyson, he found both unaccountably uncommunicative. To his right, Worthy emitted an icy coldness, his eyes hooded as he stared straight ahead of him at a blank wall. On the other side of him, the latecomer, Allyson displayed her feelings from the moment she sat down.

As Inspector Ruggiero summarized the case to that point, Father Fortis listened for any clue to his friends' opposite reactions. Yet, the inspector's conclusions struck him as similar to their own, to his knowledge, of their own. The body of Brother Sergius proved that the relic thefts were far more serious than anyone originally thought. Until that morning, Venice was dealing with a burglary case and a homicide. Now, the city had two separate homicide investigations, one centered on millionaires and the other connected with stolen relics.

If Inspector Ruggiero's summary wasn't the cause of Worthy's and Allyson's odd reactions, had something erupted between the two of them? For several days, Father Fortis was worried about how Allyson might take Worthy's characteristic withdrawal, his standard behavior when he went digging for something that only he was aware of. But Father Fortis' sense of Allyson led him to expect a different reaction from her. If Worthy's silence troubled her, would not she have been the one to don the frozen mask? And would it not have been Worthy who would have struggled to hide his vulnerability in the face of his daughter's rage?

So, if Ruggiero's summary wasn't to blame, and if there had been no confrontation between Worthy and Allyson, then what was behind their strange moods?

As he threaded his way through the narrow walkways leading from one side of *La Giudecca* to the other, he pondered other questions. With the police now fully aware of the close relationship among Worthy, Allyson, and himself, why did they need to return to this out-of-the-way island? And yet, hadn't Worthy insisted that they meet in their same secret place?

If he hoped for an immediate answer to that question, he was disappointed, as it was Allyson, not Worthy, who was seated at an outside table.

She looks burdened, he thought. Waving at her, he thought of the Biblical invitation, "Come unto me, all you who … are heavy-laden." May we say something tonight to lighten her burden, he prayed.

"Phew, Nick, I'm glad this day is about over," she said with what to Father Fortis seemed to be a forced smile. She studied his face for a moment before adding, "You look like you fell into the lion's den at the zoo. What happened?"

He explained his morning journey to Murano and Torcello, all in the hope of picking up Brother Sergius' trail. Skipping over his mystical experience in the church of Santa Maria Assunta, he described seeing her father arrive on board a police boat and his trudging cross-country through swamps, a canal, and finally through the thorny brambles of the last field.

He had the feeling that Allyson was waiting for him to say something else. After a moment, she commented, "It must have been a shock when you realized the body was Brother Sergius."

Did she not hear what he said? "No, but it was a shock to the police when they saw this," he said, pointing to the scratches on his face. "I finally made it across the fields. When I saw the police boat, I knew they must be there for a homicide. And I just knew, sad as the outcome was, that the body was be Brother Sergius'."

Over Allyson's shoulder, Father Fortis saw Worthy approaching the restaurant. His friend was wearing a sport shirt, sleeves rolled up, and looking far more relaxed than at the meeting.

"I could use a drink," Worthy said, taking the seat next to his daughter and sighing deeply. "This afternoon was like being back in Detroit, trapped in a meeting that just wouldn't end."

"I don't remember you saying a word, my friend," Father Fortis said.

"What I had to say wasn't going to be welcome," Worthy replied. "But let's order some food."

When the waiter came, Allyson ordered a salad, saying she wasn't very hungry. Worthy and Father Fortis ordered full meals, along with two bottles of wine.

Seeming to be ignorant of his daughter's quietness, Worthy leaned forward. A smile played across his face. I recognize that look, Father Fortis thought. That's Worthy's smile when he's figured something out.

"I know this is going to take some explaining, but hear me out. The last time we were here, you two were looking at the Russian's map. Remember?"

"The one with Torcello written at the bottom," Allyson commented.

So she is paying attention, Father Fortis thought.

"Exactly. When I saw you two huddled over that map, it struck me that the reason we weren't making much progress on the two cases was because they are two parts of one case."

Father Fortis felt slightly disappointed. Didn't they dismiss that suggestion at the time? "But wasn't that based on your assumption that a Ukrainian and a Russian in Venice would know each other?" he asked.

"Okay, I know I was wrong about that. But we should have paid more attention to this fact, that the first missing relic was reported stolen in Venice no more than two weeks before Lorraine LaPurcell's body was found."

To Father Fortis' surprise, Allyson seemed suddenly alert, her eyes fixed on her father's profile. What am I missing, Father Fortis wondered. None of this is new.

"There's a lot I don't understand yet, but I think the pieces begin to make sense if Brother Sergius is the link between the deaths and the missing relics."

"A middleman, that's what you're saying?" Allyson asked.

Worthy looked over with apparent gratitude. "Yes, Ally, that's exactly what I'm saying. Look, what we've never figured out is why the millionaires came to Venice. We know it wasn't to flaunt their wealth. The three lived in dives and kept very low profiles. They even wore cheap clothes."

"I thought we assumed that they were hiding out," Father Fortis interrupted.

"But why? The only logical reason for their being in Venice that makes sense is their cancers," Worthy proposed.

"I agree," Allyson added.

Father Fortis could feel Worthy's mind racing. And Allyson seemed to be following him.

"But they didn't consult any oncologist in the city, Christopher. Unless someone is lying."

"But they did find someone to cut incisions in their bodies, someone with some basic medical knowledge," Worthy replied.

"And the coroner said that those cuttings have nothing to do with their cancer sites," Father Fortis protested. "And you still haven't drawn any connection with the stolen relics. Are you saying that these millionaires, all dying of cancer, decided to become burglars before they died?"

Worthy shook his head. "No, but I do think that the relics were what lured them to Venice. And I don't think they gave a second thought to those being stolen."

After their dinners were put before them, Father Fortis poured the wine and offered a toast. "I admit to still being confused, but here's to solving this mess, whether it's two cases or one."

They took not more than several bites of their meals when Allyson put her fork down and rested her chin on folded hands. "Here's what I think." She spoke the words slowly and waited a moment before resuming. "Okay, I need to start by telling you that I did notice something out in Padua that I didn't share at the meeting." Once again, she described how her assigned interviews produced nothing definite.

"But I ended up near a church in Padua, one dedicated to a St. Anthony," she added.

"Yes, a very important Franciscan saint," Father Fortis interjected.

"When I entered the church, I saw this line to visit the crypt of the saint. I thought I should see what a real relic looks like, given all the attention they've gotten here in Venice. But when I had my turn, the crypt ended up being just a huge marble box. I guess the relics are encased inside."

Allyson momentarily looked away from the table and out over the lagoon. And when she resumed speaking, Father Fortis thought her voice sounded tighter. Is she afraid of something, he wondered.

"Anyway, when I was in line for the crypt, I had a chance to read the story of Saint Anthony. Apparently, Catholics pray to him when they lose something."

"And not just Catholics, my dear. My dear mother would ask for his help when she couldn't find her keys."

With her eyes returning to the lagoon, Allyson cleared her throat before saying, "I found out that St. Anthony is also a saint for people in trouble. I guess like St. Jude helps those with lost causes."

Father Fortis set his water glass down. "Good Lord," he exclaimed. "Are you saying … "

Allyson cut him off with a sharp glance. There was a challenge in those eyes, he realized, that he didn't understand.

"So I think you're right, Dad. The millionaires came to Venice because of the cancer. They came hoping to be cured," Allyson said. "And that's where I think they thought the relics might help. You know, maybe they were hoping for a miracle. Could relics be known for that?"

Father Fortis' hands shot to the sides of his head as if trying to prevent the thought from escaping. He laughed with such gusto that other patrons stared over at their table. He opened his eyes to see Worthy looking at his daughter in wonder.

"Of course, of course," Father Fortis said. "I've been too modern in my thinking. I was fooled by the fact that few people believe in relics these days. But in the Middle Ages, the sick who could afford it would take pilgrimages to touch relics or at least pray near them."

Worthy continued to stare at his daughter. "I guess we were put off the scent by the fact that none of our victims were known to be religious."

Allyson nodded and then picked up her knife. "And I think this is the next piece of the puzzle."

Father Fortis felt a cloud slowly dissolving, but Worthy seemed to be already ahead of him. "Go ahead, Allyson," he said, a smile beginning on his face.

"Millionaires with terminal cancer have to figure out what to do with all their money, right? Which was why you, Dad, checked to see if any of them made large contributions to charities."

"And that was a no-go," Worthy added. "They were much too self-absorbed for that, weren't they?"

"I think they were. I think they paid to have their skin cut open," she said, brandishing the knife, "so that a relic could be inserted."

Father Fortis caught his breath. "Of course. Good Lord, didn't the actor Steve McQueen do something like that? Didn't he travel to some other country and pay a fortune for some bogus cure?"

"I heard the comedian Andy Kaufmann did the same," Worthy added.

Father Fortis pondered Allyson's stunning theory. No, it wasn't a theory, he admitted. This is the truth that had eluded them. The relics, the millionaires, and the incisions. Yet, something still didn't make sense to him. "Shouldn't we have found the relics in their bodies then?"

Allyson looked over at her father. "I think you know the answer to that, Dad."

"If I do, it's only because you figured out the whole puzzle. Ally, this is really something," Worthy said. "Actually, it's remarkable. Lorraine LaPurcell, James Kuiper, and Vladimir Monsitoff were all about to die. They were desperate, and somehow they heard that relics could bring about miracles. And someone promised them unheard of access to relics here in Venice. Long story short, they were very willing to pay a ton of money to have a stolen relic implanted in hopes of forcing a miracle."

Father Fortis studied Allyson's face. She looked pleased with her father's compliment, but not as pleased as Father Fortis would have expected or hoped. Despite all the revelations, Father Fortis still sensed an unspoken block at the table.

Worthy seemed to pause and give Allyson the chance to continue. "The relics weren't found on the bodies for the same reason that the incision sites showed that they were cut twice," she said. "Their bodies were cut once to embed the relic and then the second time to extract it."

Again, Father Fortis could do nothing but laugh uproariously. "That's brilliant, Allyson, absolutely brilliant," he gushed. "But wait a minute. That explains everything about the incisions except why these millionaires would, on the one hand, pay hundreds of thousands of dollars for a relic, but then allow someone to extract it."

Allyson shrugged. "I haven't figured that out."

"I can think of one possibility," Worthy said. "Maybe those offering the relics thought that it would be too risky to let the millionaires leave Venice with them," Worthy suggested. "Family members or their normal doctors would undoubtedly see the scars and ask questions."

Father Fortis shook his head. "You two make quite a pair, you know that?" He poured the last of the wine into the three glasses and offered another toast. "Here's to the Worthys and their gifts for solving mysteries. May the Good Lord and St. Anthony be praised."

Though both father and daughter joined in the toast, Allyson noticeably stiffened when Worthy put his arm around her and gave her a squeeze.

In the awkward silence that followed, Father Fortis found himself pondering one last question. "So is the fear of eventual exposure the reason that the millionaires had to be killed, assuming they were killed?" he asked.

It was Worthy who replied. "That's as good a theory as any I can think of. What would those millionaires do when they got home to the States or the Ukraine and found out that their cancers were still flourishing?"

"Hmm. More tourists fleeced in Venice, right, Allyson?" Father Fortis asked.

She nodded. "Only this time they were taken for a third of a million dollars each. Unless, of course …"

Worthy was now the one who seemed lost. "Unless what?"

"I think what Allyson means," Father Fortis helped out, "is that they were fleeced unless their cancers were actually improving when they died."

Worthy exhaled slowly. "No offense, Nick, but I agree with the killers on this. They never considered that their ruse might actually work. That was just the line that they fed the victims."

"And I'll bet the families would never give permission to exhume the bodies to answer that question," Father Fortis mused.

Worthy nodded in agreement. "What we know from the autopsies is that their cancers were still at an advanced stage when they died. Which leaves us with this discouraging conclusion: the one person who could best reveal why they were killed was found dead this morning. Unless the other two monks were part of the scam, I'm drawing a blank about where to go from here. Any suggestions, Allyson?"

Allyson glanced at her watch before answering. "Huh? No, no ideas." Pushing her chair back, she stood up and yawned. "Maybe we'll do better in the morning."

CHAPTER TWENTY-THREE

ALLYSON MADE A POINT OF WALKING slowly with Father Fortis and her father to the *vaporetto* stand. Thankfully, her boat was different from the one that would take the other two back to Venice proper. Feigning another yawn, she waved at both of them as their boat pulled away from the dock.

"*Buona notte*," Father Fortis called to her. "See, I'm learning some Italian."

"*Buona notte, papa*," she called back.

But Allyson was anything but tired. Was she emotionally exhausted at having to keep Giovanni's name, as well as the names of the two others, out of the discussion? Yes, she would admit to that. But with adrenalin surging through her system, she felt she could swim across the expansive Grand Canal lapping in front of her.

Forty minutes later and with ten minutes to spare, she approached the dock where she was to meet Giovanni. The lights there were of little help, and so she could hear, more than see, the boats jostling at anchor just offshore. As far as she could tell, and she was cautious, she was alone at the dock. This part of Venice bordered on the industrial, so with little to attract tourists, the entire area was already dark.

When Giovanni didn't arrive at the agreed upon time, Allyson hoped that he changed his mind. That was far better than the alternative that she could imagine. Ten anxious minutes passed before she heard the faint hum of a motor. Staring out into the darkness, she found the tiny green light of an approaching boat and followed its slow progress. As the boat drew closer and closer, she could feel her heart pounding in rhythm with the motor's vibrations. The odd thought struck her that she would have been overjoyed if Sylvia were standing next to her at that moment.

Sylvia, jealous Sylvia, she thought. In the end, before leaving the apartment for the dinner meeting with Father Fortis and her father, Allyson felt the need to leave a message for Sylvia—just in case. Just in case I've misread Giovanni all along, she thought; just in case, he doesn't come alone; and just in case I'm making the worst mistake of my life.

She struggled to compose a message that was deliberately vague, something that would give the police and her father some clue if matters didn't work out, but also a message that could be easily dismissed if she were overreacting. In the end, she settled for "Don't be mad at me, Sylvia. If anyone asks, say I'm out with Giovanni."

Allyson breathed a brief sigh of relief when she saw that Giovanni was alone on the boat. As the wooden craft maneuvered around one of the moored boats, Allyson was surprised to read what was painted in gold lettering on the stern. "*Grazie G.*" What did the "G" stand for, she wondered.

Rather than tying up at the dock, Giovanni brought the craft parallel to the dock's end and reached for her hand. In one step, she was on board, and without saying a word Giovanni steered the boat back into the darkness.

And right there was the point of no return, she thought, as she looked back on the lonely dock. Giovanni's face was obscured somewhat by a hat, but Allyson was able to see in the moment that he reached for her that he hadn't shaved that day.

In the darkness, Allyson was unable to determine where they were going, but it seemed to be away from Venice itself. And despite the fact that Giovanni continued to run the boat at low speed, Allyson rejected the urge to try to talk over the motor, to ask where they were headed. Giovanni asked her to trust him, and now was not the time to panic.

In less than a half-hour, the boat approached a cluster of lights on what Allyson was sure was the mainland. Perhaps, we're in Mestre or another of the towns that face Venice proper, she thought. The motor was almost whispering as Giovanni brought the craft to one side of a dock.

"Please, Allyson, come with me," he said as he jumped onto the dock and quickly tied up the boat before reaching back for her.

And this is another point of no return, she thought, as she accepted his hand and stepped ashore. She looked around with hopes of seeing a club, a restaurant, or at least a bar, but Giovanni led her away from the lights and though a series of storage sheds until they came to a larger building made of cement blocks.

A chill that she couldn't control passed through her, causing Giovanni to glance over at her and say, "No need to fear."

Easy for you to say, she thought, but nodded that she understood. Unlocking the door of the building, Giovanni took her hand again and led her into the pitch blackness.

She heard the door shut behind her as Giovanni released her hand. Panic gripped her again as she imagined herself abandoned, bound, and locked up in this darkness. What will they say about me, she wondered. Will I be remembered as another American overseas, one who threw caution to the wind in order to have a fling with a handsome Italian, a man whose last name I don't even know? Will my father spend the rest of his life blaming himself for my disappearance—my second disappearance?

Feeling close to screaming, she nearly lost her balance in the blackness until a fluorescent light winked on. Her eyes adjusted, and she began to discern a room full of boxes as well as a small card table with chairs set up in the middle of the room. A bottle of wine and several glasses were all that was on the table.

"Please," he said, gesturing toward the table. "Would you like some *vino*?"

His voice sounded soft to her, the way it was the first time they met. She looked into his face and thought, yes, this is the Giovanni I know. I am not afraid of him.

"No thank you," she said.

"Would you mind if do?" he asked as he sat in the other chair.

She shook her head. "Of course not."

He poured his wine so slowly that Allyson was reminded of a Zen tea ceremony she'd observed at college. But the sadness in Giovanni's face suggested his deliberateness had nothing to do with contemplation.

"*Mille grazie*, many thanks for coming, Allyson." He said her name as he always did, All-ee-sown. "Believe me, I will not abuse that trust."

"Yes," she replied. "I mean, I understand."

He gazed around the room and then at his glass, anywhere, she thought, but into her eyes.

"I was told you follow me in Padua yesterday, yes?"

"Yes. I'm sorry."

He waved her apology away. "But someone else follow me."

"Don't you mean that someone was following me?" she asked.

"No, he follow me." He paused, then nodded. "And then, yes, he saw you follow me, so, okay, he also follow you."

"Why would he follow you?" she asked.

He shrugged. "He no trust me. He not like you. Please, Allyson, tell me what you see when you follow me?"

Allyson could not escape the pleading tone in his voice. What does he want from me—help? Absolution? Understanding?

"I wanted to see you again. But then I saw you meet two others. And I saw the man grab you around the neck. Oh, and I saw you kiss the woman."

She thought that she could see the beginning of a smile begin on Giovanni's face. "*Mia sorella*, my sister."

"Oh," she said with relief. Maybe I've misunderstood everything, she thought. "Oh, I see. And was the other man your brother?"

"No, no. He my sister's boyfriend." He coughed before adding, "And in the basilica? What did you see?"

She paused, trying to find the right words to describe what she observed. "I guess I will have some wine. Just a little, please."

He poured her half a glass. She took a sip and set down the glass. "I saw you at the crypt. I could tell you were suffering."

"Ah," was all he said, but he looked up to make eye contact.

They sat in silence for a moment before Allyson spoke. "You said that you needed my help. What can I do, Giovanni?"

He swirled the wine in his glass. "Are you magic? Can you change everything?"

Allyson heard the unmistakable hopelessness in his voice. "I don't know what I can do until you ask," she said.

Giovanni gazed up at the ceiling light and sighed audibly. "We have a proverb in Italia," he said. "I think in English it is 'A happy heart is better than a full purse.' My sister and I heard that our whole lives. I never believe this proverb. I think it is what poor people say, what my mother and father say. But now I know the proverb it is true. But I know this too late. You see, Allyson, I have much money," he added, as if where confessing to a disease.

"But not a happy heart?" Allyson asked.

He gestured toward the door. "I have nice boat. I have nice clothes. I need much money to buy my club."

"Yes, I remember," Allyson said. "A club out on Lido."

"Now, maybe never."

Allyson took another sip of the wine. "And so you were hoping that St. Anthony could help?"

He nodded. "If I take people where I am told, I get beautiful boat. So I get beautiful boat. Also much money. So I take these people."

So the boat was his, the "G" for Giovanni, Allyson realized. "*Grazie G*"—was that Giovanni saying thank you for the boat or someone thanking Giovanni by giving him the boat? Whichever, some exchange definitely took place. So, what had Giovanni exchanged for money?

"You say that you take people places in your boat. What people are you talking about, Giovanni?"

"Rich people. People Pietro tell me to meet, to take on new boat. They pay him much money."

Pietro, she thought. The smaller man who could grab Giovanni's throat and not risk getting beaten in return.

"You mean the millionaires, the ones who've died here in Venice."

His head drooping to his chest, Giovanni nodded slowly.

"Do you know how they died?" she asked.

Giovanni shook his head as he looked up hopefully. "Pietro say they do suicide. TV say the same."

"The police aren't so sure about that. There's a chance they were murdered."

Giovanni's head fell back down again. "I don't know this. I don't want to know this."

Giovanni looked overwhelmed by the news, and Allyson decided to back away and try a different approach. Looking around the room, she asked, "What is this place, Giovanni?"

Giovanni did not look up. "This my father's business. He find scrap metal, then he resell it. He use this place to store metal."

Not the kind of job that leads to a luxurious wooden boat, she thought. "The first time I met you, you said 'Venice is a dying lady, but a woman who needs lots of money,' " she said. "Do you remember?"

"*Sì, sì.* Money always money. Never enough. But if I drive boat, I now have money."

There was no doubt to Allyson that Giovanni's portrayal of himself as a poor boy needing money to fulfill his dreams was an attempt to gain her support. But what do I want, she asked herself. Do I want to find Giovanni innocent, or do I want the truth, even if that truth spells his doom?

"How did you know which people to take in your boat?" she asked.

"I say already. Pietro, he tell me."

"But who told Pietro? These people came to Venice from far away. Did Pietro make some sort of contact with them or did someone else?"

"No, Pietro. He very smart with computers. He know things, how to find out about somebody. Anywhere in the world."

"He's a hacker, then," Allyson said.

"*Sì, sì.* He find people with computer. He make list of those who he can bring here, people who will spend much money."

Allyson began to see how the scam could be accomplished. First, this Pietro would find lists of wealthy people in various countries. Then, if he was really good at his job, he could hack into the medical records of those on the list. From there, this Pietro could identify those with terminal cancers. The next step was easy. He would contact them, use some cover so the email couldn't be back-traced, and offer the fake history of the relics performing miracles.

The irony of what Giovanni was telling her struck her full force. Her internship required her to analyze scams that are perpetrated on tourists in Venice. But, compared to what this Pietro engineered, the scams she tracked were amateurish.

She knew that she had to approach the next question, that of the relics, with gentleness. How had the relics been obtained? Was Pietro, Giovanni's sister, or Giovanni himself the thief? And where did Brother Sergius, the Russian monk, fit in?

"Did you know that these millionaires had cancer? Did you know they were dying?"

Giovanni nodded. "Maria, she tell me this."

"Maria?"

"My sister."

A piece of a memory from Padua, the building in front of which Giovanni was waiting, came back to Allyson. "So, who is in the medical science field, Pietro or Maria?"

Giovanni looked down again. "Maria, she study biology."

"And did you know that each of the millionaires made a trip to Padua before they died? That was where Maria did something to the millionaires, didn't she?"

"She no hurt them, Allyson. She swear this to me."

"Did you see the Americans and the Ukrainian after they'd been out to Padua?"

Giovanni looked up at her with fear in his eyes. "You know very much, Allyson." After a pause, he added, "I take them to Maria's flat. I come back to take them to train station. I am on the train with them."

"What did they seem like? Were they groggy? Did they complain of soreness?"

"Senora LaPurcell, she cried. The men do not say anything, but they are sad."

That must have been when the relics were removed, Allyson thought. Was their "cure" complete, or were they asked to cough up more money for the next relic? Was that when they realized that they paid a third of a million for nothing?

"My sister, she not a killer, Allyson. I am not a killer."

She wanted to believe him. She wanted to save him if she could. But she had to know everything. "I notice that you left out Pietro," she commented.

Giovanni shook his head. "Pietro, we know each other all our lives. His father die when Pietro is young. He have five brothers and sisters. Very poor. But very smart."

One question remained, and with it she would know Giovanni's fate.

"Did you take someone in your boat out to Murano and Torcello several days ago? A Russian? A monk?"

Chapter Twenty-Four

Lent was a time when Father Fortis was often asked by one of the larger parishes in Ohio to assist with confessions. And perhaps it made sense, when he helped out in Cleveland, Columbus, or Cincinnati, that more people would come to him for absolution than to their own priest. Father Fortis did not know them, and they would not see him week after week. He accepted that he was like the bartender in a faraway city to whom strangers would unburden their souls.

Yet, Father Fortis' experience in these parishes also exposed him to those who took the opposite approach. These folks would come to him and whitewash their sins, knowing that this out-of-town monk didn't know them well enough to confront them on their evasions. Despite, or perhaps because of, their efforts, he developed a keen sense of knowing when truth was being shaded or when an excuse was being substituted for an admission.

And that was what he was feeling again when Allyson's face came to mind as he said prayers before retiring for the night. At dinner with Worthy and Allyson, the frustrating puzzle pieces of the missing relics case began to fall into place. While Worthy was the first to connect the two cases, it was Allyson who explained how the relics lured the millionaire cancer victims to Venice, what caused the incision marks, both of them, on their bodies, and why the millionaires were so reclusive as they hoped and waited for a miracle.

In some ways, Father Fortis knew that he witnessed something extraordinary that evening in the ongoing saga of Worthy and Allyson's relationship. Three years before, when he first met Worthy, Allyson was a complete mystery, another frustrating puzzle, to her father. The renowned detective who could crack stubborn cases wasn't able to find his runaway daughter. She returned home, but was careful to avoid giving her parents any explanation about where she had been or why she had gone. Worthy always assumed that she ran away to hurt him, that this was somehow his fault. And Allyson seemed perfectly content to let her father remain both confused on that point and guilt-ridden.

But then, a little over a year before, Allyson began to reconnect with her father, to begin to construct a tentative bridge of understanding. But Worthy had to accept that the flow of that bridge was strictly one-way. Allyson began to ask, no, to demand, to know things about her father, especially why he seemed more concerned about those whose deaths he was paid to investigate than his own living family. But Worthy was not given permission to respond in kind. He still reminded Father Fortis of someone walking on eggshells.

The strange deaths of the millionaires in Venice forced Worthy and his daughter together in a way that neither would have requested. But, to his relief, Father Fortis was present to see the two at least begin to establish a new footing. To Father Fortis, it seemed that neither of them knew how to be father and daughter, but they began to know how to be colleagues on a case. Perhaps, he thought, if they worked together on this case long enough, the elusive family connection might be recovered.

But that night, as Father Fortis tried to find a comfortable arrangement of his pillows, he felt that the amazing revelations of the evening could not hide this underlying truth—Allyson avoided telling them something, something important. She was like one of those who came to him for confession and who, in saying a lot, managed to avoid what was most important. For some reason that Father Fortis could not fathom, Allyson retreated from both her father and him that night.

As he tried to relax and let himself fall into sleep, he offered a prayer. "Oh, God, protect Allyson from herself."

GIOVANNI GRIMACED WHEN ALLYSON ASKED HIM about the Russian monk.

"So you did take him out to those islands?" she said.

Giovanni nodded slowly. "He come in my boat many times," he admitted.

"Where did you usually take him?" Allyson probed, believing his answer might indicate where the relics were being hidden.

"Many, many times to Torcello, to an old house. But nobody live there now. I take him there and wait. Then I take him back to Venezia."

"Did Pietro introduce you to Brother Sergius?"

"Brother Sergius?"

"That's the monk's name," she explained.

"*Sì, sì*. Pietro brings him to me maybe three months back."

"Giovanni, you have to tell me the truth about Brother Sergius."

"I do tell the truth," he countered, looking offended.

"Good, good. Did you ever see Brother Sergius with Lorraine LaPurcell, James Kuiper, or Vladimir Monsitoff—the rich people?"

Giovanni shook his head. "I see the monk many times with Pietro. Sometimes I see him with Maria."

No doubt when he brought her the relics, Allyson concluded.

"Did you ever see the monk and Pietro fight, Giovanni?"

Giovanni looked down again at his untouched wine. "*Sì.*"

"When was that?" she asked.

"Four days ago, when I take monk to Torcello."

"But you didn't take the monk back to Venice, did you?"

Giovanni shook his head. "I wait and wait, but he no come to my boat. I think maybe he come back to Venezia another way."

"Giovanni, Brother Sergius didn't come back. The police found his body this morning. He'd been tied up, strangled, and thrown into a canal."

Giovanni groaned as his head dropped into his hands. "No, no, please no."

"Did you know that Pietro intended to kill Brother Sergius?"

Giovanni seemed not to hear the question. Allyson reached over and touched his hand and then repeated the question.

"I tell Pietro I am afraid. I tell him to keep my boat. I tell him I quit."

"That's what you said to him in Padua, wasn't it? Just before he grabbed your throat."

"He tell me I am too late. That Maria will be in big trouble if I don't do what he say."

Allyson could feel the blood drain from her face. Brother Sergius was undoubtedly already dead when she saw Pietro grab Giovanni in Padua. And that meant that Pietro had already killed the monk when he followed her in Padua and the next morning in Venice. What had the killer planned to do to her?

"Giovanni, I can't help you unless you answer my question. Did you know that Pietro intended to kill the monk?"

Giovanni looked up and crossed himself. He hid his eyes as he began to cry "I swear I do not know this. *Dio Mio*, poor Maria."

Allyson breathed a sigh of relief. Giovanni would have that question thrown at him repeatedly by the police. If he was lying, they would break him down. But Allyson was almost certain he was telling the truth.

"Giovanni, listen to me," she said. "If you come with me to the police and tell them what you told me, I think I can help you. Do you hear me? I said I can help you."

He nodded that he understood. "Maria?" he asked.

"Maria will have to explain her part in all this herself," she said. "Even if she didn't know what Pietro was planning to do with Brother Sergius, she'll still have to answer for inserting and taking out the stolen relics."

"Not murder?" he pleaded.

"No, not murder. Giovanni, it's now almost two in the morning. Can you take me back to Venice and stay in my apartment? And tomorrow, we go to the police, okay?"

He nodded but asked, "Why I stay with you?"

"Because I don't trust Pietro. I think your life might be in danger."

Standing, Allyson felt overcome with fatigue. It would be good to leave this place and return to Venice, she thought.

Out of the corner of her eye, Allyson saw the doorway open slightly and a hand reach in. The light went out and they were pitched into total darkness.

Chapter Twenty-Five

Father Fortis was having a fitful sleep, and consequently the muffled tap on his door at first seemed part of a nightmare he was having. When the tapping continued, he sat up in bed and glanced at his watch. Five thirty a.m. As he rose quickly and donned his robe, he felt dread rising within him. Good news rarely came at that time of the morning.

He opened his door with some trepidation. Would his visitor be Worthy with more bad news? But it was Brother Alexei and Brother Nilus, the latter nearly hidden behind the shoulder of the former. Both struggled to meet Father Fortis' eye.

Brother Alexei, having obviously taken over Brother Sergius' speaking role, asked if they could speak with him. The arrogant disdain that Father Fortis previously felt from the Russians was gone. Brother Nilus' body was completely hunched, and Father Fortis wondered if their black robes were always soiled. In Brother Nilus' sallow right hand was a bag.

Good Lord, they're orphans, Father Fortis thought.

He offered the two Russians the only chairs in the room, while he sat on the edge of the bed. Brother Nilus stared at the floor and the bag between his legs, while Brother Alexei began to read from a sheet of paper that he pulled from a pocket.

"Our dear Brother Sergius, our brother in Christ, has died," he read and looked over at Father Fortis.

Father Fortis nodded that he already knew.

"This is great tragedy for Brother Nilus and for me. We have lost our leader."

Again, Father Fortis nodded. Certainly, he thought, the monks did not come before dawn to tell him what was obvious news.

But then Brother Alexei spoke in Russian to his companion, and Brother Nilus in response rose and handed the bag to Father Fortis.

Father Fortis looked into the bag and removed a brown hooded robe along with a rope-corded belt and a wooden cross in the form of a Greek Tau.

"I don't understand," he said. "This is the robe of a Franciscan or Capuchin friar."

Brother Alexei closed his eyes and seemed to be mouthing words. "We find robe under bed of Brother Nilus. He know not how it is there."

Father Fortis studied the robe again. "You think this is Brother Sergius', don't you?"

It was now Brother Alexei who nodded.

"I think I understand," Father Fortis said. He remembered that the police found earlier only robes and books. The police would hardly have known the difference between the Capuchin robes and the black Orthodox ones.

"This is a disguise," he explained to the two Russians.

"Please?" Alexei asked, seemingly confused by the word.

"Brother Sergius sometimes wore this to pretend, to make people believe, he was a Catholic friar."

"Maybe yes, maybe no. But why? We wish to stay away from Papists."

Then you're in the wrong country and the wrong city, Father Fortis thought. He laid the robe down next to him on the bed and placed the rope cord at the beltline.

With his uncut beard, flowing hair, and black robes, Brother Sergius would be the picture of a Russian Orthodox monk. With his constant sober expression, he looked as if he just descended from Mt. Athos. But in these brown robes and rope belt, he could be easily confused with a Capuchin or Franciscan friar. And in this robe, he would have been able to enter some of the minor churches of the city or on Murano with no one suspecting his real purpose. Yet, if Brother Sergius used this robe on Murano, he wondered, why wasn't the robe found on him when his body was discovered on Torcello?

The evidence of the robe notwithstanding, he knew that it was time to see how well these two monks knew their leader. "Are you aware that Brother Sergius took," he began, deliberately avoiding the word "stole," "relics from some of the churches of Venice?"

Both monks shook their heads. Were they denying the truth, Father Fortis wondered. He looked at the two beaten-down monks and reasoned that they would hardly have come to him at this time of the morning if they participated in the thefts.

"You said before you didn't know about Brother Sergius's plane tickets for Russia. Was that the truth?" he asked.

Brother Alexei again closed his eyes and formed words silently. "He say he be gone two weeks, then come back."

"Did he say why he was going back to Russia?"

"He say he get email from Father Sopheris, to come home."

Their abbot, Father Fortis figured. That could be the truth, which suggested the mastermind of the thefts might be back in Russia or might be just Brother Sergius' cover. If the monk was planning on smuggling the stolen relics out of Italy, Father Fortis wondered, how was he planning to do that? Then Allyson's insight of the previous night came back to him. Of course, he thought. Brother Sergius must have planned to have the relics inserted into his body, even as the millionaires did. And in Russia, the relics could be removed and hidden in any church or monastery of the country. Ingenious, Father Fortis thought, but then he remembered that Inspector Ruggiero said that there were ligature marks on Brother Sergius' wrists, but no incisions. Am I wrong, Father Fortis wondered, or was the monk killed before the incisions could be made?

"Brother Alexei and Brother Nilus, you've done the right thing in bringing the robe to me. And I will take it to the police. But I have just one more question. Did you ever see Brother Sergius meeting or talking with an Italian, someone from Venice but not from the Center?"

The two monks looked at each other before nodding. "We see him two time, three time with Italian man."

"Did you ever ask Brother Sergius who this man was?"

"Yes, I ask," Brother Alexei offered. "He say he is friend in Venice. But I see this man. He angry."

"Why do you say that?" Father Fortis asked.

"One day, I see him. He grab girl and push girl."

"And did Brother Sergius ever tell you his name?"

Brother Nilus suddenly looked up and stared at Father Fortis for a moment. "Like Russian name. Like Pieter," he said.

Worthy awakened on the next morning, a Friday, with an odd mix of feelings. He felt a kind of welcome impatience, as the previous day's events, from finding Brother Sergius' body to the dinner conversation, meant that they were significantly nearer the end of the case.

And with that realization came the knowledge that he would likely be returning to Detroit within days. He had a great deal to tell the Kuipers, certainly more than they wanted to know. He would be able to dispel their confusion about why their husband and father lied about his travel plans, for what purpose he spent the third of a million dollars, and why his body was found with the incision marks.

But what nagged at Worthy was that he still did not know whether James Kuiper was murdered or committed suicide, the very question that the Kuipers were paying him to answer. Only those who inserted and extracted the relics from his body would be able to shine light on that question, and even they, if the millionaires committed suicide, could say in a strictly legal sense that they had nothing to do with their deaths.

But the obvious murder of Brother Sergius suggested, at least to Worthy, that homicide was still a strong option. Why the millionaires were killed must have something to do with the fear that the three would eventually expose the fraud.

Consequently, while Worthy welcomed the end of this case as he did every case, he had to admit that the death of Brother Sergius left him both troubled and uncertain. It was one thing to be able to account for the intricate details of a crime, but it was another to find those behind the crime. With Brother Sergius now gone, who would be the key to find the culprits?

But Worthy was also contending with another feeling, one that he hadn't felt for nearly five years. Prior to the divorce, back when his world made more sense, he had a number of occasions when he felt—no, when he was given permission to feel—pride in Allyson. Her academic achievements and then her value to the volleyball team garnered Allyson the ribbons and certificates associated with such successes. And even when an investigation prevented Worthy from attending one of the award programs, he always let Allyson know her successes gave him great pleasure.

But with the divorce and then her running away, Allyson's awards dried up. Even her acceptance into the criminology program at Franklin College was something that he knew he shouldn't make too much of.

But that morning, as he sat at his borrowed desk in the *Questura*, he was brimming with joy. Allyson, more than he, found the critical if not the final pieces to the puzzle of the relics and the deaths of the millionaires. Having finished only one year of college, she contributed, and contributed in a major way, to the solution of a very complex case. He looked forward with a father's pride to the meeting with Ruggiero when Allyson, not he, would lay out the solution to the two interconnected cases.

But as the morning dragged on, his checks of Allyson's desk produced nothing. Remembering how tired she was after dinner the night before, he dismissed her tardiness as well-deserved rest. From ten to eleven, however, he found himself growing angry at her disrespect, and, after eleven o'clock, his anger morphed into concern.

At noon, he called her cellphone number but was told that the number was out of service. That didn't make sense at all to him. He walked away his lunch hour, trying again twice, but with no luck, to reach her by phone.

It was as he was reentering the *Questura* that he realized that Allyson never told him where she was living with her roommate, Sylvia. He would have to ask Inspector Ruggiero for that information, in the process exposing his daughter's absence as well as his embarrassment over Allyson's distrust of him.

But in walking down the hallway to his desk, he was told that he had visitors. He opened the door, hoping to find Allyson but instead saw Father Fortis sitting next to two monks in the same black garb as Brother Sergius'.

In a matter of minutes, with the brown robe now lying on his desk, Worthy grasped the essential role that Brother Sergius played in the thefts and perhaps, with the naming of Pieter, he'd discovered the identity of his killer.

"We should turn all this over to Inspector Ruggiero," Worthy advised. "But I was hoping that Allyson would be here for that. She deserves the most credit, don't you think, Nick?"

"Absolutely, my friend. Where is Allyson?"

Worthy's face reddened. "Her phone seems to be out of service, and I've been too embarrassed to ask Ruggiero where she lives. You see, she never told me."

Father Fortis paused for a moment before giving Worthy a weak smile. "I wish I could tell you that she told me, Christopher, but she didn't. But doesn't her roommate, I think her name is Sylvia, work in the emergency room at the hospital?"

Worthy drew out his phone. "Good thinking, Nick. Let me get that number and call her."

While Worthy tried one number only to be given another, the two Russian monks kept looking around the room at the chaos of police staff on phones or yelling at one another.

Finally, Worthy heard a woman's voice on the phone. "Is this Sylvia?" he asked.

"Yes, this is Sylvia. Who is this?"

"My name is Christopher Worthy. I'm Allyson's father."

"Are you calling from the States?"

Great, Worthy thought. Allyson didn't even mention him to her roommate.

"Actually, I've been in Venice for a few days," he lied. "Allyson probably forgot to mention that I'm here on business… and to see her, of course. That's why I'm calling, Sylvia. I was supposed to meet Allyson this morning, but I can't reach her."

"Allyson, she is at the police station, where she works," Sylvia explained curtly.

"Well, I'm there now, Sylvia, and she hasn't come in yet for the day. I was wondering if you could tell me how to reach her."

"I don't know. Allyson did not come in last night."

"What?" Worthy asked in disbelief. "Are you sure?"

"Sorry, I must go. Yes, I am sure. She left a note, so I know she didn't sleep in the apartment."

"Sylvia, please. What does the note say?"

Worthy could hear an exasperated sigh on the other end of the line. "She say she will be out with Giovanni. Giovanni is her boyfriend. She no tell you that? Why am I not surprised. You have a very—what is the English word?—yes, you have a very sneaky daughter, Mr. Worthy."

No lie, Worthy thought. But more than anger, Worthy felt fear. I may have a sneaky daughter, but, right now, I have a missing daughter. Good God, not again.

CHAPTER TWENTY-SIX

ISPETTORE RUGGIERO ADMITTED THAT THE CONNECTION between the deaths of the millionaires and the missing relics was very clearly advanced by Allyson, but he regretted to add that he could not officially sanction a missing person's report for Allyson until it could be established that this Giovanni, last name unknown, had something to do with the cases. Ruggiero said that he could cite at least seven cases in the past year when families of missing females, all from foreign countries, pressured the Venice police department to treat their daughter's disappearance as a crime when it turned out, usually within days, to have been a romantic fling.

That meant, once the two monks were taken away to give their statements, that Worthy and Father Fortis were left to try to pick up Allyson's trail. As the minutes dragged on with no further word from Allyson, Father Fortis was careful to say nothing about his fears, especially his feeling that Allyson was holding something back the previous night. Nonetheless, he could see that his friend was deeply troubled.

Turning to the map of Venice together only led to despair. What is this city, Father Fortis thought, recalling his earlier attempt to find Brother Sergius, but a maze of hiding places? And with so many thousands of tourists entering the city every day, how could any area or *sestiere* of Venice be said to have been thoroughly canvassed? How do you find a needle in a haystack, Father Fortis wondered, when hay is constantly leaving and new hay keeps being unloaded?

At two o'clock, when the afternoon shift was coming in to replace the morning one, Worthy sat back heavily in his chair and rubbed his eyes. "Where do we go from here, Nick? I mean, we're little better than visitors to this crazy city. We're the least likely ones to find her, aren't we?"

Father Fortis pondered the question. Are we? Had they not solved difficult cases before? What were they overlooking in this one?

"Listen, my friend," he said. "I think the past is blocking us—you, but also me."

"What do you mean?"

"Allyson ran away before, and it's hard not to think about that now. But even though we both know that this time the situation is completely different, that puzzle from the past is in the way."

Worthy nodded. "You're probably right, but I can't pretend that what happened four years ago didn't happen, any more than I can pretend that Allyson has trusted me since the divorce."

Father Fortis stroked his beard. "And I'm not asking you to do that. Let me put it this way. If you were back in Detroit, and you'd received a call from the Venice police informing you that Allyson was missing, what would you be hoping the police would be doing right now?"

Worthy leaned forward, grabbed the map, and folded it. "Certainly not sitting here staring at a map that doesn't make sense."

"Okay, then what instead?"

Worthy sat quietly for a moment. "Okay," he said, "One thing seems obvious. It's been less than an hour since I talked with Sylvia. I would hope someone in my place, someone not her father, would have the sense to interview Sylvia, see if she knows this Giovanni and if she knows this Pieter or Pietro. Where do these guys live, what are their last names, those sorts of things. God, why can't I think straight?"

"I think you're just overwhelmed, my friend. After all, she is your daughter."

"And who knows how much time we have." Worthy rose from his chair. "Wait a minute. There's something else that we should do."

"What's that, my friend?"

"I said her cellphone was out of service. That could mean that the battery has been removed for some reason."

And now is not the time to speculate on what "for some reason" means, Father Fortis thought.

"But before her battery was removed," Worthy continued, "her phone could have been located by its GPS device inside. We need to find out where her phone was just before... before it went out of service."

Father Fortis joined Worthy in standing. "Good, good, Christopher. There are two tasks, and there are two of us. Which do you want?"

Worthy opened his mouth, then closed it for a moment. Finally, he looked at Father Fortis and said, "I need to be the one to track the GPS. You should talk with the roommate, Sylvia."

Father Fortis understood his friend's choice. Of the two approaches, tracking the GPS would lead them to the last known place where Allyson was.

But that place might also be where her body would be found.

With help from the techie at the *Questura* and the cooperation of the telephone service, Worthy was able, within an hour, to trace Allyson's cellphone to an industrial area of Mestre on the water. With Castelucci and Basso accompanying him, he was soon skimming across the lagoon in a police boat.

As he leaned forward next to the pilot, Worthy tried unsuccessfully to put out of his mind what else the GPS search revealed. The last known location of his daughter was quite easily established, but almost as crucial was the knowledge that Allyson's phone suddenly went out of service at fifteen minutes after three the previous morning.

Twelve hours ago, he thought. The statistics were well known, at least for kidnappings or missing persons in the States. The first six hours in such cases were the most important. For every hour after that, the chances of finding the missing person alive went down precipitously.

The boat was now past the western edge of Venice and traveling parallel to the bridge to the mainland. He remembered a summer day five years before, when his world still made sense, a day when he was teaching Allyson how to drive their speedboat. With almost every command about the controls or suggestion about not over-steering, Allyson would say, "I know, Dad. I've seen you do that a million times." And he remembered how touched he was at the time to know she was watching when he didn't notice.

As tears began to form only to be whipped from his face by the speed of the police boat, Worthy wondered if his daughter was still alive and, if so, what trouble she was facing. Had she learned from him how to survive in a potential life-and-death situation? Would she know that her best chance of fighting panic was to will herself to think like a professional? Had she learned from him that people unused to killing almost always committed a blunder in the pressure of the moment, and the key to survival was planning what she could do if and when that moment arose?

A wave of guilt washed over him. How could Allyson have learned anything from him when he'd been absent for so much of her life while off tracking killers?

The waiting room of the emergency unit of the city hospital held the same level of chaos as Father Fortis experienced back in the States, only here the drama was in Italian or the local Venetian dialect. A mother rocked her child who was sweating heavily and moaning. An intoxicated old man was talking to himself and picking at his skin. A young man in soccer gear sat with a bag of ice on one of his knees. And every ten minutes, emergency personnel of the city brought in someone else in need of attention.

With only three medical staff seemingly on duty, Father Fortis found it difficult for his request to talk with Sylvia, last name unknown, to be understood. The young intake nurse's grasp of English was minimal, and the noise level of the room added to the confusion. He finally thought that he made his request clear by writing Sylvia's name on a sheet of paper.

But as minutes passed with no results, Father Fortis couldn't help but think of Worthy's comment about time running out. He was about to plead with the intake nurse again when a short Italian young woman, with the dark hair and eyes so common in the women he saw in Venice, approached him and identified herself as Sylvia.

"Is there anywhere where we can talk that's a little quieter?" Father Fortis asked. To his relief, Sylvia seemed to grasp his question immediately and led him outside to a bench.

"My name is Father Nicholas Fortis, and I'm a friend of Allyson Worthy and a friend of her father."

The girl frowned at him. "I already told her father. I not know where is Allyson."

"Yes, I know that. Please, it's very important that we find her," he replied. "Can you tell me where we can find this Giovanni? Or, can you at least tell us his last name?"

Sylvia shrugged. "Giovanni is Giovanni. That's all I know. Allyson is the one who knows all about Giovanni. Not me."

Father Fortis detected the hint of regret. So there is a rivalry, he thought. No wonder she labeled Allyson as sneaky.

"How did Allyson meet this Giovanni? Can you tell me that?" he asked.

"He come with Enrico to a club. Then we all go out to Lido in his boat."

"When was that?"

Sylvia paused. "Maybe week ago. Yes, I think so."

It took Father Fortis a moment to recall that part of Allyson's assignment for the police department was to visit local clubs with her roommate to learn what she could about and from the personnel of the hospital. It must have been at one of those clubs that Allyson met Giovanni.

"Does Giovanni work here at the hospital?" he asked.

"Giovanni? No. Giovanni a student."

"Here in Venice?" he asked.

"No, he study in Padua."

With the name of the town, Father Fortis remembered Allyson's report, from just the day before, of her trip to Padua. And he also remembered his own feeling that she held something back. What she was holding back, he realized, was Giovanni.

"Would this Enrico know anything about Giovanni?"

She nodded grudgingly. "Yes, maybe so. I must go back to work."

"Yes, yes, but before you go, how can I contact Enrico?"

Sylvia rolled her eyes and sighed heavily. But she drew out her cellphone, scrolled down a list of names, and hit the send button. In a moment, she was talking rapidly in Italian to someone whom Father Fortis hoped was Enrico. After a few more exchanges, she flipped the phone closed.

"His name, Giovanni Castelli," she reported. "Giovanni live with father in Mestre."

Sylvia stood and put her phone back in her purse. "You say you have second question."

"Yes, thank you. Do you know a Pieter?"

"Pieter? No, no. I know two Pietros."

Of course, Father Fortis thought. Brother Nilus didn't say the name was Pieter. He said the name sounded like the Russian name Pieter.

"Would either of these Pietros know Allyson or Giovanni?"

Sylvia shook her head. "No. Pietro is my grandfather. The other Pietro is my… what you say in English, my nephew. He seven years old."

Father Fortis thanked Sylvia for her help and took out his own phone to report to Worthy.

Then, just as Sylvia reached the sliding doors of the emergency unit, she turned and called back, "Enrico say he try to call Giovanni this morning. Giovanni's phone, it's dead."

Her words brought a blast of dread. Allyson and Giovanni together. Both missing. Both phones dead.

Chapter Twenty-Seven

The interior of the building was dark and dismal, smelling of rusting metal and oil. Worthy, along with Castelucci and Basso, approached the building cautiously, but found it empty.

In the light from an overhead fluorescent lamp, Worthy first checked the dusty floor. There was evidence of recent footprints, but no evidence, to his relief, of a struggle. In the middle of the room sat a folding table with a near-empty bottle of wine and two glasses, one full, one half-full, that being the only clear evidence of recent occupancy.

Donning latex gloves, the three moved quickly as they searched through the boxes stacked along the walls for other clues to Allyson's whereabouts or Giovanni's identity. Fingerprints could be gathered later.

The beep of Worthy's phone brought a jolt of relief. But the caller was Father Fortis, informing him of what he had gleaned from his interview with the roommate, Sylvia. The good news was that the name Castelli matched a name found on several of the invoices scattered around the room. Worthy's initial hope that Giovanni Castelli could be traced through the father was dashed when Father Fortis shared the knowledge that Giovanni's phone, like Allyson's, was dead. Worthy realized that he would have been relieved to find that Ruggiero was right, to discover that Allyson simply ran off with this Giovanni. But something far more serious happened here.

After an initial search of the room, Worthy was convinced that the deactivated phones were not there. Dejected, he sat down in one of the chairs by the small table. His hopes that Allyson had the presence of mind to leave a clue of some sort had not materialized. And Father Fortis similarly struck out, for all practical purposes. Allyson's trail led to a man's name and this room, but here it seemed to die out.

For some reason, his eye was attracted to the one glass that was full of wine. In the fluorescent lighting, its redness seemed almost black. Did Allyson drink from this same glass? Did she sit in the chair that he was now sitting in? Fingerprints on the glass would answer those questions, but that evidence would be too little, too late.

Careful not to smudge any lip or fingerprints, he picked up the glass and held it to the light. To his amazement, he could see that there was something shining in the glass. No, the glint of light didn't seem to be a reflection, but rather from something within the glass.

Carefully, he set the glass down and, not having tweezers, inserted two of his gloved fingers. He withdrew a single key on a key ring. He turned the key ring over and rubbed wine residue off its face. On the ring were the words "*Grazie G.*"

The dinner that evening was far different from the one the previous night. Then, the pieces of the puzzle were falling deliciously into place. Then, the three ate with the satisfaction of knowing that they would certainly solve this puzzle.

And now, even though more of the pieces were known, with Giovanni and Pietro being somehow connected to the thefts of the relics, the suspicious deaths of the millionaires, and the killing of Brother Sergius, Father Fortis and Worthy sat together in silence. Fifteen hours had now passed since Allyson's and Giovanni's phones were deactivated. By next morning, the number of hours would rise to twenty eight. And every moment was leaching hope.

Neither Worthy nor Father Fortis had an appetite, but both ate the bar food nonetheless, as if they realized that they would need the energy for the long night ahead.

Worthy should have been grateful that the evidence of the deactivated phones and the discovery of the key set the Venice police department into motion. While the name "*Grazie G*" meant nothing to Worthy, Castelucci and Basso found, from further interviews with Sylvia and Enrico, that "*Grazie G*" was the name of Giovanni's boat. But the boat wasn't in Mestre, nor was it moored at its slip in Venice.

Yes, there was a whirl of official action around Worthy and Father Fortis, but what could either of them contribute, Worthy pondered.

"So how many wooden boats do you think there are in Venice?" Worthy posed. "And even that's assuming the '*Grazie G*' is still in Venice."

Father Fortis nodded. "I have heard Venice described as a lady, and if so, she is a lady with an endless number of secrets and hiding places."

Worthy put down his half-eaten sandwich. "And that's what the three millionaires counted on, right? They could hide here and be almost positive that no one would recognize them."

"But, my friend, the police now have five leads to follow: Giovanni Castelli, this Pietro, the name of the boat, the connection with the University of Padua, and, of course, Allyson. The more the better, right?"

Worthy gave an exasperated sigh. "You know, Nick, why we have to sit here and wait, don't you? Why we can't do anything?"

Father Fortis didn't say anything for a moment. "If you need to say it, then say it, my friend."

A lump formed in Worthy's throat. Yes, he did have to say it. "Because my daughter doesn't trust me. Because she has to go missing before I find out about someone named Giovanni Castelli. That whatever she knows about a Pietro she chose not to share with me. And now, because of me, she could be dead. How'd you like to live with that the rest of your life, Nick?"

Before Worthy could protect himself, Father Fortis reached across the table and slapped him. For a moment, the two men just stared at one another.

"Sorry, my friend. First, I invite you to say what you need to say, and then I slap you. But I had to, Christopher. Ever since she disappeared, you've been torturing yourself. How this is all your fault for being such a lousy father. How this connects with the past, when she ran away the first time."

Father Fortis paused a moment before continuing. "You remind me of my aunt, God rest her troubled soul. Whenever anything bad happened, like an accident, all she cared about was who was to blame. Who did what? Who should get punished? To this day, my sorry cousins can't do anything with a problem but waste their time blaming someone for it."

Worthy's face still stung, but he considered what his friend was saying. "This afternoon you said that the past was getting in the way of my thinking."

Father Fortis slammed his fist down on the table. "And what Allyson needs from you most right now is for you to think clearly. You've been trying so hard to patch up your relationship and become her loving dad again that you haven't realized what she really needs. She doesn't need a guilt-ridden father right now. She needs Lieutenant Christopher Worthy."

CHAPTER TWENTY-EIGHT

WITH EACH PASSING HOUR, ALLYSON REALIZED that she was alive because Pietro still needed something from her. He was sitting on the other side of the shed, at times lecturing Maria, Giovanni's sister, while at other times staring at Allyson and Giovanni as they were trussed up in chairs, back to back, their hands tied behind them. The gun that Pietro used in the Castelli shop in Mestre, no longer needed, sat on a table near him.

That Giovanni needed to be tied up while Maria, his sister, sat next to Pietro told Allyson a lot. This was the same woman who stood by while Pietro grabbed and slapped Giovanni in Padua. How far would Maria go to please or appease the jumpy man next to her?

Allyson remembered little from the martial arts course in junior high. She certainly had no illusions that she could somehow break out of her bonds and wrest control of the gun from Pietro. But what she did remember from her two years of kicking bags was that her first step, if she ever had to fight, was to study her opponent very carefully for his or her tendencies and weaknesses.

Pietro looked to be about Giovanni's age, and, although he was smaller, his wiry build suggested a kind of intensity. He seemed the opposite of Giovanni in many ways. Giovanni moved with a kind of grace and fluidity, while Pietro's every move seemed impulsive. She remembered how quickly he grabbed Giovanni's throat in Padua. So Pietro, she realized, would be hard to predict.

She noted that his comments also seemed compulsive and jumpy. Over the fifteen hours that she'd been captive, Pietro told her a great deal about himself, and that openness scared her.

Yes, he was a hacker, of which he said he was proud. But what Allyson did not know about him was that he also studied history. And in a medieval history course two years ago, he learned of the value of relics in centuries past. He read a monogram on how relics, when linked with the promise of miracles, led to amazing riches for those who held them.

"Some Englishman once said, 'those who forget the past are doomed to repeat it,' " he reminded her that morning. "But I say something better. 'He who studies the past *can* repeat it.' Do you understand what I say?"

Needing him to keep talking, Allyson replied that she did understand. He was able to combine that knowledge with his hacking ability to produce a list.

"Yes, a list," he confirmed. "A list of rich people who soon will die. What need do they have for their much money?"

"And money is everything, right?" she asked. Behind her, she felt Giovanni squeeze her hand. Was that his apology for the same drive?

"Being poor in Mestre is terrible life," Pietro said. Behind him, Maria nodded in agreement. "Every day, what do you see? Across a bridge, you see Venezia, a dream world. Every day, you take train into city. Around you, everywhere, people from all over world come to Venezia and spend much money. More money for silly gondola ride than my mother make in a week. And every night, you take train back to Mestre. Venice, she no let you stay unless you have much money."

For a moment, Allyson caught a glimpse of how her beloved Venice could become a hellish dream for those tantalizingly just out of her reach. She remembered when she ran away in Detroit four years before with the absurd fantasy that she could find her way to Venice. What would it have been like to have that same dream, be able to walk into your dream every day, but be exiled, spewed out, every evening? That was what drew Pietro, Maria, and Giovanni together.

Which means the police department, her father, and chiefly she were clearly in the way of Pietro achieving his dream. And Brother Sergius, she figured, must have been in his way as well.

"The police are wondering what part Brother Sergius played in stealing the relics," she offered.

"What you know about him?" Maria asked. To Allyson, her voice held anger, but also fear.

Allyson decided to bluff, telling Pietro and Maria only that the monk was still missing along with another relic.

Behind her, Giovanni squeezed her hand. She held her breath, fearful that, in arguing with Pietro in Mestre, Giovanni might have already shared that the police found Brother Sergius' body. After a moment that seemed an eternity, Pietro replied arrogantly that he and he alone was behind the thefts. Yes, he admitted, Brother Sergius had helped with several of the thefts, but that was all.

"Would you like to know where this monk is now?" Pietro asked her.

"I suppose he's hiding out somewhere in Venice," she replied.

Pietro shook his head and smiled at Maria, who still looked troubled. "He is back in Russia, and the relics, they are with him."

For a brief moment, Allyson wondered if someone else besides Pietro could, in fact, have killed Brother Sergius. But then she remembered Giovanni's reaction in his father's shop the night before when she told him of the monk's murder. And once again, she felt Giovanni grip her hands tightly, as is to confirm that Pietro was lying.

As Allyson gazed over at Maria after Pietro's lie, she thought that she saw a look of relief. Was it possible that Maria still didn't know of the monk's death? If so, Allyson realized that Pietro may have made his first mistake. Pietro did not know that she told Giovanni the truth about Brother Sergius. That meant that as far as Pietro knew, no one in the room knew that he strangled the monk but him.

Yes, Pietro showed his hand in the lie. For some reason, he didn't want Maria to know that truth. Did that mean that Pietro hadn't killed the three millionaires as well? Had each of them, in fact, committed suicide? Or had she just learned that Maria still believed that they were suicides? Didn't Giovanni the night before think the same?

She could almost hear her father's voice in her head. *Pietro doesn't want Maria to know that he's a killer. Think how you can use that knowledge to save yourself.*

Allyson felt tears welling in reaction to how close her father seemed in those moments. She moaned as she admitted that she wouldn't be in the mess if she trusted him. God, she thought, he must be going crazy. Here I am, missing again without leaving a word. If I die, it will be because I broke two of the cardinal rules of police work: not letting partners know of your plans and going solo. And I broke those rules because one of my partners is my father.

But I did, she reminded herself, leave my father two clues. The first clue was leaving Giovanni's name with the jealous Sylvia. And then there was the clue of the key and key ring.

When Giovanni and she were surprised in Mestre by the gun-wielding Pietro, they were first too shocked to move. Pietro must have been listening to their conversation, as he immediately launched into a verbal barrage aimed at Giovanni. Allyson understood enough of the rapid-fire Italian to know that he was accusing Giovanni of being a traitor.

While Giovanni was trying to defend himself, he had the presence of mind to turn his back to the table. Gesturing wildly with his right hand as he yelled something about Pietro ruining everything, he lay, with his left hand, the key and key ring on the table behind him.

What is he doing, she asked herself. When she saw the words "*Grazie G*" on the key ring, she thought she understood. He wanted her to hide the key, thereby forcing the three of them to stay right where they were.

Just at that moment, Pietro advanced toward them, and Allyson was able to do nothing but grab the key and hope that he didn't see the exchange. With gun in hand, however, Pietro asked only for their cellphones. It was after Pietro opened her phone to remove the battery that she realized that she would have about the same amount of time, no more than three seconds, to hide the keys when he opened Giovanni's phone. She glanced around the room and saw nothing within reach. At the last second, when Pietro's eyes were diverted, she slipped the key and key ring into Giovanni's glass and saw it disappear beneath the wine's surface.

But she was wrong. When Pietro asked for the keys to the boat, Giovanni reluctantly reached into his pocket and pulled out an identical set. And with that, Pietro forced them back to the boat. Left behind in the room was a boat key hidden in a glass of wine. How long would it take the police and her father to find that?

Pietro loaded both of them onto the boat and forced Giovanni to serve as pilot. In the gloom of the lagoon, Allyson realized that they were not returning to Venice, but motoring farther out into the lagoon. An hour later, they came ashore on what Allyson saw in the earliest light of day to be a sparsely-occupied island. This isn't Lido, she thought. Across a field, she saw the tall bell tower of a church. Where have I seen that before, she wondered. Remembering the book of Venice that was with her for at least the past ten years, she realized that Pietro had taken them to Torcello. Did he know that the monk's body was already found?

On landing, Pietro forced Giovanni and her to pull a camo tarp over the boat. He then marched them to an old warehouse, where Maria was waiting with water, a bag of food, and the ropes.

Now, hours later, with only one guarded use of a makeshift bathroom in the warehouse, Allyson felt that her hands were past the tingling stage into near total numbness. It was painful to even attempt to move them against the tightly bound cord, but she tried nonetheless. I'm not going to die here, she told herself.

Two clues, she thought. I left my father two measly clues: Giovanni's name and a spare key to the *Grazie G*. And now that boat was on a nearly deserted island and covered with a tarp.

For the past ten years, she had heard of her father's reputation for solving convoluted and even impossible cases. But had she left him too little to find her before it was too late?

✝

FATHER FORTIS DID NOT KNOW HE would slap Worthy until it happened. Not that this was the first time that he felt like slapping someone. Often, when a person came for confession, only to dance around what really needed to be said, Father Fortis had the urge to slap the person. He remembered thinking how sensible was the practice of Zen masters who routinely hit their disciples on the head, shoulder, or hands to awaken their Buddha mind.

But in the case of striking Worthy, his intent was nearly the opposite. Worthy carried so much guilt over his divorce and broken family that he fell into the pit of despair whenever Allyson merely sneezed. He first met Worthy soon after Allyson ran away. Worthy was so paralyzed at the time that he'd nearly lost his job.

The danger now was horribly worse. If Worthy fell into that same pit now, Allyson would surely die. But if Worthy could detach himself from that painful past, he, more than anyone in Venice and maybe in the world, had a chance to save Allyson's life.

His impulsive act at least seemed to loosen the hold of guilt on Worthy. Worthy was now occupied making a list of everything that he remembered Allyson saying in police conferences or over dinner. All that is to the good, Father Fortis thought, but I might need to slap him again, and again, and again.

"Here's what I have on my list," Worthy said. "Tell me if you remember anything more from our dinners. I have Ally investigating scams against tourists, visiting clubs with Sylvia to pick up anything she could about the millionaires' deaths, going to Padua, figuring out the value of the stolen relics to the three with cancer, and figuring out the meaning of the incisions and the scars."

"I agree, but that's still too narrow, Christopher. We also know that here in Venice, she met a young man named Giovanni Castelli, and she probably met up with him again in Padua, where he's a student."

Worthy added that to his list. "Well, going even wider, we could say that Venice is Ally's favorite city, although I'm not sure that helps us much."

Father Fortis sat up. "Let me see that map again," he asked. Laying the map out again on the table, he continued. "We both know this looks like a crazy maze to us. But, when Allyson was looking at it in the restaurant, she knew it like it was Detroit. I mean she knew immediately where Torcello was."

"I think she knows this city better than Detroit," Worthy agreed. "But how does that help us?"

"Hmm. Well, for starters, we can admit that Allyson very likely knows where she was taken on the *Grazie G.* We may be lost, but she's not."

Worthy frowned. "All that tells me is that the situation would be a lot better if one of us was lost, and Ally was looking for you or me."

He's dancing close to the pit again, Father Fortis thought. He can't even see that this gives Allyson an advantage if she somehow manages to escape. "Don't prejudge anything, my friend. Just write it down. You never know when it might help us."

With a paper in his hand, Castelucci approached Worthy's desk. Father Fortis saw evidence at the last meeting of this officer's antipathy to the Americans' presence, but he now wore only an expression of concern. "*Scusi*, please. I check at the university in Padua. Giovanni Castelli a student in business. Also, he have sister there. Maria Castelli, she study medical science."

Father Fortis shot a glance at Worthy and, with relief, saw that his friend also understood the significance of the information.

"She could have done the incisions," Worthy said. "What do you think, Nick?"

"My thought exactly, my friend." Father Fortis turned toward Castelucci. "Did you check to see if there is a Pietro studying computer science?"

"*Sì, sì*. Three students named Pietro study computer. One from Padua, one from Chioggia, one from Mestre."

Worthy stood and started to fold the map. "Giovanni Castelli is from Mestre. Let's bet on him. What's the last name of the Pietro from Mestre?"

"*Sì, sì*. Pietro Portocelli."

"Castelucci, I can't thank you enough," Worthy said as he reached to shake the officer's hand. Castelucci blushed with the attention.

"Is there any way we can trace their cellphones?" Worthy added.

"*Certo*, certainly. I will call university again. I hurry, okay?"

"The offices won't be closed?" Worthy asked.

"No problem, no problem. I find out."

Though Worthy's jaw was set, Father Fortis could see the fire in his eyes.

"Granted that this may lead us nowhere...," Worthy started to say, but then emotion overcame him.

"I know, I know, my friend," Father Fortis said. "Isn't it what you've always said—'Sooner or later, even the cleverest makes a mistake?' Let's pray that one of them left his or her phone on."

"You pray, Nick," Worthy said. "I can't."

Father Fortis glanced over to see if his friend was mocking him. But no, he thought, this time Worthy means it. In years past, he would have said, "I won't."

CHAPTER TWENTY-NINE

PIETRO WAS QUIET, TOO QUIET FOR Allyson, while Maria was in an adjoining room taking a nap. Given her predicament, Allyson was surprised that her own head dropped several times before she jerked awake. And Giovanni's heavy breathing behind her suggested he dozed off as well.

Why am I still alive, she wondered. She imagined that Pietro was asking a very similar question, why am I letting this American live? All that she could conclude was that Pietro backed himself into a corner by hiding Brother Sergius' death from Maria. He did not want Maria or Giovanni—too late for that—knowing that he had crossed a line, moving from fraud to murder. Now he had to find a way to dispose of her while hiding his true potential from his childhood friends. And that was why Pietro's silent brooding troubled her. He was still hatching his plan.

So, if Pietro is finalizing his plan, what's mine, she asked. Her only advantage was that she and Giovanni knew Pietro's secret. Somehow, she had to use that against him when the time was right.

And if ever the time would be right, she realized, that would be when Pietro needed a nap. But even that normal human need assumed that Pietro, in his undoubtedly agitated state of mind, would give in to fatigue.

Plan it out anyway, she told herself. The elements of her plan formed in her mind piece by piece. If and when Pietro took his turn on the mattress in the adjoining room, she would begin her "campaign of truth" with Maria. Allyson would tell her about the monk's body being found. She would explain that the police already knew Pietro's name and were looking for him. And, most important of all, she would try to open Maria's eyes to the fact that Pietro planned to kill her, Allyson, next. And finally, Allyson would explain how, if that happened, Maria would be considered under the law his accomplice in the murder.

The unknown in her plan? Well, that's easy to see, she thought. Just how devoted was Maria to Pietro? He already convinced her to risk her career in medical science by performing the incisions. Was his hold over Maria so strong that she would reject everything that Allyson would say?

IT WAS A LONG HOUR, NOW nearly eight in the evening, for Worthy and Father Fortis as they were forced to sit by and watch Castelucci and then the computer wizard, Foligno, try to track the cellphones of Pietro Portocelli and Maria Castelli. The results, however, when they appeared, left no doubt as to the action that Worthy and Father Fortis should take.

Maria Castelli's phone was deactivated. But the GPS in Pietro Portocelli's cellphone was active. All we need is one phone on, Worthy thought. In five minutes, Foligno tracked the GPS device to the southwestern side of an island of the lagoon called San Erasmo.

Within minutes, Worthy and Father Fortis, along with Castelucci and the pilot of the police boat, were speeding out into the lagoon. Worthy had just enough time before their departure to open the map to find the island. Once the home of a monastery, the island was now nearly deserted. Not a bad center of operations, Worthy thought.

Beside him as he stood by the pilot of the speedboat was Father Fortis. My man of hope, he thought. He's standing by me to keep me from dwelling on the worst that could await us on this island.

And Nick is right, he conceded. It was too late to wonder what he could have done differently with Allyson over the past three weeks. He tried to give her space, to not have his presence smother her. And only Allyson could say if that was his mistake. He longed for a time when Allyson would blame him for that or for anything.

Castelucci, with his own phone in contact with the computer wizard at the *Questura*, led the way once they arrived at the small island. Beyond a narrow strip of rocks and sand, brush overran the hillocks and swamps of the island. Tall, sprawling trees, maples it seemed to Worthy, rose up like scattered sentinels above the briars and bushes. In whispers, Castelucci repeated the directions he was receiving over the phone as he led them along an overgrown path into the interior of the island. Rounding a grove of trees, they saw in the distance a cluster of stone buildings, no doubt the abandoned monastery, most with caved-in roofs, but several still intact.

With the evening light diminishing, the place looked deserted to Worthy. Broken windows revealed only greater darkness inside. And yet, Worthy considered, would I expect anything else of a clever hideout?

Castelucci pointed in the distance to the larger of the intact structures. As the Italian slunk forward, Worthy felt as if his legs were frozen in place. The seemingly-deserted building fifty yards ahead of them was the needle in the haystack of the confusing maze of Venice. There, one way or another, the search would end.

Castelucci wisely turned off his phone and motioned for Worthy and Father Fortis to wait. In a whisper, he indicated that he would circle the building to determine the best place of entry.

As the Italian moved toward the building, Worthy felt a debt of gratitude for how Castelucci stepped forward. The once seemingly hostile Italian had done an about-face. Perhaps he has a daughter himself, Worthy thought.

Behind him in the tall brush, Father Fortis breathed heavily. Worthy did not expect his friend to say anything, as there was truly nothing to say. But Worthy knew his friend hadn't stopped praying since they received the message about Pietro's active cellphone.

Worthy tried to recall how other cases ended, when the killer was surprised. His own experience told him that anything could happen, from the person surrendering peacefully to the killer instantly turning on the hostages. What they had to assume, Worthy was convinced, was that Pietro had some weapon on him. How else could he force Allyson, or maybe Allyson and Giovanni, to obey him?

After the longest ten minutes that Worthy ever experienced, Castelucci crawled back to them. Using hand signals, the Italian indicated that there was only one doorway, being both entrance and exit. They would have to go into that one and hope that Pietro didn't panic.

Now, it was all Worthy could do to keep himself from sprinting through the door and facing what had to be faced. Maybe Pietro will turn his weapon on me, he thought, and Castelucci, also armed, would subdue Pietro before he could kill anyone else. I will take that ending, he thought. Gladly.

Father Fortis seemed to sense all this, as Worthy felt his friend's hand on his shoulder. In his ear, Worthy heard Father Fortis whisper, "We go with God."

Staying as low to the ground as they could, the three advanced toward the door. There was still no sound, but what most caught Worthy's attention was that the ground did not look disturbed by footprints. And Worthy's trained senses noticed something else. There was no smell of human presence, neither the odor of death nor a telling smell of food or human waste.

Castelucci and Worthy took opposite sides of the door. After a moment of listening, Castelucci, with gun drawn, motioned for Father Fortis to wait there and prevent anyone from escaping. He then motioned for Worthy to push on the weather-beaten door. Even before the creaking of the door subsided, the two were inside the room. They heard nothing as they moved from one room to another. Worthy guessed that the small rooms were once cells for the monks. It was when they were in next to the last cell and still having heard nothing that they saw the tiny blinking light. Worthy stood back, his legs too weak to move forward, as he guessed what they were looking at.

Castelucci reached for the cellphone. He turned on his own phone and soon was talking with Foligno at the *Questura*. Even though Worthy didn't understand Italian, he did understand the unmistakable sound of disappointment. Pietro, the scam artist, had outfoxed them.

Allyson squeezed Giovanni's hand as hard as she could when Maria took over the role of guard. Pietro? He didn't go into the other room for a nap but outside. Allyson listened as the sound of his footsteps faded. She had little doubt that Pietro was planning how he would dispose of her.

Giovanni coughed, as if to let her know that he was awake. "Do what you can to help," she whispered. "I'm going to try something."

"No talk," Maria commanded. "Else, I gag you, yes?"

"Just listen to me, Maria. You haven't been told the truth by Pietro," she said. "But you need to know… "

"Now I gag you," Maria said, coming toward them.

Giovanni spoke rapidly to his sister in Italian, but Allyson understood enough to know that he was begging his sister to listen. Maria approached her brother and leaned down. Allyson listened as Giovanni repeated the request.

"You need to know that Brother Sergius is dead, Maria," she said.

"No, no, he in Russia. Pietro get him to Croatia. From there he go to Russia."

"That's what Pietro told you, Maria, but he killed Brother Sergius."

Maria stepped back but kept staring at her brother. "No, no. Tell her, Giovanni. Pietro no kill anyone."

Giovanni's voice was low as he confirmed what Allyson said.

Allyson felt a wave of panic. If Maria challenged everything, then Pietro would surely return before Allyson convinced her.

Giovanni spoke again softly to his sister. Allyson could understand that he was asking if she trusted him, her brother.

"I trust you, but I trust Pietro, yes?"

"No, do not trust Pietro. I am family, Maria. I am family. We always trust each other, you and me. We never lie to each other."

Maria didn't speak for a moment, but there was little force in her voice when she answered, "But I love Pietro, Giovanni. I love him."

"He lie to us, Maria. He kill the monk here on Torcello, and he now plan to kill Allyson."

Maria shook her head, but tears were in her eyes. "How you know this, Giovanni? You see body of monk?"

"I know it is true. Trust me, Maria. Pietro, he change. We both know this. You must free us before Pietro come back."

Maria gasped. "I no do that. Pietro has plan, but he kill no one. I no believe that. She," Maria said, pointing at Allyson, "she lie to you."

"Why does he have us tied up, Maria?" Allyson added.

"I tell you. Pietro has plan. Always plan. How to bring rich people to Venezia. His plan work. How to take relics. His plan work. How to get monk to Croatia. His plan work."

Giovanni seemed to sense as well that time was running out. "Do you trust me, your brother, Maria? Do you trust me?"

Maria bent down and touched her brother's face. "Yes, I trust you, Giovanni. But I cannot cut ropes. I cannot."

Allyson heard the finality in her tone. Maria may doubt Pietro, but she would not act on that doubt.

A sudden thought struck her. "Maria, do you have your phone with you?"

"Yes, but I no make call for you."

"But is it activated? Is it turned on?" Allyson pressed.

"No, Pietro ask me to take battery out."

Allyson felt she was near to choking. "All we ask is that you put the battery back in. You don't even have to turn it on, Maria. Just put the battery back in."

"Why I do this?"

"If Pietro didn't kill Brother Sergius, the police right now are thinking I've run away with your brother. And they'd have no reason to be tracking your phone. But if Pietro did kill the monk, I think the police are not only looking for Pietro, but also Giovanni and you."

For a moment, Maria didn't move.

Giovanni spoke slowly and almost in a whisper. "You no have to believe Allyson. Believe me. Turn your phone on."

Chapter Thirty

Father Fortis took the end of the line as Castelucci, Worthy, and he retraced their steps to the boat. Castelucci and Worthy said nothing as they exited the abandoned building. No, the worst didn't happen, but perhaps the prelude to the worst possible outcome.

When the two entered the building, Father Fortis asked for all the departed souls of the monks who ever lived on this island to pray for Allyson's life. Now, as he walked behind Worthy, his friend's gait slow and methodical, he asked again for the monks' prayers. With no hint of where to pick up Allyson's trail, Father Fortis knew that he was asking for more than help. He was asking for a miracle.

I'm no different from the three millionaires, he realized. We all want a life-saving miracle. Perhaps if Worthy knew of his prayers for Allyson, he would lump me in with the three who'd been scammed. Only in my case, Worthy would probably say that God was the scam artist.

They were soon at the dock where the boat awaited. The silence that the pilot, Castelucci, and he were giving out of respect for Worthy was broken by static cracking from Castelucci's cellphone.

"*Pronto*," Castelucci said. The dejection in his voice was palpable. The Italian behaved like a guardian angel, first getting the cellphone numbers of Pietro and Maria and then shepherding Worthy and himself to this island. The disappearance of Allyson seems very personal to him, Father Fortis thought.

Father Fortis was aware that Castelucci was listening to a long comment from Foligno back at the *Questura*. But then Castelucci replied with "*Sì, sì*," and bounded onto the boat. Swiveling around, he called out to Worthy and Father Fortis on shore. "Maria Castelli's phone. Someone turn it on. She is on

Torcello. *Andiamo*, we go. Hurry."

Pietro reentered the room and surveyed the scene. Did everything look the same to him, Allyson wondered. She was still tied to Giovanni, and Maria was once again standing by the window.

"*Problema?*" he asked Maria.

She shook her head. "*Nessun problema*."

Pietro pulled out a cellphone and showed it to Maria. Allyson had no trouble understanding his Italian. "It's a cheap telephone I got in Padua. I just finished talking my friend, the one who took the monk to Croatia. He'll be here in a few minutes to take the American to the same place, to Croatia."

Maria looked straight at him but said nothing.

"My friend promises to drop her in the hills over there. So before she can ever get to a phone, he says we have time, maybe three days, for him to take us out of Venezia. Good plan, yes?"

Maria now looked from Pietro to Giovanni as if she were in a trance.

"What's the matter?" Pietro asked Maria as he moved closer to Allyson and Giovanni. He reached down to check the ropes binding them before returning to stand face to face with Maria. "Why you say nothing?" he asked.

Maria seemed to snap out of her spell. She threw her arms around Pietro and kissed him over and over again. "The boat's coming soon? They'll come here," she gazed around the room, "to take Allyson?"

Pietro shook his head. "No, I'll take the American to the boat. You stay here and watch Giovanni."

"Pietro, let me take her to the boat, okay?"

"Why?" Pietro asked, a coldness in his voice.

Maria looked down at the ground and shrugged. "I want to see that she's okay."

"No!" Pietro said as he grabbed her. "I said you stay here."

"*Sì, sì*, okay," Maria said, kissing him again. "When does the boat come?"

"Soon," Pietro said. He placed the gun down on the windowsill and turned toward Allyson. From his front pocket, he took out a camping knife. "We go now, you and me. You go on boat," he said in English.

No need to speak to me in English, Allyson thought. The nearness of death seemed to activate unknown resources in her brain. She saw Maria looking over at the gun on the sill. She can stop this right now, Allyson thought, and she knows it. "Just pick up the gun and order Pietro to stop," she whispered.

Maria's eyes were frantic as she looked from the gun to Pietro's back.

"No talk," Pietro ordered. He stooped down and began to cut Allyson's cord. When she was free, she looked pleadingly at Maria.

"Do it now," she said.

Pietro yanked her to her feet. "I say no talk."

Allyson looked behind her to see that Giovanni's hands remained bound. Pietro pushed her in the direction of the door.

"Give me the gun, Maria," he ordered.

Maria picked up the gun and stared at it. Giovanni called out something to her that Allyson didn't understand, but Maria shook her head and with a determined look handed the gun to Pietro.

Now what, Allyson thought. She rubbed her hands together to get the blood flowing. If she had no other option, she would take off running and hope that Pietro was a poor shot.

Pietro pushed her through the door and out into the darkness. The only lights on Torcello were those illuminating the bell tower of a church a half-mile away. She stopped, knowing that once Pietro marched her far enough away from Maria and Giovanni, he would kill her. Does he intend to strangle me, as he did Brother Sergius, stab me with the camp knife, or shoot me, claiming I tried to run away?

But she had one other plan.

"Maria, Giovanni, come out here," she called back. "I want to say goodbye."

"No talk. I say no talk," Pietro hissed, again pushing her.

"Just let me say goodbye," she asked in her best begging voice.

Pietro hesitated and then said something to Maria. In a moment, she led her bound brother through the door.

"Before I say goodbye to you both, I think we better let Pietro know that the police already found Brother Sergius' body. And they know that Pietro killed him. What did the Russian want—for you to keep your end of the bargain and actually give him the relics?"

Like a rabbit, Pietro jumped to the side so that he could face all three. "She lies," he countered in Italian. "I swear the monk, he is in Russia with the relics."

"And Giovanni, maybe you should tell Pietro the truth, that you know that he plans to kill me too."

Giovanni slowly nodded. "No more, Pietro," he said in Italian.

"*Stai zitto*, shut up," Pietro ordered.

But Giovanni continued. "You've changed, Pietro. You're no longer the friend we know."

" 'We?' " Pietro asked, sneering.

Maria took a step toward him. "Pietro, tell me Giovanni is wrong."

"You too? Of course, yes, he wrong," he said, switching back to English. "I swear I put the monk on the boat."

"So where is this boat that's coming, Pietro?" Allyson challenged. "This is a flat, lowland island. Where are its lights?"

Pietro looked like he'd been bitten. For a moment, he seemed to not know how to answer. "The boat is coming with its lights off. *Andiamo*, we go."

Allyson faced Pietro and the gun leveled at her. "It's too late. The only boat that's coming is the police boat. And you'll probably hear a helicopter in a few minutes." If only that were true, she thought.

"She lies. Don't listen to her. The police don't know we're here."

"Tell him, Maria. Go ahead."

Maria folded her hands as if she were praying to Pietro. "I turn it off. I swear, as soon as you came back, I turn it off."

Pietro turned the gun on her. "What are you talking about?"

Maria seemed unable to answer, her face twisted in agony.

"She's telling you that she turned her phone back on for a few minutes," Allyson explained in English. Was she accomplishing anything more than getting herself shot more quickly by the desperate Pietro?

Maria pleaded with Pietro in rapid Italian, but the adrenalin boosted Allyson's understanding of the language. "If the monk is in Russia, it doesn't matter. Pietro, it doesn't matter. She said the police would only be listening to her phone if you killed the monk. So, we're safe, Pietro. We're safe. Tell me we're safe." An animal growl exploded from Pietro as he took three steps toward Maria and hit her in the mouth with the butt of the gun. For a few seconds, the three stood without moving as Maria slumped to the ground, her mouth a bleeding mess.

Just as Pietro stepped back to train the gun on Allyson again, Giovanni, hands still tied behind his back, rammed Pietro full force from the side. The gun flew out of Pietro's hand in an arc and landed ten feet away.

Allyson didn't hesitate. She had too much respect for the power of Pietro and his desperation to try for the gun. Instead, she ran across the field toward the distant, illuminated bell tower.

For the first twenty yards that brought her to a stone wall, her knees nearly buckled several times. Even though she felt nothing, she knew that she was dehydrated and hungry. And her joints, which had been locked into the same position for nearly twenty-four hours, seemed out of her control.

At the stone wall, she risked taking a quick look behind. Giovanni, probably equally weakened by the ordeal, was lying next to his sister. But Allyson could see him struggling to stand. Pietro reached the gun and, in what seemed like only seconds, was running in her direction.

She no longer feared that he would be able to shoot her in the back. The ground was too uneven, and the gap between them gave her the advantage. There was, however, a much more likely outcome, she realized. He looks fast, a runner, she conceded, and that means he'll probably catch me before I get to the church.

And even if I do beat him to the church, what do I do then?

But her knees now seemed to remember their role. She zigzagged slightly, not enough to impede her progress but enough to discourage Pietro from using the gun.

So what's the plan, she asked herself again as she ran through brambles and felt them catch on her jeans. She heard no sound of a helicopter, but did think, or was she dreaming, that she heard a boat in the distance.

I have no plan, she admitted, other than to live one minute longer, and then another minute. If I am going to die on this island, I swear I won't make it easy for Pietro. There will be no pleading, she promised herself.

She was running full speed when, without warning, the ground disappeared below her. Somehow she willed her body to rise up, not fall down, as she leapt as far as she could, coming down on the other side of a narrow canal. I'm halfway to the church, she encouraged herself, as if the church were the goal of safety in a children's game of tag.

As her breathing became more labored, she pushed herself ahead and listened for Pietro behind her. She could have screamed with relief when she heard a loud splash in water. Pietro fell into the canal that she somehow soared over.

She gained a second wind and began to believe that she would beat Pietro to the church. What then, she wondered. How can I break into a church that's sure to be locked?

The sound of the boat was now louder and, as she risked turning around, she could see lights progressing up the canal near where Maria and Giovanni were waiting.

Should I try to circle back, or should I count on Giovanni pointing the police in my direction? She had no time to ponder each possibility, but found her legs still moving forward. To try to circle back, she understood, would take her closer to Pietro and the gun. He must know now, she reasoned, that his chances of escape were decreasing with every second. And yet she was not surprised to hear his heavy breathing as he continued to pursue her. Pietro, having killed at least one person already, would not let the person who ruined his clever plan go free. Or perhaps he knows that his only chance of escape is to catch me and, instead of killing me on the spot, use me as a hostage.

A final stone wall brought her to the courtyard surrounding the church. In the flood lights aimed at the church, she realized that there were two churches side by side. For no reason that she could explain, she raced toward the larger and better lit of the two. From the halo around the building, she began to picture its floor plan. Romanesque in style, the church, she knew, would be in the shape of a rectangle, with two rows of pillars running the length of the structure from the apse at the far end to the back wall. The door, if her memory of the style was accurate, would be found on the right side.

She turned the corner of the church and ran toward where she expected the door to be. To stop and try the door would be to lose precious seconds, but she also knew that her energy was flagging fast.

In the shadows, she spotted the door ahead of her. She reached for the handle and pulled. Nothing. Without a second thought, she pushed on the door instead and, and, to her surprise, felt it give way.

Once inside, she realized that the light from the outside floodlights barely penetrated the room. And what light was filtering in, in accordance with Romanesque design, was trapped in the upper third of the nave. Great, she thought. My last thoughts are going to be about architecture.

Again, without knowing why, she edged her way toward the altar and the concave apse behind it. Her breathing was so heavy that she thought she heard it echoing off the walls. I have to hide, she thought. Maybe not for long, just long enough for the police to find their way to the church. She suppressed the logical objection that the island was quite large and there was no guarantee that the police would search for her here and in time. That would all depend on what Giovanni told them.

I have no more than ten seconds to find a place to hide, she reasoned. Just as she was feeling her way toward the altar, her knee struck something hard. In pain, she reached down and felt the cold marble edge of a box.

Her fingers told her that the box was a sarcophagus. She felt for the top of it but realized that this sarcophagus was without the stone lid. She didn't know whether to be angry or relieved, but she did know what she had to do.

She climbed over the side and nestled herself in the bottom of the empty sarcophagus. Her feet hit the end immediately, and she realized that she was taller by several inches than the body or bodies that had inhabited the sarcophagus in the centuries before her.

Just as she curled her legs up, she heard the door creak. Pietro, she knew, was now in the church, standing just inside the door. He too was breathing heavily, and as if by instinct, she realized that the only way for her own breathing not to give her away was for her to breathe in rhythm with her pursuer. She heard him inhale noisily and then exhale. When he next inhaled, she did the same and then waited. She had the advantage of the darkness and hearing of his progress. At first, he seemed to be moving away from her, as if he was headed to the other side of the nave. Live a minute longer, she told herself.

Her breathing calmed sooner than Pietro's, so she could hear him change his direction and begin to move along the far wall toward the altar. In a flash, she realized the chance before her. Pietro had the gun, but with every step he took toward the altar on the far side of the room, he was moving another step away from the door. And the nearer he came to the altar and her hiding place, the more she, not he, had the advantage of being nearer the door.

If I stay here and no one intervenes, I will surely die in this box. She repressed an hysterical fit of laughter as she realized that hers would be the last relics to use this sarcophagus. Relics, always the relics.

But if I run for the door, she realized, I have a chance of getting there ahead of him. And with my recovered wind, I might be able to make a dash for the police boat.

As she struggled to raise herself without making any noise, she felt coins on the bottom of the sarcophagus. She gingerly gathered four of the larger ones that were apparently tossed there for good luck, and as silently as possible stepped outside the confining box. With all her might, she threw the coins as far to the opposite end of the nave as she could.

She waited a heartbeat after the coins clanged and bounced on the mosaic floor before sprinting toward the door. The first gunshot seemed to explode over on the other side, where the coins landed, but a second whizzed by her head.

He knows my plan, she thought, as she heard him crashing into chairs in pursuit. Just as she reached the oak door, she heard the bullet strike it and make the door ring. No time to wait for another shot, she realized.

But just as she reached for the door handle, the door shot toward her as if it had a mind of its own. She ended up flat on her back, the wind knocked out of her. She knew she would die, but her only thought was how beautiful the light was that played off the ceiling rafters.

It was then that she felt someone stooping over her, a hand feeling the contours of her face. She heard the voice whisper something to Basso and then yell to Pietro that the police had arrived and that he was trapped. And, in a moment of shattering relief, she smelled the cheap aftershave of Castelucci.

The church of Santa Maria Assunta was empty except for Father Fortis and Worthy, who sat together as the light of dawn began to peek through the clerestory windows. Worthy slumped over in his chair while Father Fortis patted him on the back.

"She could have died," Worthy said in little more than a whisper. "What terrifies me all the more is that if just one or two tiny aspects of this case had gone differently, Allyson *would* be dead. If that had happened, I don't think I could have …"

Feeling the sob pulse through his friend's shoulder, Father Fortis said nothing. He did not know what Worthy needed most from him, so he settled for what he needed to say to his friend.

"I'm not sure how I could have carried on, either, having gotten to know Allyson so much better the last few weeks."

Worthy reached over and patted Father Fortis's knee. "If you hadn't slapped some sense into me, Nick, she very well would have died. You saved her life."

"Well, I would say that Allyson did a lot to save her own life. You should be proud of how clearly she thought under pressure, my friend. And, about that slap. Always remember that I didn't know I was going to do that until I did."

Father Fortis couldn't tell if Worthy's reaction was another sob or a laugh. "What you would call providence, right, Nick?"

Father Fortis chose not to respond. His friend articulated what Father Fortis considered to be the truth better than he could with a sermon. No, a sermon was not what Worthy needed now. He didn't have to tell Worthy that he had never stopped praying for Allyson over the past two days. Worthy would know that.

"My friend, as a parent and especially because of how Allyson reacted to your divorce, you can't help but be grieving something that could have happened. But it did not happen, Christopher. She did not die."

"Are you going to slap me again?" Worthy asked, still looking down.

Father Fortis's laugh echoed through the empty church. "No, I won't slap you. But I would encourage you to say something to Allyson besides 'you could have died.' What do you most want to tell her?"

"Do you mean besides saying that I forbid her to work in law enforcement or criminal justice?"

"I hope you're joking," Father Fortis replied.

"Yes, partially, at least. I know my forbidding Allyson anything is not going to work. But I think you can understand how much I wish she would wake up today and announce that she's changed her career goal to accounting or organic farming."

"Of course, I can. Let me ask you a different question, probably a much better question. What do you think Allyson needs from you right now?"

Worthy sat up and looked toward the church's altar. After a few moments, he replied, "I've never been good at guessing what she needs. I'll have to think about that."

Father Fortis nodded. "She made some serious mistakes, my friend."

"I'm sure she knows that and doesn't need me to list those for her. But she made some amazingly good decisions as well. As you said, she did a lot to save her own life."

"And probably the lives of the Giovanni and his sister."

"Hmm. You're right, Nick. In the end, Pietro would have been forced to kill them."

The two sat in silence for a few moments before Father Fortis spoke. "I loved this church from the first moment I stepped into it. Despite what transpired here a couple of hours ago, I'll always remember this church as a gift to me, giving me a sense of what God wants."

"And what is that, Nick?"

"Peace. Not the peace of nothing bad happening, but the peace of life overcoming death."

The two men stood and walked slowly to the door. Father Fortis reached for the handle, expecting the quirky door to resist him as it had days before. But the door opened with ease, bringing a smile to his face.

He waited for Worthy to exit first before he realized that Worthy had stopped. "What is it, Christopher?"

"You said the word 'gift.' I just realized the gift that I should give Allyson before I leave. It will cost me a lot, but it's the right thing to do."

Chapter Thirty-One

Dizzy. That is what Allyson felt as she awoke the morning following the capture of Pietro Portocelli and, with that, the solving of the case. Perhaps, she thought, the dizziness is what people feel after the adrenalin slowly ebbs.

As she turned over in her bed, her muscles ached and she could feel where she cut herself in her escape from Pietro the night before. Slowly, she managed to sit up and dangle her bruised legs and feet over the edge of the mattress.

I should be feeling joyous, she thought. Pietro could have caught me, but he didn't. Had Pietro's aim been better, I could easily be dead, but I am not. So why the sadness?

She hobbled to the bathroom and took a hot shower, wincing when the water hit the cuts on her arms and legs. She saw only the sad faces of Giovanni and Maria as they watched the struggling and handcuffed Pietro being led onto one of the police boats. Giovanni then hugged the weeping Maria as they were escorted onto a second police boat.

What would happen to them now, she wondered. No doubt the two of them, in working with Pietro, committed various crimes, although murder would not be one of them. She dried herself off and slowly dressed before heading for the *Questura*.

Castelucci was the first to greet her at the police station with kisses on both cheeks. Although his aftershave seemed even stronger this morning, Castelucci deserved, in Allyson's opinion, a genuine hug in return. He escorted her to *Ispettore* Ruggiero's office and opened the door for her.

She was surprised to see her father and Father Fortis in her supervisor's office and then wondered why she was surprised. When she was younger, she often waited impatiently for her father to come home after he'd closed a case.

As she grew older, she learned that the end of a case was the beginning of the paperwork. Today, Allyson realized, the deaths of the three millionaires, the death of Brother Sergius, and Pietro's attempted murder on Torcello had to be accounted for on forms—Italian forms, to boot.

Her father hung back and let the inspector be the first to greet Allyson and ask if she felt fit enough to be at the station. He drew a chair up for her even as he gave her permission to take the rest of the week off to recuperate. After she declined and sat down, Ruggiero took his own seat before saying, "If you wish to return to your country, we understand."

She glanced at her father and at Father Fortis before shaking her head. "I think the best medicine for me right now is to get back to normal work. Pickpockets and scam artists, I mean."

"*Brava, brava,*" the inspector said with a broad smile. "Your staying is my wish, too, but this must be your decision."

Allyson paused, wondering if her father would declare his own wishes for her, but he said nothing. Father Fortis was smiling as broadly at her as Ruggiero, but he also said nothing.

"It is my decision, *Ispettore*," she said, rolling the final "r." "Besides," she added, "I want to do what I can to help Giovanni and Maria. I wouldn't be alive if it weren't for them."

She thought she heard a slight sigh from the direction of her father, but she did not look over at him.

"The *Publicco Ministero*, our prosecutor, will decide on charges to file for them, but yes, I see that they played a part in closing this case, not to mention, in saving your life, Allyson."

The inspector pronounced her name exactly as Giovanni did, and a wave of sadness washed over her. Whatever the police decided about Giovanni, she knew that his dream of opening a club on Lido was over. And what would happen to Maria's dream of a career in medicine? Unless the Italian system was more compassionate than the American one, Allyson was sure that Maria's performing surgeries without a license on the three millionaires would end her dream as well. In a crushing image, she saw both Giovanni and Maria living out their lives in Mestre, looking across the lagoon to the lady Venezia, who would never embrace them.

"There is nothing harder," Worthy said, "than knowing that you can't save all those caught up in a murder case, especially when they're your friends."

Allyson wondered if her father somehow read her mind. The truth of what he said brought tears to her eyes. She accepted the offer of a tissue from Ruggiero and fought to regain control.

"I guess I'm feeling a bit fragile today," she explained.

"*Certo*, certainly," Ruggiero replied. He paused before asking Worthy,

"Have you communicated with the families?"

"I managed to reach the Kuiper family last night—it was afternoon in Detroit. I haven't reached any of Linda Johnson's relatives, nor do I have contact information for Vladimir Monsinoff."

Ruggiero offered to contact the Monsinoff family as Father Fortis said, "I don't suppose the Kuipers understood what happened any more than they did three weeks ago."

Worthy shook his head. "No, they can't accept that the father and husband they knew would take his own life."

"Hmm. I wonder if it's fair to conclude that he did," Father Fortis said. "I don't for a moment think the loss of the money bothered any of the three of them at all. No, but what do people do when their last thread of hope is severed? Surely, it was Pietro Portocelli who killed them, as surely as he killed Brother Sergius. I will pray that their families will forgive them. They deserve that."

Chapter Thirty-Two

On the night before Worthy was to fly back to the States, Allyson asked her father to meet her on the promenade by the Doge's Palace, the same place where she stood just four weeks before. She remembered telling herself that night that everything was perfect. And now? What would she tell herself tonight?

She still loved Venice. That hadn't changed. The canals, the voices echoing down the watery corridors from gondolas or from windows, the churches by Palladio that seemed to float on the water, the leaning bell towers that seemed the work of careless children, the balloon salesmen competing with the pigeons for tourists in San Marco Square, the wavy mosaic floors in San Marco—she would change none of that.

But there was so much she wished she could change. Giovanni and Maria would go on trial for offenses, even though the Pubblico Ministero recommended leniency. Both cooperated fully with the authorities and answered the remaining questions about Pietro's inventive scam. Pietro, the hacker, having identified millionaires with terminal cancer, lured them to Venice with medieval accounts of the fabulous healing power of relics. In Padua, Maria met the desperate millionaires, made the incisions, inserted the stolen bone fragments, and then, weeks later, removed them. Although Pietro wasn't talking, it seemed likely that the millionaires placed so much hope in the miracle cure that they asked for, maybe even demanded, a second operation. Pietro either offered to accommodate for a now higher price or laughed at them. Either way, the millionaires saw through Pietro and lost all hope.

Father Fortis supplied what was likely to be the rest of the story. Brother

Sergius, masquerading as a Capuchin monk, stole the bones of Eastern saints for Pietro, with the assurance that he would eventually have them inserted into his own body so he could transport them back to Russia. Perhaps because of Father Fortis' arrival and investigation, Brother Sergius concluded it was time for him to abandon his fellow monks and make that trip. He met Pietro on Torcello to demand the relics, but Pietro apparently wanted his profitable scam to continue. They fought, with the wiry Pietro overpowering the thin Russian monk and killing him.

Giovanni's part in the plot was minor, transporting the millionaires and Pietro with his boat. Maria's part, however, was more significant and damning for her. Even with the promised leniency, Allyson knew that Giovanni's and Maria's lives would never recover. In many ways, Venice was a small city, and their part in the "Millionaire Relics Case," as the newspapers were calling it, would never be forgotten. Perhaps the only hope the two had for a future would entail the two moving farter away than Mestre.

Giovanni and Maria were not Allyson's only regret. She would also wish to change what she needed to talk to her father about before his departure. Father Fortis left three days earlier, first going to Rome to make his report to the Vatican and then home to the quiet of his monastery. The Orthodox Center where he and the three Russian monks had stayed in the city did not even bother to thank him for helping solve the mystery of the missing relics. They wanted him to clear the name of the Orthodox community in Venice, and in that he failed.

Allyson realized that for her father, the case was not over. In Detroit, the Kuipers would undoubtedly be waiting for him to tell them, once again, how their father and husband willingly went along with the thefts of the relics, hoping that they had miraculous power, and how he was fleeced by Pietro Portocelli. Worthy would explain once again how their father and husband was so devastated by Pietro's apparent subsequent demand for more money in order to have a second relic inserted that he decided to empty the bottle of sedatives. The open Bible at his bedside was, in the end, proof only of the man's desperation. The Kuipers would not find much comfort in the knowledge that two other millionaires with terminal cancer also came to Venice in hope of a miracle, no doubt also knowing that the relics were recently stolen, but in the bitter end could not endure the mockery of Pietro's ultimate desertion. Perhaps there were other relics missing and other millionaires who experienced the same scam and decided to slink home to await a natural death, if terminal cancer could ever be considered natural.

But before her father faced that ordeal, she wanted, with more tension pulsing through her body than she had felt before, to speak with him. She hoped he wouldn't question her need to look away from him out toward the darkening lagoon as she talked.

She turned to see him walking slowly toward her. He approached almost shyly as if he might once again be rebuffed by her.

"Thanks for coming, Dad," she said. Her voice sounded shaky, and she decided she was not ready. "What time does your plane leave tomorrow?"

Worthy looked out over the water as if he, too, had the same need. "Five-thirty in the morning. That takes me to Amsterdam, and then I fly out to Detroit at noon. I should be home by ten at night, Detroit time."

"That's four in the morning, Venice time, isn't it?"

Worthy nodded but did not say anything.

Allyson cleared her throat. "I wanted to tell you something, something about Giovanni and Maria that I didn't share at the *Questera*. Dad, I don't think I'd be here—alive, I mean, if Maria hadn't trusted Giovanni."

Out of the corner of her eye, she saw her father nod again. "Activating her phone, you mean," he said.

"Right. She did that because he told her that families trust one another. And in the end, I knew that she would never believe me. And I think she didn't so much believe Giovanni in those moments as much as what he said about family."

This time she could tell that her father, hands in pockets, was bracing himself for what could come next.

"Even at the time, when I was hoping Maria would do what her brother asked, I knew, if I was in her place, that his argument wouldn't have worked on me."

She paused for a moment, relieved that the quaver in her voice was gone. Perhaps, she thought, I've wanted to say this for a long time.

"Maria had to trust her brother more than she trusted Pietro, the man she loved. And here I was, tied to that chair, because I placed more trust in Giovanni, an Italian whose last name I didn't even know, than I did in you, my own father."

Worthy coughed, but did not say anything.

"Before you leave, I want to be honest with you." She found that she could now look at her father, although Worthy, his eyes lidded, was still focused on the water.

"When I first got here, I thought everything in my life was as perfect as it could be. I was in the city that I loved, and still love, I had an internship with the *Questura di Venezia*, I had a roommate and a nice apartment, and I had my freedom. I was here alone, just as I wanted."

"I sure changed that, didn't I?" Worthy interrupted, almost below his breath.

She nodded. "I didn't want you here, Dad. I didn't want Mom or Amy here either, but you most of all. I guess I didn't want you here anymore than Castelucci and Basso wanted me here. But look what I owe to Castelucci," she added with a short laugh.

Worthy offered a weak laugh himself. He's still waiting for me to stomp on his heart, she thought.

"But I was wrong," she said, and waited. There was no response.

"This goes back a few years, doesn't it?" she asked.

Her father nodded.

"When Mom asked for the divorce, I felt that I'd never trust you again. Your holy crusade of a career destroyed our family, and it seemed that it destroyed me. I wanted you to suffer, and so I made you suffer. And even after I came home, I saw making you suffer as the way to keep you at a distance.

But in working on this case, I found myself trusting you. Not as my father, but as a cop. I mean, I never worried about you squashing me, or making me feel invisible. I guess I found that you trusted me—as a colleague, I mean."

She was relieved to see her father's shoulders relax a bit. "But I should have told you about Giovanni. Except, I didn't trust you with that. It was like, if we were colleagues, rather than father and daughter, I wouldn't be expected to tell you what I was doing on my off-hours. Even in Padua, when I figured out that Giovanni could be involved in the case, I wanted to keep him from you. And that almost cost me my life."

Thinking her father was about to say something, she held her hand up. "I can only imagine how my going missing—again—affected you. I didn't intend to be so cruel to you, but that's what happened anyway." She paused for a moment and felt as if her whole body might liquefy at any moment and drain into the lagoon.

"What I'm trying to say, Dad, is that I'm glad you came to Venice, and I'm glad that we ended up working together. Okay, now you can talk."

Worthy looked down at his hands and for several moments didn't say anything. Finally, with a tremor in his own voice, he asked, "Is it wrong for me to hope that we won't have to work together on another homicide for us to trust each other?"

She moved closer in the dark. Worthy's arms hung uselessly by his side. Five nights before at the restaurant, she thought, he tried to show his pleasure in her detection by putting his arm around her and trying to hug her. She had pulled back, her entire body stiffened by the touch. There was still a distance between them, and she knew that whatever would happen from now on was up to her alone.

She crossed the barrier and kissed him on the cheek, tasting his salty tears. "Call me tomorrow night, Dad, even if it isn't night but four o'clock in the morning here. I want to know you got home safe, okay?"

Worthy held on to her for a moment. "You used to accuse me of bringing gifts home to you and Amy when I finished a case. I think you called them guilt offerings. I want to give you a gift now, but it has nothing to do with guilt."

"Okay," Allyson whispered as her own tears began to flow. She drew back and looked her father in the eye. "What is it?"

Worthy said, "All that I will ever tell your mother or anyone else, for that matter, about our working together on this case is that it proved you're a natural, and, without your help, a murderer would never have been caught. And Allyson, I will say that because that's the truth. You're very good at this … this business of detection, and I want you to know … to know you have my blessing."

Photo by Leif Carlson

David Carlson was born in the western suburbs of Chicago and grew up in parsonages in various cities of Illinois. His grade school years were spent in Springfield, Illinois, where the numerous Abraham Lincoln sites initiated his lifelong love of history. His childhood hope was to play professional baseball, a dream that died ignominiously one day in high school.

He attended Wheaton College (Illinois) where he majored in political science and planned on going to law school. Not sure how to respond to the Vietnam War, he decided to attend seminary for a year to weigh his options. To his surprise, he fell in love with theological thinking—especially theological questioning—and his career plan shifted to college teaching in religious studies. He earned a doctorate at University of Aberdeen, Scotland, where he learned that research is a process of digging and then digging deeper. He believes the same process of digging and digging deeper has helped him in his nonfiction and mystery writing.

Franklin College, a traditional liberal arts college in central Indiana, has been his home for over four decades. David has been particularly attracted to the topics of faith development, Catholic-Orthodox relations, and Muslim-

Christian dialogue. In the last thirteen years, however, religious terrorism has become his area of specialty. In 2007, he conducted interviews across the country in monasteries and convents about monastic responses to 9/11 and religious terrorism. The book based on that experience, *Peace Be with You: Monastic Wisdom for a Terror-Filled World*, was published in 2011 by Thomas Nelson and was selected as one of the Best Books of 2011 in the area of Spiritual Living by Library Journal. He has subsequently written a second book on religious terrorism, *Countering Religious Extremism: The Healing Power of Spiritual Friendships* (New City Press, 2017).

Much of his time in the last three years has been spent giving talks as well as being interviewed on radio and TV about ISIS. Nevertheless, he is still able to spend summers in Wisconsin where he enjoys sailing, fishing, kayaking, and restoring an old log cabin.

His wife, Kathy, is a retired English professor, an award-winning artist, and an excellent editor. Their two sons took parental advice to follow their passions. The older, Leif, is a photographer, and the younger, Marten, is a filmmaker.

For more information, please visit: www.davidccarlson.net.

CPSIA information can be obtained
at www.ICGtesting.com
Printed in the USA
LVHW041734261121
704539LV00025B/3679